# BURNING RIDGE

## ALSO BY MARGARET MIZUSHIMA

*Hunting Hour*

*Stalking Ground*

*Killing Trail*

# BURNING RIDGE

## A Timber Creek K-9 Mystery

*Margaret Mizushima*

CROOKED
LANE

NEW YORK

Published in the United States by Crooked Lane Books, an imprint of The Quick Brown Fox & Company LLC.

Crooked Lane Books and its logo are trademarks of The Quick Brown Fox & Company LLC.

Library of Congress Catalog-in-Publication data available upon request.

ISBN (hardcover): 978-1-68331-778-4
ISBN (ePub): 978-1-68331-779-1
ISBN (ePDF): 978-1-68331-780-7

Cover design by Melanie Sun
Book design by Jennifer Canzone

Printed in the United States.

www.crookedlanebooks.com

Crooked Lane Books
34 West 27th St., 10th Floor
New York, NY 10001

First Edition: September 2018

10 9 8 7 6 5 4 3 2 1

To my daughters and son-in-law,
Sarah, Beth, and Adam

# ONE

## Saturday Night, Mid-May

If Deputy Mattie Cobb had eaten supper at home with her K-9 partner, Robo, she wouldn't have noticed the rig parked illegally across the street from the Main Street Diner. But there it was, a charcoal gray truck and horse trailer parked parallel in front of the Watering Hole Bar and Grill, taking up more than their share of the diagonal parking spaces. A rack full of rifles filled the back window of the truck. California license plates, probably someone passing through town.

Being off duty didn't really matter in Timber Creek, Colorado. The sheriff's department was small enough that the entire staff needed to assume they were on call any time of the day or night. Besides, Mattie felt more ownership of this town than some, since it was the only place in which she could ever remember living. She'd grown up here, she'd struggled to survive here, and she now worked here to protect citizens, especially kids, from threats that lurked outside the sheltering mountains of their little community.

But this vehicle didn't pose much of a threat. As Mattie stood and stared at it, wondering if she should write a citation, one of the horses inside the trailer neighed. Four horses tied on the near side peered out, shifting their considerable weight enough to make the vehicle rock.

When Mattie'd left work, she'd agreed to meet her friend Detective Stella LoSasso for a bite to eat. Main Street consisted of only six blocks, and it was hard enough for businesses there to thrive without the sheriff's department ticketing their customers. The rig's owner had probably stopped for dinner and would be leaving soon. She decided to let it go until after she ate. If parking filled up and it became a problem, she'd deal with it then.

Inside the diner, Mattie found Stella already seated at a table near the window, her head bent over the one-page, laminated menu. The detective had taken down the ponytail she wore for work, and the slanting rays of early evening sunlight touched the highlights in her auburn hair. She glanced up and made a little grimace as Mattie sat down. "I don't know why I keep thinking I'll find something new on this thing. I have it memorized by now."

Mattie smiled her agreement. "I'll just have my usual."

Stella went back to frowning at the menu. "Burger, fries, and a vanilla shake. I swear, Mattie, I don't know how you stay in shape eating the dinner of champions as often as you do."

"Running up and down the hills with Robo every morning before work."

"Yeah, but still. It's all about nutrition, girl."

Mattie eyed the empty beer bottle in front of her friend. "And the nutritional value of your favorite beverage would be?"

The waitress approached to take their order.

Stella gave Mattie one of her too-sweet smiles, picked up her empty beer bottle, and tapped its end against the tabletop. "I'll have the chef salad. And go ahead and bring me another beer."

After Mattie ordered and the waitress left, Stella settled back in her chair. "It's been a while since we had a chance to catch up. Have you been in touch with your brother lately?"

Although Mattie didn't like to share information about her family, Stella had become a trusted friend, and Mattie felt safe with her. "We've been talking on the phone once a week for about a month now."

Stella paused while the waitress set down their drinks and then left. "And?"

"It's been okay." Her vague reply hid the trepidation she'd felt upon contacting Willie and inviting him back into her life. "We're talking about getting together some time. Maybe meet halfway between Los Angeles and here, like in Vegas. In about a month."

"Sometime in June? We're usually not too busy then. You should be able to get the time off." Stella gave her one of her penetrating looks. "How do you feel about seeing him again after all these years?"

"Nervous. I mean, it's been almost twenty-five years, you know? And our lives are so different." Truthfully, she feared Willie might say more that would dredge up memories that could haunt her for months.

"Has he ever heard from your mother?"

When Mattie was six and William eight, their father had beaten their mother badly enough for her to be hospitalized. He'd been sent to prison, only for their mother to abandon them when she was discharged from the hospital. They'd been raised in separate foster homes and had lost touch with each other until seven months ago, when Willie called out of the blue, releasing memories of abuse that Mattie had repressed for years.

Mattie reached for her shake. "He hasn't heard from our mom either, but he'd like to help me look for her. Since Willie is older, maybe he can remember something that can point us in the right direction."

Stella adopted an innocent expression as she changed the subject. "How are things between you and Cole?"

Warmth crept upward from Mattie's throat. The local veterinarian, Cole Walker, and his two daughters had become an even more important part of her life during the past month. "We . . . uh . . . we're getting along fine."

Stella suppressed a snort of laughter. "Well, that says it all. You've got a definite tell behind that poker face. Do I sense romance in the air?"

"We're taking it slow." Mattie couldn't help but smile. Thinking of Cole, Angela, and Sophie gave her heart a much-needed lift. "We're with the kids most of the time."

"And when you're not?"

Thoughts of snuggling on the couch while they talked and

good night kisses made her blush deepen. "You know, Detective, some things might not be your business."

Stella laughed full out. "Okay, Mattie. I'll let you plead the fifth."

Mattie sipped her shake, hoping to damper the heat that infused her face. Despite guarding her feelings, she'd surprised herself by falling in love with Cole. She sensed that he might feel the same, though neither of them had said the words.

Flashing lights from down the street caught Mattie's eye, and she leaned forward to watch a Timber Creek sheriff's cruiser pull up and park across the street. Her radar spiked when Deputy Garcia exited the vehicle and sprinted toward the bar. "Garcia must've been called to the Watering Hole. I'll go see if he needs backup."

Vaguely aware that Stella was speaking to the waitress, Mattie dashed out the door and headed to her SUV. She was still wearing her uniform, but she'd left her utility belt locked in her car, which held some vital peacekeeping equipment. It took mere seconds to unlock the door, strap on the belt, and zip across the street.

When she cracked open the bar door, raucous cries and shouts greeted her, and she knew she was in for it. Two burly men dressed in western shirts and jeans were pounding their fists into each other's faces while local citizens cowered against the walls. A small woman, her long black hair worn in a braid down her back, jumped onto one of the men's backs and rode him like a bronco, boxing his ears while he roared and whirled away trying to shake her off. A third big cowboy with a bushy red beard had grabbed Garcia by the shirtfront and was yelling and shaking a finger in his face.

She radioed dispatch to request help, then pulled her tactical baton from its strap and snapped it into extension, feeling it click into place.

"Sheriff's department! Halt!" she shouted as the guy with the red beard threw a punch at Garcia's face. Everyone ignored her, so she dove in and used her baton to whack Redbeard on the muscle at the back of his calf.

Redbeard grabbed his leg, giving Garcia room to twist free and get the upper hand. A roar from behind them made Mattie turn. While the one guy was still fighting with the woman, the other—a tall blond cowboy with a military buzz cut—picked up a chair and hurled it at Mattie. She ducked, and the chair whizzed by before crashing into a table.

He lowered his head and charged. She stood her ground until the last second when she dropped low to the floor, shot forward, and rapped him hard with her baton on the muscle outside of the thigh and above the knee.

During almost eight years of experience on the force, she'd found that old adage to be true: "The bigger they are, the harder they fall." This one crashed down, grabbing his injured thigh as he howled. Though Mattie hadn't seen her arrive, Stella jumped in to take over, cuffing the guy before he recovered. A quick glance told Mattie that Garcia had twisted Redbeard's arm behind his back and appeared to have him under control.

The bald man with the woman on his back yelled obscenities while he used his body weight to slam her against the wall. Air wheezed out of her lungs and her eyes glazed over. She released her grip from his neck and slid down the wall until she collapsed onto the floor. The guy bellowed and launched himself toward Mattie.

She stood her ground, intending to use the same tactic. She crouched, but before she could drop low to strike his leg, he used his head to crash into her full steam. She took the blow squarely on her chest. Gasping for air, she clutched her baton as she fell.

She hit the floor on her backside, the big guy on top of her. She drove her left fist into his Adam's apple, and he reared up, grabbing his throat and giving her those few extra inches she needed. She thwacked her baton as hard as she could on the muscle at the base of his neck. He let out a roar, his breath tainted with the smell of liquor, and pinned her to the floor.

Unable to breathe, she pushed at the guy feebly. She was seeing stars when all of a sudden he flew off her. As her vision cleared, she could see her boss, Chief Deputy Ken Brody, dragging the man away and yelling, "Cobb! Are you okay?"

She struggled to prop herself up on one elbow, filled her poor lungs with enough air to say, "Yeah," and scanned the room for Garcia. He'd gotten the better of his guy and had him in cuffs.

The bald one glared at Mattie while Brody cuffed him, arrested him for disorderly conduct and criminal mischief, and read him his rights.

As Mattie struggled to regain her feet, the guy spat at her, splattering her boots. "I'll get you, you bitch."

"Add assault in the second degree to that one's charges," Stella said, as she escorted the man she had cuffed toward the door.

After Deputy Johnson arrived and a large part of Timber Creek's entire sheriff's department had loaded the gang of cowboys, including the woman, into the backs of cruisers to drive to the station, Brody returned to where Stella and Mattie stood on the sidewalk.

"Damn, Cobb," he said in his growly voice as he approached. "If I'd known you were here kickin' butt and takin' names, I might not have hurried so fast to get here."

Mattie rubbed her sternum, where she'd taken the brunt of the head butt. "Could've used you sooner, Brody. What took you so long?"

He gave her a half smile. "Do you need medical care, Cobb?"

"Nope. I'll be okay."

He looked at Stella. "Shame. Can't make the assault charge stick."

She gave Mattie a once over. "If I took a headbutt like that, I'd be heading to the doctor's office."

"Cobb's tough." Brody started to walk away but turned back. "Where's your partner? He would've made short work of those guys."

"Home, eating."

"That's where we should all be. Damn dog's smarter than the bunch of us." Brody laughed as he headed toward his cruiser.

"Do you want me to call the Humane Society to take care of

these horses?" Mattie called to him as she gestured toward the illegally parked horse trailer.

"Nah, Garcia will handle it from here." He got into his vehicle and drove off.

Stella's face showed her concern. "You took quite a blow, Mattie. Do you feel like going back to eat?"

"I'll get it to go. I'll feel like eating later."

They stepped off the sidewalk and headed toward the diner.

"I don't know why the guy singled out *you*," Stella said, "and not Brody for arresting him."

"He was the one scrapping with the woman. Might be a macho thing."

"They'll probably all bond out by tomorrow. Watch your back until you know he's well out of town."

Mattie nodded in agreement, though she wasn't too worried about it. These things were all in a day's work. No big deal.

★

When Mattie drove home, she spied Riley Flynn sitting on the edge of the front yard by the street. She was tossing a pile of pebbles, one at a time, into Robo's empty water dish, which she'd evidently moved off the porch. Her shoulders were slumped, her long brunette hair trailing to her chest in a side braid.

Riley and her father had moved to Timber Creek only a few weeks earlier, and since then she'd been somewhat at loose ends. Making friends at the end of the school year was a challenge for anyone, but Riley appeared to be more reserved and quiet than most other fifteen-year-olds. And though Mattie had connected with her quickly, having once lived at the fringe of a high school peer group herself, the girl struggled to connect with kids her own age.

Riley perked up when Mattie drove in and parked. Her amber eyes lit and a grin bunched her lightly freckled cheeks. She was a cute girl who always seemed eager to please, and Mattie's heart had gone out to her when they'd first met at the school. But this was the first time Riley had shown up uninvited.

Riley gave a little wave as Mattie grabbed the bag that contained her meal and exited the car. "Hey, Mattie!"

Robo, Mattie's German shepherd, stood at the front window, paws on the sill, barking at them from inside.

"Hey, Riley. I'm surprised to see you here."

Riley avoided eye contact as she dumped the pebbles out of Robo's bowl and stood. "I hope you don't mind. I was out riding my bike, and I thought I'd come by to say hi to you and Robo."

"How did you know where I live?"

"Everyone knows where you live." Riley gestured toward the backyard. "You're the one with the razor wire at the top of your fence."

"Oh." The county had added the wire to the top of Robo's seven-foot-high enclosure after someone had tried to poison him during a nasty case last summer. "I suppose it does sort of stand out."

"Uh, I'll put Robo's bowl back on the porch. I guess I'd better go home now."

Mattie paused. Battered and tired, she didn't feel up to hosting a guest, but she didn't mean to act unfriendly. Word at school was that Riley's mother had died of cancer about six months earlier, and at least Mattie could make the girl feel welcome. "Have you had any dinner yet?"

"I had a sandwich before I left."

"Does your dad know where you are?"

"He's at work. He started working nights at the bar in Hightower."

As they walked toward the house, Robo popped in and out of the window to bark. Mattie could picture him beating a path from window to door as he eagerly willed it to open.

Riley put his bowl back on the porch and gave a shy smile. "That's why I moved out into the yard. He was pitching a fit to get out."

Making a decision, Mattie raised her bag of food. "Why don't you come out to the backyard and we'll watch him play while I eat my dinner? I have part of a vanilla shake here that I could offer you. Or a soda from the fridge, maybe?"

Light returned to the girl's face. "I'd love that. Robo's the best."

"Yes," Mattie said, leading the way to the door, glad that she could make both her dog and this girl happy while she did nothing more than sit on her back porch and eat. "Yes, he is."

# TWO

## Sunday Morning

Cole Walker leaned forward in the saddle as his horse, mud sucking at his hooves, lunged out of a stream swollen from spring snowmelt. He kept an eye on his two daughters riding in front of him. Sixteen-year-old Angie led their three-pony string while sitting astride Cole's roan gelding, Mountaineer, who could be trusted to stick to any trail you set him on. Nine-year-old Sophie sat atop a mount named Honey, an aged palomino mare borrowed from Cole's dad. Cole also rode one of his dad's horses, a tall, bay gelding called Duke.

The family's Doberman pinscher, Bruno, ranged off trail, often loping out front and then trotting back. Much to Sophie's disappointment, Cole had decided to leave Belle, their Bernese mountain dog, home because of a gunshot injury to her hind leg from last summer. Though her wound was nine months old and well healed, Cole thought a long trek through mountain terrain would be ill advised, since she still walked with a limp that he feared might be permanent.

He wanted to show his kids the mountain sheep that he and a crew from Colorado Parks and Wildlife were going to relocate in a few weeks. The sheep lived on Redstone Ridge in the national forest west of Timber Creek, an area still recovering from a major fire from decades earlier, and the herd had grown too big for the available food supply. Cole had signed on to help sedate and trap about half the herd so they could be moved to a range farther west near Durango.

"How ya doing, Sophie-bug?" Cole asked for the umpteenth time as they breasted the steep incline that led them out of the draw. He would be the first to admit that he'd grown overprotective of this child—his baby—since she'd been kidnapped a month ago.

"My legs are getting sore," she replied over her shoulder, her brown curls jostling as Honey made the last hump up the hill. She clutched the saddle horn.

"We're almost there, and then we'll stop for lunch. Look at how green everything is up here and how big the trees are getting. Twenty-five years ago this part of the forest was entirely black." Although the forest still lacked density, healthy evergreens topped out at about twenty feet here in the old burn area. He wanted the kids to develop an appreciation for how long it took a forest to recover.

"There's still plenty of black skeletons," Angie called back from in front. She'd worn an olive green baseball cap to protect her fair skin from the sun, and her blond ponytail swung out the open notch at the back.

"There *are* still some skeletons." Cole passed one of the hollowed out, blackened trunks, settling in his saddle as their horses climbed upward on a lesser grade.

Since talk was difficult, they rode in silence for a bit, the rocky trail winding through the evergreens, their horses' shod hooves clicking against stones. Bruno trotted beside them, occasionally loping ahead but always returning. The pecking sound from a woodpecker echoed through the still forest, a balm to the soul. Cole's back loosened as he swayed in the saddle, the sun warming his shoulders.

He wished Mattie had come with them. He'd thought she was going to say yes when he invited her, but after telling her he planned to round up a string of horses for them to ride, she'd begun to look apprehensive.

He smiled as he thought of her, a small package of dynamite with twice the power. Deputy Mattie Cobb with her intense, brown eyes and dark hair. He'd believed she wasn't afraid of anything, but he was beginning to suspect that her fearlessness didn't apply to horseback riding. In the end, she'd declined going on their trail ride, saying she needed to spend time with her foster mother on her day off.

An occasional clump of young aspen shot up toward the cloudless blue sky. Spring leaves, bright green and as yet unblemished by summer dryness, quivered at the ends of branches, their spade-like shape seeming to catch even the slightest of breezes.

"Look at the aspen leaves, girls. They're dancing."

Sophie tilted her head back and watched the leaves while she rode through the grove, and Cole watched *her* to make sure she didn't get dizzy and lose her balance. Briefly, he regretted saying anything to distract her from paying attention to her seat, but she righted herself soon enough, and he relaxed his vigilance.

When Angie topped the rise, she reined Mountaineer to the side of the trail and pulled him to a halt. "Take a look at this."

"Oh, wow!" Sophie said as she rode up beside Angie.

Cole angled Duke to the left of Sophie. In a meadow covered with bright green grass lay a carpet of red and pink blossoms. A soft breeze tossed the tiny, bright colored flowers back and forth on their stems. Heading into the wind, Bruno streaked through the foliage, his glossy black coat creating a brilliant contrast against the red flowers.

"That's fireweed," Cole said. "Sometimes it grows thick in burn areas like this. It helps hold the soil and prevents it from washing away."

"It's gorgeous," Angie said.

"Do the sheep eat it?" Sophie asked.

"They could, but I bet they prefer the grass." On the other side of the meadow, the solid cliff face and rocky spires that made up Redstone Ridge towered over the evergreen forest. Cole gazed upward, searching the rocks and boulders, and noticed movement at the top. "Look, girls."

A bighorn ram with impressive curled horns scrambled to the top of a red-colored granite promontory and stood, apparently observing the human intruders from his perch. A group of four females, part of the ram's harem, were scattered on various outcroppings below him, one with a small kid at her side.

Cole let out a quiet "huh" as the sight confirmed a thought that he'd expressed earlier to Ed Lovejoy, one of the wildlife managers. There would be ewes and babies to keep together during the relocation, and no pair should be broken up. Ed had assured him they would target younger animals to transfer and leave the pairs alone.

"Look at the baby," Sophie squealed.

Cole unsnapped the leather case holding his binoculars and fished them out, then swung his leg over his horse's rump to dismount. "Let's get off here and stretch our legs. You guys can get a better look through these field glasses."

After tying their horses to trees, they spent the next few minutes passing the glasses around, adjusting the eyepieces to the different sizes of their faces, and learning how to zoom in on the sheep. Sophie giggled with delight as she watched the tiny lamb hop from rock to boulder, while the more-reserved Angie smiled with contentment.

He couldn't tell which made the bigger splash, the big horned ram with the full curl or the tiny but sure-footed baby who could keep up with its mom despite the rocky terrain.

When Cole focused in on the ram, he noticed a fully healed, jagged scar on his right shoulder. In his mind's eye, he pictured the deadly force created when two rams collided, locking horns until one skidded off and then backing up to explode toward each other and crash heads again. He wondered how many battles this old guy had fought in his lifetime.

"Look at all the pretty red-and-pink rocks," Sophie breathed.

"There's a strain of rose quartz and red shale that runs through this ridge. That's what the ridge is named for," Cole said.

"Redstone," Sophie murmured.

It warmed his heart to see how much fun his daughters were having. It had been a tough, emotional month since Sophie had been kidnapped in April, and his family had been in recovery mode. If there were a bright side to the experience, it would be that it had drawn them closer, especially the two sisters. They seemed to appreciate one another more now.

Angie drifted into the field of flowers, picking a handful as she went. Cole watched her from the corner of his eye as he squatted near Sophie, helping her focus on the ridgeline. Things were safe enough up here in the mountains, but he kept his guard up at all times with the kids. They were no longer allowed to come home from school alone. Either he or their housekeeper, Mrs. Gibbs, had to be there to meet them at the bus stop. He'd set a rule that he needed to know where the girls were at all times; everyone had a cell phone now, Sophie included, and they were expected to check in with one another if plans changed during the day.

Their family counselor had told him he should probably lighten up a bit, but he'd be hanged if he could do it. Maybe in time.

Coming out from the tree line, Bruno bounded across the meadow, carrying a brown chunk of wood. The dog seemed to be having as much fun as the girls.

"Oops, I lost the focus," Sophie said, fiddling with the adjustment dial.

Cole reached for the glasses. "Here, let me see if I can get it back for you."

After placing the binoculars against his eyes, Cole could see that the sheep had moved away from them enough to become a blur. He concentrated on bringing back the sharp detail of the ram's head, the huge brown horns, the fathomless depths of his golden eyes.

A shriek made him snatch the glasses from his face and search out Angela, finding her about forty yards away. She was backing away from Bruno, her mouth open in horror, her hands raised.

Bruno dropped his shoulders into play position, rump still up, but then he lay down, watching Angie in confusion.

Cole rushed toward her. "What is it?"

Angie kept backing, her eyes glued to a spot between her and the dog.

"Is it a rattlesnake? Angie, stay still!" Cole ran toward his daughter, pulling his Smith & Wesson .38 Special revolver from a concealed holster under his jacket, extra protection for his daughters that he'd decided to carry today.

Hand to her face, Angie whirled and ran toward him. Holding his pistol ready at his side, he opened his free arm and caught her up against his chest. She collapsed into him.

Bruno picked up the piece of wood and began trotting toward them.

Angie yelped. "Stop him! Make him put it down."

"Bruno, down!" Why was she so upset? Angela wasn't the type of kid given to hysterics.

Bruno dropped down, looking at Cole for his next command. Cole was close enough now to see that the object the dog held in his mouth was not a chunk of wood. He spoke quietly to Angela. "What is it?"

She trembled as he held her tightly against his side. Her voice quivered. "It's a boot. Th-there's a foot inside it."

"What?"

"It's b-burned. But it looks like a foot."

For a moment, his mind couldn't process what she'd said. The fire was decades ago. There was no way a human foot could still exist without being completely decomposed.

Sophie came up beside them and latched onto Angie, looking frightened. "What's going on?"

Cole squeezed Angie and studied her face. She'd reached out to hold Sophie, but she was looking up at him as the three of them stood together in a tight little knot. "Can you take care of your sister for a minute?" he asked.

She nodded as she released him and put both arms around her sister. Cole swept a quick glance around the meadow while he approached Bruno, but saw nothing out of the ordinary.

"Bruno, drop." Bruno released what Cole could now see was a boot blackened by fire. The dog looked up at him with a panting grin. "Stay."

With his toe, Cole nudged the boot away from Bruno and set it topside up so he could peer inside. Charred flesh. And the flash of white bone. Now he could smell the stench of decomposition. Horror twisted his stomach.

"Bruno, leave it. *Komm her.*" For emphasis, Cole told Bruno to 'come' in German, the language of his original training.

The bilingual dog looked at the boot longingly, but obeyed and left it.

"Come with me." Cole gripped Angela's arm with his free hand and guided the kids back toward the horses. Angie held tightly onto Sophie, their faces pale beneath their previously rosy cheeks. He scanned the area as he rushed them toward the cover of the trees. He called Bruno back when the dog tried to split away and reclaim his prize.

Once they reached the edge of the forest, Cole turned to Angie. "I'm afraid some animal might come and take it away, so I need to bag it and take it to the sheriff's office. I've got a trash bag in the pannier. You and Sophie stay here."

Sophie started to cry softly. Although typically not susceptible to tears, his youngest had suffered some tough times, and she was clearly terrified. "What is it?" she said. "What are you guys talking about?"

Cole bent over her and drew her into a one-armed hug. "It's a burned boot, and it might be evidence that there's been some sort of a crime. We don't know, but we need to be cautious, okay? You don't need to be frightened."

"B-but Angie is." Sophie looked up at him. "You look scared, too, Dad. And you've got your gun out."

He realized that his fear for his daughters' safety might be getting the better of him, but he didn't know what he could do about it. His mind had already jumped to the worst. What if this guy had been killed? And what if the killer was still up here?

# THREE

Once again Angie led their small party through the forest, but this time Cole clutched Sophie on the saddle in front of him rather than allowing her to sit on her own mount. If they needed to run for any reason, he feared she wasn't experienced enough to control a horse and keep her seat. He'd holstered his pistol, but had taken off his jacket so that he could easily access his weapon if necessary.

Without touching the boot, he had scooped the grisly object into a garbage bag and had tied it onto Honey's saddle for transporting down the mountain. He'd thought about leading the mare, but eventually decided to let her follow the other horses, and he'd tied her reins around her neck loosely so that she could travel unencumbered. If someone came after them, he was willing to risk losing the horse.

A branch snapped behind him, making him turn and search the trees. Nothing. Now every sound felt threatening. Even the white thunderheads building in the sky seemed ominous.

"I'm hungry," Sophie murmured.

Cole remembered that she'd been the only one who hadn't seen and smelled the foot—of course she was the only one who still had an appetite. "I'll get you some food from our picnic when we get down to the truck."

After they rode away from the old burn site, the pine and spruce grew dense and tall, shutting out sunlight and sending a chill down Cole's back. *Who was this person, and how did he die?*

Angela was scanning the area as she rode, her face white and tense. Mountaineer rarely needed guidance, and he plodded down the trail through rocky footing and across streams with the sure-footedness of a mountain pony. Dirty patches of snow dotted the north side of the hill, with rivulets of pure water trickling downward. His horse splashed through another muddy stream and climbed the bank on the other side. Honey followed, wanting to stick with her herd-mate.

A crow cawed from the top of a lodgepole pine off to the right and then swooped down in front of Mountaineer, soaring along the trail before beating its wings to land in a spruce on their left. The trail wound between huge boulders, which rose up as if to block their escape. Cole cringed as he watched Angela disappear into the split, imagining some human monster jumping out to snatch her away. He nudged Duke to quicken his step through the boulders, and he released his breath when he saw her moving safely down the trail ahead of him on the other side.

The ride downhill seemed to take forever. At last they reached a spot where there was a vantage point overlooking the parking lot at the trailhead.

"Stop here for a minute," he called to Angela.

She reined in her horse and he drew up beside her. Honey edged in beside Duke and stopped, crowding near.

Although the parking lot was still over a mile away, from up here he had a clear view of it. Rolling forest stretched off to the horizon in every direction, with the tallest mountains behind him.

There were two other rigs parked in the lot beside his, rigs that hadn't been there when they'd unloaded this morning. Cole took out his binoculars and glassed the pickups and trailers, but they didn't tell him much. One was a forest-green truck pulling a long, silver, four-horse trailer, and the other a dark blue pickup with a white, two-horse trailer hitched behind it. He didn't recognize either of them. Could one or both belong to the person who dumped the body?

He put away the field glasses and made a decision. If there were newcomers on the trail, they'd be ahead, not behind.

"Angie, can you take Sophie on the saddle in front of you?"

"Sure."

He dismounted and reached toward Sophie. "Come here, Little Bit. I've got you," he said as she hesitated before allowing him to lift her from the saddle. He hefted Sophie up high so that Angela could grasp her and help settle her into their shared seat. The saddle accommodated the two skinny kids well, and Sophie would probably be more comfortable here than sharing a saddle with him.

Cole stepped back up into his saddle. "I'll take the lead now, Angie."

Reining Duke onto the trail, he noticed Honey try to take second position. "Go ahead and get right behind me, Angel. Make Honey follow us. Stay close to me."

Angela nudged Mountaineer into second place, jostling the mare back into third on the narrow trail. The docile mare accepted her position and didn't try to push forward.

"Do we know who the trailers belong to, Dad?" Angela asked, fear evident in her tone.

"I don't, sweetheart, but I'm sure everything will be okay."

He glanced behind to give the girls a reassuring smile, but saw that Sophie was nibbling her thumbnail. Not a good sign.

Whenever Cole reached a gap in the trees, he strained to scout the trail ahead. It crisscrossed the mountain at this point, traversing the steep grade in a series of switchbacks. This afforded him an occasional peek at the trail below.

Soon he saw them—two men together on horseback, heading up the trail. His body tensed. Should he leave the kids here and ride down to meet these men? Or should they stick together in case someone was coming from behind, too?

He recognized one of the horses before he recognized the rider. It was a big sorrel gelding with a wide white blaze and three white stockings. The large man who wore the broad-brimmed Stetson and sat astride the familiar gelding would be its owner, Ed Lovejoy, the local wildlife manager who was leading the mountain sheep relocation project and who was also one of Cole's clients. He breathed a sigh of relief and reined Duke over at the nearest switchback. "I know one of these guys, kids. Let's stop here and wait for them."

Ed's mouth turned up at the corners in a tight-lipped smile of recognition as he drew near, and then he spat a stream of saliva, which was darkened by the pinch of snuff that bulged beneath his bottom lip. He had unusual grey-blue eyes and a ruddy complexion that looked like he suffered from chronic sunburn despite the hat that covered his sandy hair. As he pulled his horse to a stop, Cole caught a whiff of the mint-flavored tobacco, a scent that reminded him of his dad.

"Doc Walker." Ed greeted him with barely moving lips as he spoke around the wad of chew. "You been up to check the site?"

"We have. I suppose that's where you're headed."

"That's right." Ed turned in his saddle, cocking one hip so that he could gesture toward the tall, lean man who'd pulled up behind him. "This is Tucker York from the state office in Denver. He's going to be supervising the project."

Cole tipped his head in a nod as the two of them exchanged hellos. He got an impression of keen brown eyes that assessed him from under a broad-brimmed felt hat. A man that looked to be in his fifties, Tucker York wore the standard Colorado Parks and Wildlife khaki uniform. Turning back to Ed, Cole said, "I'm hoping you can help out with a problem we've discovered up above."

Ed raised a brow.

"Our dog found some partial human remains at the site."

Now both eyebrows raised in shock. "Human remains?"

Cole nodded. "I need you to turn back and go down to the trailhead to keep everyone out until I return with the sheriff. It's a crime scene up there, and we need to stay out of it."

York spoke up. "What did you find?"

"Our dog brought us a boot with a foot inside."

He narrowed his eyes. "Did you find a body?"

"I have the kids with me. My first priority is to get them back home. Then I'll take the boot to the sheriff's office."

Both York and Ed peered around Cole, their eyes drawn to the bag tied on Honey's saddle.

"You're right," York said. "We need to secure the area. We'll go on up and take care of it."

"I think the sheriff would want you to stay clear of the area until he arrives," Cole said. "And it could be dangerous."

"We've got rifles."

Cole saw that they did, in scabbards attached to their saddles. He crossed his arms on his saddle horn and leaned forward. "It's possible the sheriff will want you to ride with us. But for now, I think it's safer to stay away until we can return with a larger party."

Ed glanced at York, and Cole knew who held the authority.

"Ed, you go down the trail and stop the public from coming in," York said. "I'll ride on up, but I won't disturb anything in the area. While I wait, I can scout the sheep and still get on the road in decent time to head back to Denver today."

So this was more about keeping his schedule than anything else, but as a Parks and Wildlife officer, this man had the authority to take over if he wanted to. Cole tried one last time. "I don't know what happened up there, but I think it's likely that the owner of this boot didn't die of natural causes. The boot's charred and burned, and I didn't see any sign of recent forest fire in the area."

Ed's ruddy complexion had flushed a deeper red, apparently torn by the conflict between his superior and his veterinarian. "I reckon we'd better do as he says, Tucker."

After giving Ed a brief study and taking into account his discomfort, York apparently made a decision. "I'll be all right. You go on down, Ed, and close the trail. Wait for the others and come up with them."

He kneed his horse and it sidled by, continuing up the trail.

Ed reined his gelding in a tight turn. With a final glance at his supervisor, he nudged his horse and started back down the trail.

Cole waved Angie forward. "You go next, and I'll follow with Honey."

The kids still looked frightened, and he worried about them. Would they be traumatized by this experience? Would they develop a fear of riding into the high country, a place he loved more than any other on earth and wanted to share with them?

He thought about his own reaction during their flight through the forest. By drawing his handgun, had he frightened them even more?

Probably. But he couldn't help it. He'd do anything to protect his children. Even so, as he descended the trail he couldn't help but feel responsible—for the whole darn mess.

# FOUR

Stiff and sore from the brawl at the bar, Mattie jogged slowly toward her foster mother's house. Since Mama T's home was only a few blocks from hers, it seemed silly to drive her car the short distance.

Despite it being her day off, she'd risen at daybreak to take Robo for a run. He didn't recognize opportunities to sleep in, but he did enjoy morning naps in a spot of sunshine, which is what she'd left him at home to do now.

Later, Rainbow, the sheriff's department dispatcher and a woman who had—against all odds—become her friend, would stop by Mattie's home to give her a weekly yoga lesson, something she'd come to enjoy. At first, the still poses had driven her batty, but she liked the moving poses and was beginning to catch on to what it meant to feel "centered." They planned to fix a light lunch together at Mattie's house.

Later still, there would be dinner at the Walker home, and she planned to go early to help the family housekeeper, Mrs. Gibbs, cook the meal. Mattie had never been handy in the kitchen, but she enjoyed conversation with Mrs. Gibbs, and she was picking up tips on how to prepare simple things.

She arrived at Mama T's tidy yard, its flower beds splashed with the bright reds, oranges, and yellows of spring tulips and dots of deep-purple hyacinths. Plaster-of-Paris chipmunks and squirrels scampered about in frozen poses that reminded Mattie of the game

Freeze Tag that she'd once played with her brother Willie. She hadn't thought of that in years.

She skirted around the side of the house and let herself into the kitchen. Mama T, a stout woman with graying black hair drawn back in a bun, greeted her with a warm hug, and soon Mattie found herself seated at the table with a bright red mug of steaming coffee in front of her. Mama stood at the stove, adding seasonings to a large pot of chili con carne, its spicy aroma teasing Mattie's taste buds.

"Where are the kids today, Mama?" she asked, referring to the bunch currently in residence for foster care.

Mama T had lived in Timber Creek for decades, but she still spoke with a thick Spanish accent. "They went for ice cream. That new place on Main Street. I forget what it's called."

"Oh yeah. I think it's called Happy Shack or something like that."

"*Si.*" Mama T bobbed her head in agreement. "Silly name for an ice cream shop."

"I heard they have old fashioned video games and stuff. They want to provide an after school hangout for the kids. Timber Creek really needs something like that."

"The games are free today." Mama T put down her spoon and closed the pot with a lid. "Get those kids hooked and then *boom!*" She threw both hands in the air. "Prices will go up!"

Mattie chuckled. "You're probably right about that."

"At least my little ones can enjoy the day today. They shook out their piggy banks for ice cream money before they left."

Mattie remembered back in the day. No one received allowance without working in Mama T's house. They earned their pennies by doing chores, and with a houseful of kids, there were always plenty of those to go around.

Mama T poured herself a cup of coffee and came to sit beside Mattie, pressing her arm with loving fingers. "So tell me. What do you hear from your brother?"

Mattie told her about her plans to meet Willie in Vegas.

"Las Vegas," Mama breathed. Mattie could tell the city heralded something magical for her foster mom. Not so much for Mattie.

"I'm not thrilled about going there, but I want to take Robo with me, and it's a lot closer than driving clear to L.A. I'll have to find a pet-friendly motel to stay in."

"When do you leave?" It was no secret how Mama T felt. The sooner Mattie and Willie could reconnect, the better.

"I have to ask for some time off, but we're talking about a month from now."

"Then sign up for the time off tomorrow. Don't you wait, or you'll miss out."

"Yes, Mama." Mattie smiled as she lifted her mug to her lips. Some things never changed. "What have you been up to lately?"

"Did I tell you Doreen is coming to see me?"

"I don't think so. Now remind me, who is Doreen?"

"She once lived at my house, like you. Only before you came here."

*Another foster child.*

"Now she's all grown up." Mama T grinned, showing the gap where she was missing a tooth. "Also like you."

"I don't think I've ever met her."

"You must come over when she's here. She'll be here on Tuesday, and I think she will stay for two days," Mama said, holding up two fingers for emphasis.

"I'll try for Tuesday or Wednesday evening then."

Mama T beamed. "That's real nice. Come for dinner."

"Thank you. I hope I can work it out." Mattie changed the subject. "I have a new friend, Mama. She's a kid I met in one of my antidrug classes at the high school, and her name's Riley. She seems to be at loose ends after school. Her father works two jobs, and he isn't home in the evenings. She stopped by my house last night and waited for me until I got home. I think she's lonely and needs something to do after school."

"Where's her mother?"

"She died about six months ago. Riley and her dad just moved to town last month. Kind of starting over."

"Poor girl."

Mattie nodded agreement. "So I was wondering—could you use her help with the kids a couple days a week? Maybe she could be like a mother's helper for you." When Mattie had lived here, Mama T had assigned a youngster to each teen, making the older ones help the younger ones get ready for school in the morning and bed at night. Though it caused resentment at times in the older group, it also helped build responsibility. "I remember you saying that your house was filled with young ones right now, and no teenagers."

Concern etched Mama's brow. "I don't have money to pay her."

"Oh, I would pay her. I always wish I could help you more, and this is one way I could do it. Besides, I think it would be good for her to be around you and the kids."

Mama T continued to frown as she thought about it.

Mattie offered further reassurance. "I'll stay in touch with you about her. If it's not working out, I'll take care of it and find something else for her to do. But she does seem like a nice kid, so I think you'd enjoy having her around."

"Can you bring her by the house tomorrow after school? Then we'll see."

"I'll try, Mama. If I can't do it tomorrow, we'll wait until Doreen leaves, so we won't disturb your visit."

"But come by to meet her."

"I will."

Mattie's cell phone beeped, signaling an incoming text. She removed it from her pocket and checked the screen. It read: Emergency Alert—Call the Sheriff's office.

"I have to call the office, and most likely I'll need to go into work." Groaning as she stood up from the table, she drained the last of her coffee, and carried the mug to the sink. "I'd better say goodbye now, but I'll call you tomorrow about bringing Riley by."

"Why are you in pain today, *mijita*?"

"Oh, I tangled with a guy I had to arrest last night. It's nothing."

Frowning with concern, Mama T followed her to the door. "Take care now," she said after giving Mattie a last hug. "*Vaya con Dios.*"

While Mattie jogged toward home, she tapped the screen on her phone to dial into the office.

Sam Corns, the weekend dispatcher, answered. "We've got a problem, Mattie."

"I figured."

"Dr. Walker found human remains up near Redstone Ridge."

Her stomach twisted. Cole had taken his kids with him on a trail ride up there today.

Sam continued. "Sheriff is getting a party together to go up. He wants you and Robo in on it."

"All right. I can get to the office in fifteen minutes."

"You've got a half hour. Dr. Walker is arranging a string of horses to carry you all up there, and he needs that much time."

Again, she felt a tug of queasiness in her midsection. She wanted nothing to do with riding a horse. "Did Dr. Walker have his kids with him?"

"He didn't say." Sam paused. "Oh yeah, the sheriff said Doc had to take his kids home before he loaded up more horses."

"I'll be in soon." Mattie ended the call, remembering next to call and cancel her yoga lesson with Rainbow.

Cole's kids were beginning to deal with the trauma of Sophie's kidnapping last month, and now this. He'd looked forward to this trail ride all week; how quickly things could go wrong. Human remains—she hoped the kids hadn't been exposed to them. She loved those kids as much as if they were her own, and they'd suffered their share of hardship this past year.

She frowned as she picked up her pace.

# FIVE

Robo's throat squeaked, making Mattie look at him in the rearview mirror. He stood behind her on his carpeted platform and yawned, his pink tongue curling, distinct against his black muzzle.

"You still tired?"

He gave her a lazy tail wave and stared out the windshield.

"Looks like you're ready to go to work."

A black German shepherd with tan markings and weighing in at one hundred pounds, Robo was a credit to his breed. He'd been her partner for a year now, and Mattie couldn't imagine being without him. Although the county had bought him for narcotics detection, he'd also proven himself worthy in patrol and search and rescue, finding people both alive and dead.

Best of all, he'd become her trusted friend.

She drove the few blocks to the sheriff's station and pulled into the lot where several cars were already parked: Sheriff McCoy's silver Jeep, Chief Deputy Ken Brody's cruiser, and Detective Stella LoSasso's personal car, a silver Honda. Mattie unloaded Robo and went inside to find them.

They were in the briefing room, clustered around a plastic cooler marked BIOHAZARD that sat on one of the tables. Although the contents inside the container would be sealed, Robo was already sniffing the air in the room and he quickly homed in on the ice chest.

"Good, we're all here." A large African American man with a

deep voice and an unflappable manner, Sheriff McCoy was quick to take charge. "How much do you know, Deputy?"

"Very little. Sam said that Cole Walker found human remains up at Redstone Ridge."

"He and his daughters went there to scout mountain sheep for a relocation project he's doing in a few weeks. When they arrived at the burn area, their Doberman found a charred boot with the remains of a foot inside."

"Skeletonized?"

"No, fresh."

Mattie cringed. Once again, she hoped the kids hadn't seen it.

McCoy gestured to the cooler on the table. "We have it on ice, ready to send to the forensic lab in Byer's County."

"Did Cole find the body?"

Stella answered. "He wanted to get his kids downhill to safety. He didn't search for a body."

Mattie stared at the ice chest. "We need to take it back up there with us."

"Why?"

"To use for a scent article, so Robo can find the rest of the body."

Her three colleagues looked at each other in silence.

Brody cleared his throat with a harsh grunt. "Makes sense."

It seemed like the chief deputy was beginning to support her suggestions for how to use her dog on the job. He'd been her worst opponent when Robo was added to the department a year ago, but he'd done a complete about-face when she'd been able to show that she was up for the job.

Stella remained skeptical. "What about contamination? This is the only evidence we have that someone died recently. We need to get its DNA into the system as soon as possible."

"Could we take a sample from it and send that over for DNA matching?" Mattie asked

Stella considered it. "I suppose so."

"Does it smell like decomp?"

"Oh yeah," Brody said.

Mattie unclipped the lid from the cooler and lifted it enough to peer inside at the evidence—a scorched boot encased in a plastic bag, lying on bags of frozen, blue gel. She glimpsed jagged bone and blackened flesh at the boot's opening.

Closing the lid, Mattie looked at Stella. "If Dr. Walker's dog brought it out of the forest, it's already been removed from any crime scene we might look for, and there's already been uncontrolled contamination. I'll keep the boot inside the chest, and I'll control any sniffing that Robo does. Since it's ripe, he won't need to get too close."

Sam Corns rapped at the door and peered inside. "Dr. Walker is here."

"Send him in," McCoy said, and then he looked at Mattie. "We'll take it with us as you suggested, Deputy."

"I'll take care of the DNA sample and be ready to go in fifteen minutes." Stella took the ice chest with her as she left the room.

Cole came through the doorway, a grim expression on his face, his eyes searching out Mattie. A warm feeling washed through her as their eyes met, even though they kept their greeting low key. Although they'd deepened their relationship over the past few weeks, they'd kept it private.

Robo jumped up, and Mattie let him go to greet Cole.

"I have five horses loaded in the trailer and ready to go anytime," he said, bending to ruffle the fur between Robo's ears.

*A horse for everyone in the group.* "I can go on foot if you need to use one as a pack animal," Mattie offered, hoping that would be the case.

Cole looked up from petting Robo and seemed to be studying her.

"We'll all go up on horseback," McCoy said. "It'll be faster. If we need to pack something out of the high country, you or Deputy Brody might have to come down on foot." He went on to explain to Cole that they were taking the ice chest with them so they could use its contents as a scent article.

Cole nodded. "I'll strap it on behind one of your saddles. I've already got tarps and short-handled spades behind mine."

"I'll take it," Brody said.

"We'll leave in fifteen minutes," McCoy said.

The others filed out of the room while Mattie and Cole held back. "Did the kids see what was inside the boot?" she asked.

Cole's expression darkened. "Bruno brought it to Angie. Sophie didn't see it."

Mattie released her breath. "Poor Angie."

"She's really shaken."

"And you?"

"I'll be all right. I'm more accustomed than the kids are to dealing with flesh and bone, though it's a sight I wish I could unsee." As they followed the others from the room, Cole continued in a low voice. "I'll put you on Mountaineer. He's sure-footed and he'll stick to the trail without you having to guide him. You'll be okay, Mattie."

She glanced up and read the concern on his face. She hated to mention that she was afraid, but she was glad that he cared. "Okay. It's just that I'm not used to riding horses, you know."

"You'll be fine. Mountaineer will take care of you." Cole pressed her forearm with a light touch of reassurance, releasing it as they passed through to the lobby. Mattie left him there to go to her office to pack the supplies she might need.

★

With Stella in the passenger seat, Mattie drove third position in their four-vehicle caravan to the trailhead. Cole led the way, finally pulling into the parking lot and drawing his trailer up alongside another rig that was already parked. A tall, beefy man, whom Mattie had known for years, got out of the cab and marched toward the sheriff's Jeep as she pulled up beside it and parked.

"I wonder who that is," Stella mused under her breath.

"Ed Lovejoy, Parks and Wildlife manager," Mattie said.

Stella exited the SUV and introduced herself to Lovejoy while

McCoy gathered his things and got out of his vehicle. Mattie went to the back of her Explorer to get Robo.

"Cole said you'd want to ride with us to the site," McCoy was saying to Lovejoy.

"That was my plan. My boss, Tucker York, is already up there, securing the area."

"I heard that, too." McCoy gestured toward Lovejoy's horse and trailer. "Go ahead and get ready. You can ride with us."

Mattie raised the hatch and Robo met her at the opening. He danced on his front paws with his mouth open in a silly grin, waiting for her to tell him he could jump down.

She took a moment to pat him and give him a hug. This dog had become her comfort zone during the past few months, and she wished she could cover the ground on foot with him as they climbed the mountain. Since she used the foothills around Timber Creek for exercise and training, both she and Robo were capable of handling the rugged terrain. She thought she could keep up with a party on horseback, but didn't want to argue about it with the sheriff.

Stella came to get her pack from the storage compartment. "I guess it's time to bite the bullet and climb onto the back of one of those beasts," she muttered, apparently unconcerned about showing her own discomfort with the situation.

They exchanged knowing looks, Mattie somehow consoled by the fact that she wasn't the only one who was afraid.

Stella gave her a wink. "At least you can make the most of it. Have that man of yours flex some muscle and make him lift you up onto your trusty steed."

Mattie made a face at her before switching her attention back to Robo and the preparation of her supplies. While they strapped packs behind saddles and drew cinches up tight and secure, Robo ranged around the parking lot sniffing everything he came across and marking truck and trailer tires. Before Mattie could psych herself up, it was time to go.

Cole helped Stella mount Honey and gave her brief instructions. When he approached Mattie, her knees felt weak, but she pasted on a game face as she turned toward Mountaineer. Cole helped her put her foot in the stirrup and before she knew it, he'd boosted her into the saddle.

He adjusted the stirrups so that her weight rested on the balls of her feet. "Keep the stirrups out here on the toe of your boot. Don't let them slip back into your arch."

She'd worn hiking boots with a heavy tread, and she could feel the stirrup hang up as Cole scraped it along the sole.

"We'll get you some riding boots with a smooth sole before your next trail ride," he said. "But you'll be fine for today."

*As if there'll be a next time*, she thought.

He brought the reins back along either side of Mountaineer's neck and tied them in a knot as he gave her an encouraging look. "When you want him to turn, just pull the reins toward the direction you want to go. Pull back when you want him to stop. For the most part, I think you can relax and enjoy the ride."

She nodded, and Cole raised his brows and smiled, trying to reassure her before turning toward his own mount. Robo bounded up, looking at her with excitement as the riders formed a line and headed toward the trailhead.

That was Robo, always ready for something new.

Once they reached the narrow trail, Brody took the lead, his Colt AR-15 rifle slung across his back. The sheriff followed him as Lovejoy, Stella, and then Mattie and Cole fell into line. Mattie clutched the saddle horn with both hands, the ends of the reins clasped between her fingers. An experienced trail horse, Mountaineer seemed to know what to do, and he followed Honey without guidance.

Mattie felt small and helpless sitting atop such a large animal, and she held herself stiff and rigid in the saddle. When the trail broadened, Cole rode up beside her. "Keep the weight of your legs balanced on the balls of your feet and let your hips relax, so that you sway with the saddle. When we reach a steep section, lean forward. Lean back slightly on the downhill."

She did her best to follow his instructions and sometime during the first half hour on the trail, her heart rate slowed to normal. Although Robo frequently darted ahead, he always came back to look for her. After a bit, he settled in line and seemed content with sticking close.

The forested foothills closed around them as they climbed, blocking their view of the ridge and diffusing what was left of the sunlight. Despite it still being early in the day, towering cumulus clouds had risen from the western horizon and boiled above them, finally opening to splash down huge cold raindrops. Brody guided his horse off the trail into the shelter of some trees, stopping so they could pull rain jackets out of their packs and put them on. Cole dismounted and hurried forward to help Mattie with hers while Ed Lovejoy turned back to help Stella.

They headed upward again while the rain continued to fall, making Mattie worry about the integrity of their crime scene. Rivulets formed everywhere as the mountainside shed the runoff, small streams rushing across the trail and down the middle, turning it slippery and treacherous. Mountaineer continued his steady plod, and when Mattie observed Lovejoy's horse brush his rider into a low pine bough that her own mount avoided, she realized what Cole meant when he said Mountaineer would take care of her.

It didn't take long for the damp cold to seep in and steal warmth from her body. If she'd been on foot, she could've maintained her body heat. She shivered as she withdrew her running gloves from her jacket pocket and pulled them on. Water resistant instead of waterproof, they offered only slight protection from the icy spring rain.

It seemed like it took forever, but when they came to a swollen streambed, Mattie saw the beginning of the old burn area on the other side. Mountaineer eased down the bank, his hooves sinking into the mud. He picked his way across the stony bed, and then lurched up the bank on the other side. By this time, Mattie had practiced leaning forward and back, and the movements seemed to come more naturally. Still, she kept both hands tightly around the saddle horn, her fingers stiff from holding on.

This region wasn't entirely new to her since she'd hiked up here years ago, but this trip felt eerie, knowing that she was headed uphill to look for human remains. Charred human remains.

New forest growth had filled in the open spaces between blackened trees, their crooked limbs twisted like bizarre dancing skeletons. Their destination was only a short distance farther up the trail, and she was glad for it. This place had begun to give her the creeps.

# SIX

When Mountaineer topped the last hill, the meadow with its carpet of red flowers took Mattie by surprise. The rainfall had let up, and sunlight warmed the scene. It seemed an odd contrast that they had arrived to search for a body in such a beautiful place.

The rose-tinted ridge rose up sharply ahead, rocky crags jabbing skyward above the ridgeline, while pine and spruce skirted its base.

"Hello," a male voice called as they broke through the tree line.

Mattie searched out the sound and saw a rider coming from the direction of the trees at the base of the ridge.

McCoy rode forward, and Cole kneed his horse around Mattie to join him. She tightened the reins to hold Mountaineer back while Stella and Lovejoy drew up beside her.

She called Robo and told him to stay. He edged forward before going into a down, pushing the boundary so that he could get a clear view of the action. He waited there, his tongue lolling in a pant, watching the newcomer.

She could hear Cole introduce Sheriff McCoy and Brody to Tucker York.

"Have you seen anything?" McCoy asked.

"Nothing out of the ordinary. I didn't do much of a search, because I thought you'd want to head that up. I just secured the area." York waved a hand toward the evergreens at the base of the ridge. "I moved over there so that I could watch both the meadow and the sheep. There's no sign of a body where I've been."

"How about a recent fire?"

"Not even a campfire. I didn't see any signs of human activity in that direction."

"I appreciate that you didn't disturb the meadow," McCoy said. "We don't know what we're going to find out there."

"It's wet. I figured you didn't want me tracking it up. And my main concern was to scout the sheep. I have an appointment back in Denver tonight and didn't want to delay my return."

"Well, I'm glad you didn't run into any trouble, coming up by yourself," McCoy said. "You're free to go whenever you need to."

"Then I'll be leaving after I finalize some plans with Ed for our project." York turned away to consult with Lovejoy.

Mattie's sore legs told her she'd spent more than enough time in the saddle. She knew that she should dismount on the left side, so after securing the knotted reins at her saddle horn, she swung her right leg over Mountaineer's rump and stretched it way down, reaching for the ground.

Cole dismounted and led his horse back to join her.

"We might as well get ready to search," Mattie said, feeling unsteady as she straightened her knees.

"Walk around and stretch," Cole said. "It'll help with the soreness. That'll get better with more experience."

Mattie followed his suggestion while she scanned the blood-red meadow. "Where did Bruno come from when he brought the boot?"

Cole pointed off to the left. "He came from the far end over there. I think he might have entered the forest, but I don't know for sure. I thought he was bringing back a chunk of wood."

She began to untie her pack from behind her saddle.

"I'll tie the horses here in these trees." Cole moved to help her, his closeness sending a rush of warmth to her face. She hoped the others wouldn't notice, and if they did, that they would think the cool air had reddened her cheeks.

Brody came up, leading his horse. "Where do you want to start the search?" he asked Mattie.

She gestured toward the left of the field. "The remains came from that direction, but we don't know how far out. So here's as good a place to start as any."

Brody began untying the ice chest from behind his saddle.

"Robo's never done something like this before, Brody. We've always been tracking someone we thought was still alive and used clothing for a scent article. I've never asked him to find a body based on decomposed remains."

Brody acknowledged her concern with a nod as he worked out the knots in the leather ties. "I expect he'll know what to do. It's close enough."

The rain had most likely affected the scent. A trail from a living human could have been washed away, but the odor of an exposed body might well be enhanced. "I plan to give him the scent and then cast him out into the meadow. We'll let him search the area without putting too much pressure on him. If he doesn't find anything out here, I'll take him into the woods."

"Sounds like a plan."

By this time McCoy and Stella had dismounted and tied their horses with the others. Cole had placed Mattie's pack on the ground nearby.

McCoy was scanning the meadow with a pair of binoculars. "When do you want to start the search, Deputy?"

Mattie slipped off her rain jacket, turning in a partial circle as she tested the feel of the air on her face. "There's hardly any breeze, so now's a good time to start. I want to give Robo a chance to search with only me and Brody following him. Later, the rest of you can go in and do a thorough visual search."

"All right." McCoy swept the lenses toward the left, adjusting them to zoom in on the tree line.

Mattie opened her pack, removed Robo's collapsible bowl, and filled it with water from her own drinking supply. He'd drunk freely from streams on the way up, but she wanted him to moisten his mucus membranes now to enhance his scenting ability. Besides, it was a valuable part of their routine.

After he lapped at the liquid, she took off his collar and put on his tracking harness, his signal that it was time to search. Robo assumed his all-business face, adopting a serious attitude for the first time on this outing instead of acting like he was along for a picnic.

"Robo, heel." Taking the ice chest with her, she led him a short distance from the rest of the group and began to tousle his fur and pat his sides. She used the high-pitched chatter meant to rev up his prey drive. "Robo, are you ready to work? Are you? Let's find something."

He waved his tail and looked into her eyes, telling her he was ready to go.

Mattie bent to open the container about two inches, holding the lid firmly so that Robo couldn't push his nose all the way in. "Here Robo. Scent this."

The odor of rotting flesh wafted out, attracting Robo like a fly to a carcass. He poked his nose into the open crack as far as Mattie would allow. Then she gently closed the lid, forcing him to withdraw.

She secured the lid on the ice chest and straightened. Raising her hand above her head, she said Robo's name to draw his attention. After he lifted his eyes to her face, she flung her arm out in a gesture toward the meadow, at the same time telling him, "Search."

Robo dashed into the meadow with its red flowers. She swallowed the tension that had tightened her throat and jogged after him, Brody following behind.

The grass was slick from the rain, and the ground beneath it uneven and muddy. Very soon, she realized she wouldn't be able to keep up with Robo on this type of terrain. Placing her feet carefully on tufts of grass rather than sinking into the sometimes swampy muck in between, she did her best to keep up with her swift-footed dog. She'd take a rocky hillside over this any day.

With his larger feet and heavier build, Brody struggled even more than she did. They fell into a strung-out line as they crossed the meadow, Robo out front and Brody bringing up the rear. Robo quartered the area back and forth while his humans stayed on a straight line down the middle. Mattie kept her eyes on her footing, glancing up frequently to see if Robo had hit upon something.

Most of the time Robo held his head up, nose in the air, telling her that he was air-scenting rather than following a ground-track. Occasionally he put his nose down to sniff, boosting her heart rate as she wondered if he'd found a corpse or other remains, but then he would raise his head and dash forward, continuing in a general trajectory toward the forest at the meadow's far edge.

He reached the tree line when Mattie was about halfway across. She didn't want him to disappear within the woods before she got there, so she called to him. "Robo, wait!"

He paused at the forest's edge, watching her pick her way forward.

"Good boy," she said as she neared. Then, not wanting to slow his momentum more than necessary, she once again sent him on. "Go ahead. Search."

Robo entered the forest with her not far behind. She could still see him as he slipped through the sparse pine, but lost sight of him where the evergreens grew dense. When the footing became less soggy, she pushed herself into a sprint.

Sunlight dimmed as the forest closed around her. Mattie pressed forward, searching for Robo as her eyes adjusted to less light. She spotted him about thirty yards ahead following a faint trail, his nose in the air. She raced after him, using the firmer footing to catch up.

A Steller's jay, its blue feathers iridescent in the filtered sunlight, flashed ahead and then landed high in a pine to scold her, its chirrup echoing in the stillness.

*Too still?* When they'd reached the meadow, they'd ridden out of the sounds of the forest—the murmuring twitter of birds and jabber of squirrels. Were the animals and birds aware of forbidden human activity back in here? Did they avoid this area?

Her feet thumping on the trail, Mattie closed the distance from Robo to about twenty feet. Her proximity did nothing to slow his pace—in fact, he held his head high and broke into a lope, his gaze straight ahead, his attitude purposeful.

The trail rose up and dipped back down, winding around boulders, current bushes, and mountain juniper. She heard Brody's footsteps at her back and saw that Robo remained intent on what lay ahead. They rounded a curve where a stream rushed beside the trail, and Robo veered to cross it. He apparently thought nothing of splashing through the clear water. Mattie slowed to pick her way on stones where she could, but when her foot slipped, cold water filled her boot.

She hoped Robo knew what he was doing and wasn't leading them on a wild-goose chase. She pounded after him, one foot squishy inside her wet sock.

Robo breeched a short rise and shot into a small clearing that contained a circle of rocks surrounding a campfire. The brook burbled behind her while he paused to sniff the blackened ash inside the fire ring. The pit was soggy and wet, no warm coals left to indicate a recent fire.

He sat and looked at her, his signal that he'd found something. And in this case, it appeared to be something outside of the environmental norm—one of Robo's basic search skills, well practiced and highly accurate.

Her hopes fell. Had he been chasing the odor of ashes instead of decomp? Although disappointed, she followed him into the clearing, bent over and patted his side, telling him what a good boy he was. She needed to reinforce what he'd been trained to do, not be discouraged over his failure to perform a brand-new task.

Looking up into Mattie's eyes and waving his tail, Robo accepted his praise and then stood and faced the forest, ears pricked.

"What else has he got?" Brody said, arriving at the campsite behind her.

Both of them had worked around Robo enough to know what his posture meant. Full alert. He'd hit on the scent she'd given him earlier.

"Let's see," Mattie murmured. And then, in an excited voice

meant to encourage him, she said to Robo, "Go ahead, buddy. Search!"

Robo launched himself away from the stone-lined fire ring and dashed into the woods beyond the campsite. Mattie stayed close on his heels and Brody kept a short distance behind. He always covered her back, and she'd come to count on him.

She followed her dog through the trees for another fifty yards, the odor thickening as she traveled. The air grew heavy with the stink of rotting flesh. Robo picked up speed, dashing down into a hollow and then slowing. He pinned his ears, slinking up to a mound of dirt and debris.

Mattie raced to catch up. By the time she reached him, Robo had sat down and was waiting for her. His mouth opened in a pant, and he wore a smug expression as though quite satisfied with himself.

She squatted beside him and hugged him close, giving him lots of praise and pats for doing such a remarkable job. Since the stench was so bad, she wondered if this had been his destination all along, and he'd shown her the fire ring just for kicks.

"Here's the big prize," she said to Brody.

A shallow grave that had been ravaged by predators lay before them, putting on a partial display of its contents. Mattie's stomach clenched as she took in the sight. The upper body of a burned corpse had been exposed, its arms bent like those of a boxer, its wrists flexed, its fingers curled into blackened claws. Roasted flesh had been harvested from the bone by the animals that had dug into the gravesite, and the face had been uncovered enough that Mattie could see the disfigured lower half—its jaw thrust open by its charred, protruding tongue.

In all her years of law enforcement, it was the worst thing Mattie had ever seen. She controlled her need to retch and scanned the lower half of the grave.

One leg was exposed, foot and boot missing. She forced herself to think analytically. Could Bruno have done this damage when he'd found the body? No, this couldn't have been his handiwork. A pack of coyotes or foxes must have dug up the grave, one of them had dragged away the boot, and Bruno had merely found it.

Charred pieces of wood were scattered about and there'd been enough digging to see that the body had been buried inside another fire pit—this one huge.

"A burning pit," Brody said, scanning the area around them. "For getting rid of a body. Plenty of wood for fuel, but not enough heat to do the job."

Mattie struggled to remain as detached as Brody. Who was this poor man? At least she thought it was a man. What kind of a horrible death had he faced? Who was his family, and had they reported him missing? "Why bury him way up here?"

Brody shrugged. "Slim chance of being interrupted. Besides, he was probably killed up here."

She forced her eyes away from the desecrated corpse. "We need to preserve this scene the best we can. This one's going to get complicated."

Brody straightened, thrusting his thumbs under his utility belt. "That's for damn sure."

# SEVEN

Brody left to bring back the others while Mattie remained at the gravesite. She squatted beside Robo as he nosed the pocket in her utility belt that held his tennis ball. He didn't seem to be depressed that he'd found a dead person. Since he'd tracked the odor of decomp this time, rather than a scent article from a living person, perhaps he'd known what he would find.

When Robo successfully completed a mission, he expected playtime, his reward at the end of the search game. Mattie scanned the area, trying to decide what to do. She couldn't play with him here and risk destroying prints or other evidence. She wrapped an arm around him and hugged him close, putting her cheek against his. She told him what a good job he'd done and offered a treat. Looking expectant, he backed away, shifting his eyes from the pocket that contained his ball to her face.

Her heart went out to him, and she decided to distract him with work, perhaps the only thing he loved more than play. "We're not done yet. We've got to go back to work."

She took a short leash from her utility belt and attached it to the dead ring on his collar. She intended to do a grid search to see if she could find anything outside the environmental norm, anything the killer might've left behind.

Mattie stood, asking Robo to sit at heel so that he would settle down. In her mind, she laid out a grid of the area in front of her and then raised her face to determine the direction of the breeze. The odor of decomposing flesh filled her nostrils.

The forest remained silent.

A chill lifted the hair on her neck, and she scanned the area. New forest growth blocked her visibility. Fresh evergreens of all heights grew scattered among the blackened husks of trees burned long ago. Brush, deadfall, groves of aspen with their bright green leaves hanging motionless. Granite boulders, huge towering monoliths, and rocky outcroppings. Other than the gravesite, she could see nothing but normal mountain terrain.

She glanced at Robo. His hackles remained flat. Her dog hadn't sensed anything, so it could be her imagination getting the best of her. She glanced at the violated grave and saw the raised arms, their joints contracted by the fire, and the charred fists. Who was this victim? What happened to him?

She shook off her hinky feeling and focused back on the task at hand. Bending forward, she hugged Robo against her leg, patted him briskly, and while she led him to the right side of the grid she intended to walk, she began the chatter that told him it was time to get to work. Then she gave him his command for evidence detection: "Seek!"

With Robo's nose and Mattie's eyes on the ground, they started the painstaking task of walking a grid, searching about two feet of space at a time, working in strips back and forth between the gravesite and the brook. She marked faint horseshoe prints and boot prints with a short spike topped with orange flagging tape. Though disappointed that the rainfall had crumbled the imprints' edges so they were no longer clear and sharp, she could tell they were made by large-sized cowboy boots, not a work boot like the one found on the body.

They were finishing up when Mattie heard the clack of steel horseshoes against rock, a signal that the others were approaching. There was still a large area around the gravesite to search, but at least she'd completed the important part where their group would be walking back and forth. The rest could wait.

Brody and the others must have tied the horses, because they came in on foot. She told Robo to sit beside her and turned to watch them pick their way across the brook on large stepping-stones that Brody had placed to fill in the gaps.

She called a warning. "I've marked some prints here that we need to preserve, although none of them are very good."

Her gaze connected with Cole's, and they checked in with each other silently. He seemed to be holding up all right. On the other hand, some retching noises escaped from Ed Lovejoy's throat that didn't bode well.

Brody reacted at once. "If you're gonna puke, get back on the other side of the creek. Now!"

Ed scurried across the water, holding a hand over his mouth. He disappeared into some bushes down the trail, and heaving noises emanated from the spot.

Stella and McCoy approached the gravesite while Cole kept his distance. Stella leaned forward and McCoy squatted down next to the body, both taking a closer look.

"We're going to need a team to excavate this body," Stella said. "Maybe a forensic anthropologist, or some kind of specialist in managing burned remains."

"I'll call in the CBI," McCoy said, referring to the Colorado Bureau of Investigation.

"That's the way to go." Stella made eye contact with Mattie. "What do you still need to do?"

"Search the area. See if Robo hits on anything." Her dog had been known to find cigarette butts and bullet casings that eventually helped solve cases in the past, small things that a human eye might overlook.

"All right." Stella turned to Cole. "Dr. Walker, let's get the tarp you brought and cover this body."

Cole nodded and left to go back to the horses.

"We'll need an overnight watch," Stella said. "Chances are it could be tomorrow before we can get someone from the CBI up here."

"I'll stand guard," Brody said.

Mattie recalled the eerie feeling this site gave her and hated to leave Brody up here alone. "I'll stay, too."

Brody shook his head. "Not necessary."

McCoy stood. "I'll activate the sheriff's posse to organize horses to transport people and their supplies up to this area. We should be able to get tents, food, and whatever you need here by later this afternoon. Deputy Brody, you'll be in charge of securing this site and supervising the team I send up."

"All right."

"I'll assign several posse members to stay with you until we can get the investigation team up here." McCoy paused, obviously still thinking. "Deputy Cobb, you'll conduct the search around the area now before everyone else comes in. Once you finish, I want you to go back to town. You and Detective LoSasso can escort the investigative team up here whenever they arrive."

His plan made sense. Many members of the sheriff's posse were crack shots with rifles. Brody would be safe with them backing him up here at the site.

Stella spoke up. "We need to get down to telephones soon."

"You and I will go down as soon as we get this site secure," McCoy said.

By this time, Cole had returned, carrying a tarp, two shovels, rope, and a hatchet.

"You can set those things right here." Mattie indicated an area that she and Robo had cleared near the gravesite.

"I'll cut some stakes," Brody said, picking up the hatchet and going toward some deadfall to find suitable branches.

Cole began to unwrap a large sheet of green plastic. "This is new tarp, Sheriff. Never been used."

"Perfect." Sheriff McCoy moved to help him unfold the tarp without letting it touch the ground.

Mattie and Stella each took an end and the four of them stretched and lowered it, stepping carefully to avoid debris around the grave. Mattie felt relieved to have the charred remains covered and hoped the tarp would help contain the odor. Even a little bit would help.

Brody brought over several wooden stakes and joined Cole and the sheriff while they attached short lengths of rope to the tarp's corners. They anchored it to the ground by tamping in the stakes with the blunt side of the hatchet's head.

McCoy studied the gravesite and evidently decided all was in order. "Detective LoSasso and I need to leave. Cole, can you stay and go down with Deputy Cobb when she finishes?"

"Sure."

"What should we do with the horses when we get to the parking lot?"

"Tie them to the trailer. I'll take care of them when we get back," Cole said. "Could one of you call my family and tell them I'll be late getting home?"

"I'll take care of it," McCoy said.

Stella caught Mattie's eye and tilted her head, signaling that she wanted to talk privately. Mattie followed her, fording the stream by stepping on the large stones, while Robo splashed through the water and gamboled beside her. He still had his eye on that tennis ball pocket, and she knew she couldn't put him off much longer.

"I'm going to take the boot back with me and get it sent to the lab," Stella said. "Okay with you?"

"I guess we're done with it now."

"Do you need anything before we leave?"

"I've got everything I might need in my pack."

"Cole tied it back on your horse." The horses were in sight now and Mattie could see her pack tied behind Mountaineer's saddle. Ed Lovejoy leaned on a boulder, waiting, and he raised one hand in greeting when he spotted them.

"Are you going to be all right on that horse going down?" Stella asked.

"I can handle it. You?"

Stella shrugged. "Piece a cake. You'll check in at the station when you get back?"

"I'll call on my way and stop in as soon as I get to town."

"Good." Stella studied her for a few beats. "Take care going through these trees when you search. Make sure someone stays with you. This place makes my skin crawl."

Mattie nodded, glad she wasn't the only one. "Will do."

The party of three mounted up and left while Mattie untied her pack. Slinging it over one shoulder, she headed back toward the gravesite. Robo darted in front of her, whirling to face her and then trotting sideways.

She could deny him no longer. Setting aside her determination to get the job done, she put down her pack and removed his ball from her utility belt. Finding a relatively flat place and utilizing the space on the trail, she tossed Robo's ball out about twenty feet. He dashed forward and pounced on it, looking ecstatic as he brought it back, clutching the neon-yellow ball between his sharp teeth.

She tried to forget the grisly reason they were here so she could give Robo his due. After all, this was his version of a coffee break.

# EIGHT

Even though Mattie was an expert at hiding her feelings, Cole could still read her anxiety. She scanned the area constantly and jumped at the slightest sound. Something was bothering her. The grotesque corpse certainly qualified as enough to disturb anyone, but he could tell there was something more that had her on edge.

After Cole finished a search of the upper trail near the stream, he stood watch at the gravesite while Mattie and Brody combed the area for further evidence. They'd been at it for hours and hadn't yet come up with anything. He glimpsed Robo running through some willows off to his left and then saw Mattie following close behind. She looked tired, her brow etched with a frown.

She wouldn't like it, but he couldn't help but worry about her. A few months ago, she'd withdrawn from him and his kids. He didn't know the details, but she'd told him that she was working with a counselor on issues from her past and she needed a little space. She was a hard woman to read, and he was trying to respect her need for privacy by not pushing too hard. He didn't want to spook her and make her shy away from him again.

Since Sophie's kidnapping, Mattie seemed most comfortable spending time with the kids and him at their house. She accepted his casual embrace and even his kisses, but she avoided talking about their relationship. He could tell her past still haunted her.

Mattie turned away and directed Robo back out from the gravesite, with Brody trailing behind. It looked like she was making giant loops, giving her dog freedom to run and sniff wherever his nose would take him. By now they'd almost completed a circle around the gravesite, searching everyplace the rugged terrain would allow. The brook that separated the crime scene from the trail flowed toward the south, spilling over a sharp drop-off into a steep-sided canyon that defied penetration, but it appeared they were combing through the rest of the area.

Last fall, Mattie had told him that her father had been an alcoholic, and he'd frequently smacked his family around when he drank. One night the abuse had gone too far, and six-year-old Mattie had called the police. Cole winced when he imagined such a thing happening to a little kid, but he believed it said something about Mattie's fortitude, even as a child.

Mattie's father had been killed while serving time in prison—Cole's vengeful side couldn't help but rejoice a little bit about that—but she'd never heard from her mother again, and that seemed to be the root from which her pain stemmed.

Lately, her pain had become his, because he'd found himself falling in love with her, and whatever affected her affected him as well.

Cole spotted her again, approaching through the trees. This time she kept coming and made eye contact, so he put his thoughts about her past away. She gave him a shrug, telling him she'd found nothing.

Brody materialized through the thick pine soon after and followed her and Robo into the clearing. He unslung his rifle from his back and carried it in his hands the last distance.

"That was damn disappointing," Brody said. Cole had grown used to the man cutting right to the chase, his words often sharpened with a sarcastic edge.

Mattie nodded her agreement, her face showing her fatigue. Knowing that she battled insomnia most of the time, Cole wondered if she'd been able to sleep last night. He was glad the sheriff had told her to return to town instead of spending the night with a corpse.

Cole checked the time. "It's about four o'clock. I expect some-one will be arriving with supplies soon."

"You two might as well start back down the mountain," Brody said. "I can take it from here."

A shadow of concern flickered across Mattie's face, Cole catch-ing it before it disappeared. "I need to play with Robo again," she said. "Even though he didn't find anything, he still worked hard and needs his reward."

Brody shrugged. "Do what you need to, and then you can go."

Mattie started to leave the gravesite, but turned back to face Brody. "I think we need to do one more search between here and the stone ring of the campfire. And I want Robo to sweep the sides of the trail, just in case he can find something in the foliage."

"Are you trying to delay so you don't leave me here alone?" Brody asked, his brow furrowed with a scowl.

Mattie looked at him. "You wouldn't leave me without backup."

"I did once, remember?"

Brody must've been talking about last fall, when he'd left Mat-tie guarding a gravesite while he went down the mountain to orga-nize an investigative team. Cole took a step back. This was between the two of them, none of his business.

"That was different. You had to," Mattie said. "But I've got this strange feeling, Brody, like we're being watched. I'm not going to leave until backup arrives."

Brody stared at her with that measuring look he tended to give people.

Mattie turned away, leaving no space for argument. As she departed, she spoke over her shoulder. "I'm going to play with Robo, and then we'll finish a sweep of the trail. By then, someone will have arrived with supplies."

Brody shot a glance at Cole. "She's always been stubborn like that," he grumbled. "But you can't argue with protocol, and it's best to keep two people together if possible. We're taking over your whole day."

"Don't worry about me, Ken. I'm prepared to stay up here as long as you need me."

"Appreciate it." Brody picked up his rifle, shouldered it, and put his eye to the scope. He raised it high and used the telescopic lens to scan the ridge and crags surrounding the area. "What do you think about eyes watching us out there?"

"Hard to say. I haven't felt it, but I wouldn't discount it either. It might not necessarily be a human. Maybe an animal . . . a cougar or another predator."

"The more Cobb works with that dog, the more she seems to sense things. You got a set of binoculars?"

"I do. I'll go get them."

Cole crossed the stepping-stones and headed downhill on the trail. The horses were tethered fifty yards away and about halfway there, he found Mattie and Robo. The large dog was scampering after the tennis ball like a puppy, taking it back to Mattie with a jaunty wave of his tail.

"I'm headed to the horses to get binoculars. You want me to bring you anything?"

She was opening her mouth to answer when a sharp crack echoed from a distance, coming from the direction of the meadow. Mattie whirled to look, but forest and slopes hid the meadow and the lower part of Redstone Ridge from view. "Rifle shot?"

"Sounds like it."

Brody came running down the trail behind them, holding his rifle ready. "You two okay?"

"It came from farther away." Mattie pointed toward Redstone Ridge. "From over there, I think."

They took off toward the horses, Mattie and Robo outdistancing Cole and Brody. Handler and dog didn't ease up when they reached the horses, but kept running down the trail toward the meadow. Cole knew he couldn't keep up on foot, so he snatched the ends of Duke's reins and jerked the slipknot free from the branch they'd been tied to. He swung into the saddle with one smooth vault.

Brody opted to go horseback as well, slinging his rifle onto his back and mounting up quickly. They headed after Mattie.

Cole nudged Duke into a fast trot, cantering when the rocky trail allowed. As the trail dipped and rose, circling around boulders, trees, and other obstacles, he caught glimpses of Mattie ahead. They were catching up to her.

"Cobb, wait up," Brody shouted when they drew close enough for her to hear.

She slowed and looked behind her. Robo dashed on ahead.

"Don't enter the meadow alone," Brody called.

"I won't," she yelled back before turning and following Robo.

With his heartbeat thudding at his throat, Cole hoped she would slow down and stay back, but he knew she wouldn't. It wasn't in her nature. K-9 handlers were injured on the job at a higher percentage than regular officers. The very nature of their work—following their partners out front while they chased the bad guys—made them particularly vulnerable to ambush and sniper shots. He hated that about her job.

The trees thinned and when they came to the edge of the meadow, Mattie and Robo were waiting.

"See anything?" Brody said as they came to a stop.

Mattie was scanning the tree line on the other side of the large, empty meadow. "Not yet."

Cole removed his binoculars from their pouch and focused in on the ridge. He scanned back and forth, noting the sheep had all disappeared. A flash of scarlet on a patch of green shale caught his eye.

He homed in on the bright color and found its source. A sheep carcass, lying in a heap, halfway down the slope. Fresh kill. The carcass bore a scar on its shoulder that Cole recognized.

He handed the binoculars to Brody. "Dead mountain sheep, halfway up the ridge at two o'clock. It looks like the old ram with the full curl that I saw this morning."

Brody passed the binoculars to Mattie, and she focused on the dead ram. "I might be able to climb up to where it is. Maybe Robo could get a scent of the person who killed it and follow."

Brody wore a grim expression. "Not within our purview. The gravesite is our top priority. Let Ed Lovejoy handle this when he comes back."

Mattie gave the binoculars to Cole and looked at Brody. "Strange coincidence. You have to wonder if this shooter had something to do with our dead guy back there."

Cole zoomed in on the carcass again. Shale and slide rock littered the area below it, creating hazardous footing. A more suitable pathway lay farther below, and as he followed it downward with the lenses, he figured the shooter could have used it to descend from the cliff face and disappear into the forest. He told the others what he was thinking. "We might be able to pick up a scent on that trail."

"I doubt if we can climb that shale to get to the ram, but if we go up partway, we might be able to see where the shooter is, or at least where he's headed," Mattie said.

Brody thought about it. "All right, see what you can find. One of us needs to go back to the gravesite and make sure this isn't some ruse to lead us away from it."

"I'll go with Mattie," Cole said. "You can keep watch."

Brody nodded.

"Robo, heel." Mattie jogged off with Robo at heel, skirting the edge of the meadow, avoiding the soggy middle.

Cole followed, keeping Duke at a trot in order to stay up with them. It took the better part of a quarter hour to make it to the other side. Mattie led them to the grove of pine where Tucker York had been earlier. Cole followed her to the base of the rocky, steep slope and dismounted, taking his binoculars with him.

"Let's climb here." Mattie headed uphill with Robo, leaving Cole to keep up as best he could. His slick soled cowboy boots were ill designed for this activity, while the rugged boots on Mattie's feet that concerned him earlier now gave her an edge.

By the time they'd worked their way up about a hundred yards, he was drenched with sweat and puffing hard. Relieved, he saw that Mattie had stopped, and as he climbed toward her, he could hear her heaving for air, too.

She leaned against a pile of boulders, using it to brace herself against the slope's steep angle. At this vantage point, she held one hand above her eyes, shielding them from the penetrating angle of the lowering sun's glare, and scanned the meadow and forest below. Cole handed her the binoculars.

"Thanks," she said, raising them to her eyes. She adjusted the focus and continued scanning the area. Cole searched with bare eyes but turned to watch her face when he heard her breath catch. She caught her lower lip between her teeth as she focused and rescanned, the binoculars trained in a direction that appeared to be the meadow.

"Take a look, Cole," she said, handing him the glasses. "The far edge of the meadow, about one o'clock. What do you see?"

He expected to see a human and was surprised that she was directing him back toward the area from which they'd come. Had they missed something when they'd rushed through there a half hour ago?

He swept the edge of the meadow, focusing on the ground. And then he saw it—the pattern she must be asking him to confirm. "Ovals at the edge of the trees. Depressions in the soil filled with darker grass. Is that what you see?"

She nodded, and her face was grim. "What does that make you think of?"

"Something buried. Other graves?"

"Let's take note of where the irregularities are and get a closer look when we go down." She scanned the area between the dead ram and their position. "I don't think the shooter came up this far. We would have spotted him before he could get down."

"Maybe he took a shot from the pine down below."

She absently rubbed Robo's ears while he leaned against her. "Let's go back, and I'll see if Robo can pick up a scent."

Cole focused the binoculars on the ram and then swept them

upward toward the crags where he'd seen the sheep earlier. At this shorter distance, he thought he could see a trail leading away from the ledge. "I think the guy could have been on top when he shot that ram."

Mattie took the binoculars and focused on the cliff where Cole was pointing.

"I think he could have come over from the back side of the ridge. And escaped that way, too," Cole said.

"What's on the other side?"

"Nothing but wilderness. Lots of game trails. It's easier to get up on top from that side rather than trying to climb up this cliff face here."

"How long would it take for us to get around to the back side?"

"At least a couple hours. We'd have to ride down to the fork in the trail and go around. And we're almost out of daylight."

Mattie frowned with disappointment. "I'll see if Robo can pick up a scent down at the base of the ridge, but I think you're right about our shooter being up on top."

"I'll contact Ed Lovejoy about this when we get back to town," Cole said, pausing to think. "If I can come back up tomorrow, I'll ride to the backside of the ridge and try to get to that ram so I can post him. See if I can retrieve a slug from his carcass. I'm not sure how much help that will be, but it's the best I can do for the poor fella now."

# NINE

Mattie was tired enough that she felt grateful to have the gentle giant, Mountaineer, carry her down the trail. Four posse members had arrived, all rigged out for the night, which eased her mind about leaving Brody at the gravesite.

There'd been nothing to see on the other side of the meadow except for a few ground depressions, which Cole thought might have been made by elk bedding down. If she hadn't viewed the area from up above, she wouldn't have even noticed them. Still, she couldn't dismiss them and thought they warranted further investigation when the team arrived to excavate the gravesite.

She and Cole rode home in shadow. The sun set early behind the mountain peaks in the high country, but its subdued light still spread throughout the sky. The chill evening breeze lifted her jacket, generating a shiver, and she released one hand from the saddle horn to tug it closed.

Cole rode ahead. When they neared the bottom part of the trail and the steepness of the grade lessened, he turned, balancing halfway in the saddle on one hip. "Come over and grab a bite to eat at our house. The kids were hoping to see you."

It would be good to visit with the girls, and see how they were doing after their terrible experience this morning. "Do you think it's okay without asking Mrs. Gibbs first? I mean, she's the one doing the cooking."

"She was expecting you to come before all this happened.

Besides, you should know she doesn't care when you show up. She's always glad to see you."

"All right, but I have to go home and clean up first."

*And get rid of the stench of death.*

"Sounds good. I have to do the same thing."

With Cole riding sideways, they gazed at each other a moment. "I worried about you today, Mattie," he said. "It's made me realize how dangerous your work is."

His words surprised her. "I wasn't in any danger today. Not real danger anyway."

"The threat is still there . . . in just about everything you and Robo do."

"It's the nature of the job. But maybe no more so than when you work on these big horses."

Cole looked skeptical. "Can't recall a horse ever taking a shot at me."

"You know what I mean."

He shook his head, giving her a look as he turned in the saddle, returning to his seat while his horse started down a rough patch on the trail. As they approached the trailhead and civilization, her cell phone came alive in her pocket, signaling voicemails and texts. Her messages would have to wait until she was sitting inside the safety of her SUV, because there was no way she could free up her hands to check them now.

Cole didn't seem to have that problem. He'd fished his phone from his pocket and checked messages while he rode. "Here's a text from Mrs. Gibbs," he said, turning his head to speak over his shoulder. "'Tell Miss Mattie to come to dinner when she gets down from the mountain. We have plenty of food.' There, that takes care of that."

"It does."

Mrs. Gibbs was a gem, an Irish lady in her sixties who loved Cole's daughters, cooking, and—believe it or not—house cleaning. As the Walkers' housekeeper, she seemed to have taken over the much-needed role of mothering Sophie and Angela without overstepping boundaries set by their father, and much to Mattie's surprise, Mrs. Gibbs even seemed to be extending that mothering role to include her.

And it felt good.

They reached the end of the trail and rode into the parking lot, Cole leading her toward his trailer where Stella and the sheriff had tied their horses.

Cole dismounted and hurried to help Mattie. After she slipped from the saddle, he turned her so that she was facing him, and he held her close. "I know you're perfectly capable of handling yourself on the job," he said. "I worry about you because I care."

Mattie melted into the warmth of his embrace, savoring it. He'd begun to show that he cared in many ways—the depth of his gaze, his touch, low-toned quips meant only for her that made her laugh. She could feel herself beginning to respond as she opened to the idea of loving him, and she desperately wanted to trust that he would love her in return.

One more squeeze, and then he released her to take Mountaineer's reins. "You did a great job on your first trail ride today. You looked more relaxed when we were coming down."

Mattie couldn't think of a way to reply. She'd recently become an expert at projecting relaxation in the face of anxiety.

Cole unhooked the trailer's back gate and began loading the horses. "I'll have to unsaddle and feed these guys and get them set up for the night, so you don't have to rush to get over to the house. Maybe shoot for an hour after we get back to town?"

"Sounds good."

As she walked toward the Explorer, Mattie stretched her sore legs. She loaded Robo into his compartment and then stifled a groan as she grabbed the steering wheel to pull herself up into the driver's seat. Cole waved as he steered his rig out of the parking lot and drove away.

She noticed a call from Riley and several missed calls from an unknown number. She dialed into voice messaging. Riley's message came up first, saying hello and asking where she was. Mattie frowned, realizing the girl's father must be working again, even though it was Sunday. She needed to find a place for Riley to hang out, because obviously, she herself couldn't be counted on as a reliable companion for the teen.

The second message, left by an unfamiliar female voice, came as a surprise. "Hey . . . uh . . . Deputy Cobb? Mattie? This is Tamara Bennett. I'm your brother's friend. Could you call me back as soon as you can? I need to talk to you." She left a number, which matched the calls from the unknown number listed in her call log. Evidently she'd tried to reach Mattie several times that day.

Thinking it strange to hear from Willie's girlfriend, Mattie went ahead and checked her text messages. She recognized Tamara Bennett's name from listening to her brother. He was crazy about her. But Tamara had sounded stressed in her message, and Mattie guessed that she wasn't making a social call. Tamara wanted to talk to her about something gone wrong. And when you made the choice to live with an addict, that something was most likely him falling off the wagon.

*Damn it.* She didn't feel prepared to deal with addiction issues. All she wanted was to reconnect with her brother and see if they could establish some type of relationship. That's it.

Pulling out of the parking lot, she mulled things over and decided to return Tamara's call after she checked in with Stella.

The detective answered on the first ring. "Are you back in town, Mattie?"

"On my way."

"Things are going well here. I reached a CBI agent and he's pulling together a team of specialists to bring with him, a forensic anthropologist and assistants. They'll arrive later tonight. I reserved rooms at the Big Sky Motel, and they'll be ready to roll out of here with us by seven tomorrow morning."

"And the transport up the mountain?"

"Garrett Hartman has it under control. He has some volunteers from the search and rescue team lined up to go with us. We should have plenty of people-power. How was your ride down?"

"Uneventful. Yours?"

"I'm getting used to it."

"Someone shot and killed a ram up on the ridge," Mattie said. "Left the carcass and then disappeared."

"You're kidding me!"

"The timing made me wonder if it's related to our case."

Stella was silent for a few moments. "Our victim's killer should be long gone. Why would he hang around to shoot a ram?"

"But how many people go up to that area to begin with? Outside of the wildlife team, you could probably count them on the fingers of one hand," Mattie said.

"This is one of those strange things that makes me crazy at night. We need more information about it."

"Cole wants to ride to the other side of the ridge in the morning to try to do a postmortem on the ram and see if he can retrieve a slug. He'll contact Ed Lovejoy this evening, and maybe he'll go along. After all, it's Ed's responsibility."

"Maybe you should go, too."

"Actually, I'd like to. Robo and I searched all around the gravesite without finding a thing this afternoon. Maybe we can find some piece of evidence up there. Something the shooter left behind."

"I'll talk to the sheriff and clear it. We'll meet here at six in the morning to be ready to leave by seven."

"Got it. I'm a mess and headed for the shower."

Stella's reply carried a smile. "By all means, don't let me get in your way."

"Oh, one more thing. While we were up on the ridge taking a look at the ram, Cole and I spotted some indentations in the soil at the far side of the meadow, where it meets the trees. The grass is a darker green. They might be places where elk bed down, but the grass wasn't smashed and they didn't look typical. I think these spots deserve a closer look."

"Well, we have the right people joining us to cover that. We'll have them check it out. Try to get some sleep, Mattie. It's going to be a huge day tomorrow."

"We'd better pack some extra clothes in case we stay up there tomorrow night."

"Good point."

They said their goodbyes as Mattie reached the edge of town. She turned toward home, noticing that Robo was sound asleep on the cushion she kept for him in his compartment. He must be exhausted. Typically, he spent several hours per day asleep at the station while Mattie did routine computer searches and paperwork.

When she parked in front of her house, she spotted Riley on the front porch, once again tossing pebbles into Robo's bowl, a game that seemed to be turning into a habit.

"Hey, Mattie," Riley called out, a smile lighting her face.

Although Mattie wasn't sure it was a good idea for Riley to hang out at her house, she couldn't help but return the girl's smile as she exited her car.

"Hey! I just got your message a little bit ago. I was up where I didn't have cell phone service most of the day." Mattie went around to the back where Robo had awakened and was shoulders down in a long stretch, his mouth open in a huge yawn. The thought of her missed yoga lesson flitted through her mind as she viewed his version of downward dog.

Riley came out to the car, and Robo jumped down from the back, greeting her with wagging tail. She bent to pat his sides. "I was hoping we could grab some dinner together. My treat."

"You don't have to buy dinner for me, silly. When we go out, we'll go Dutch. But I'm sorry, I've already made arrangements for dinner tonight."

Riley's face fell before she tried to cover her disappointment. But then she sniffed, took a step back, and lifted her hand to her nose to smell it. "Yuk! What's Robo been into?"

Mattie realized she'd adapted to the odor of death and forgotten how much the two of them must stink. "Geez, Riley. I'm sorry. Come into the house and wash up in the kitchen while Robo and I take a shower."

Robo trotted ahead and Riley followed as Mattie went to the

house, unlocked the door, and let them all into her small living room.

She pointed toward the doorway that led to the kitchen. "You can wash up in there. I'll be out in a few minutes. Go ahead and grab a soda from the fridge if you want."

Mattie took Robo into the bathroom with her and shut the door. He loved to watch her shower and get ready for work in the morning, but he wasn't so fond of hopping into the tub himself. She took off his collar, and he knew what was coming. He tucked his tail and hung his head while she ran warm water into the tub.

While the water ran, she took a moment to text Cole to see if it was okay to bring Riley to dinner, and then she put her cell phone up high on the medicine cabinet to protect it from splashes. When she turned off the water, Robo's brow puckered with concern.

"You need a bath, sweetie. Go ahead, jump in here." He turned and faced the door, staring at the knob. She snapped her fingers. "Robo, come. Don't be such a chicken."

He hugged the door with his whole body.

Mattie bent, grasped him under the chest to pick up the front half of his body, and lugged his one hundred pounds over to the tub. "Get in there now," she said as she placed his front feet into the water, and then reached to lift his hind half in, too. He started to pant, and she stroked his head. "That's right. Now relax, big guy. This will all be over in a minute."

She made short work of the bath, lathering and rinsing his luxurious coat. Even though he looked like a whipped pup, he cooperated for the most part. He tried to shake a couple of times while still in the tub, so Mattie was pretty well drenched by the time she drained the water and toweled him off.

"Now you wait in here with me so you don't get the whole house wet."

She hurried to finish her own shower, wrapped a towel around her wet hair, and slipped on a terrycloth robe. Robo rushed out of the bathroom, shaking and grinning as he trotted over to greet Riley, who was sitting on the floor in front of a bookshelf. Mattie didn't have a television, so the girl must have resorted to books for entertainment.

Riley hugged Robo against her. "Ew, you're wet," she said, crinkling her nose and then burying it in his damp fur. "But you smell better."

Mattie left the two together while she dressed and combed out her hair. After tucking the wet strands behind her ears, she reached for her cell phone and saw that Cole had answered her text. "Bring Riley, too," it said. "What was it Mama T used to say? Little piggies eat better when there are more at the trough."

He'd remembered Mama T's words from when she'd told him weeks ago. Hard to believe he cared enough to recall such a trivial thing.

When she went back into the living room, Riley had moved onto the sofa and was looking at one of Mattie's old high school yearbooks. Robo wriggled gleefully on his back on his dog bed.

"I see you were a jock," Riley said, lifting up the book to show Mattie a picture of herself holding the state championship cross-country trophy she'd won her senior year.

Mattie shrugged and then allowed herself a grin. "I could run . . . so I did."

"I saw your picture at school."

"Yeah?" She knew Riley was referring to one of the photos in the school trophy case, but decided that was enough talk about her. "You have an invitation to dinner now."

Riley's face brightened. "You're free?"

"Sort of. Do you know Angela Walker?"

"I met her in band. She's a year older than me."

"We're both invited to dinner at the Walkers' house. You wanna come?"

Riley snapped the yearbook shut and stood to put it back on the shelf. "Sure," she said, looking like she was trying to control her eagerness.

"Do you need to call to see if it's okay with your dad?"

"Nah, he left early this morning with the horses. Said he was going on a ride." A shadow of sadness crossed the girl's face. "I think he has a girlfriend. Anyway, he said he wouldn't get home until late. I'll text him to tell him where I am."

Mattie felt sorry for her. Her father certainly appeared to be inattentive and self-involved. "Then let's go ahead and load up. Robo's coming, too. We'll load your bicycle into the back and he can sit up front with us. I'll take you home after we eat."

Mattie flipped on the porch light as they left the house. Robo dashed ahead while Riley wheeled her bike out to the Explorer. It felt strange to act so normal after the day she'd had. Whenever she'd been faced with a homicide before, she'd focused on nothing but solving the case.

She knew she needed to learn how to do this—compartmentalize her life—and perhaps she could develop that skill in time. But as she helped Riley load up her bike, the grim memory of a half burned corpse slipped into her mind to haunt her, its charred fists poised and ready to strike back.

# TEN

When they arrived at the Walker home, Sophie and Angela hugged Mattie and welcomed Riley. Mattie hoped Riley would find a new friend in Angela, but knew better than to push.

After Cole greeted Riley, he gestured toward the next room. "Let's go into the kitchen, so you can meet Mrs. Gibbs. She cooked quite a dinner for us this evening."

The girls led the way while Cole pulled Mattie aside. "I rescheduled my day tomorrow so that I can ride up with you," he said.

She thought she could tackle her qualms about riding Mountaineer in the morning by herself, but she was relieved she wouldn't have to. "We appreciate your help."

"I aim to please." Cole gave her a look that tugged her heart, and she turned away to follow the kids.

Mrs. Gibbs had set large bowls of salad and spaghetti on the table alongside a basket of freshly baked French bread, but when Mattie entered the room, the housekeeper turned away from her preparation to greet her with a hug. After they were seated, Sophie appeared delighted to have Riley as a guest and dominated the conversation, sharing a multitude of details with the newcomer about her half grown chickens. The girls made plans to go see them after dinner.

"Slow down, Sophie-bug," Cole said, as he helped himself to more bread. "Let our guest get a word in edgewise."

Used to gentle reprimands about her chatter, Sophie pretended to lock her mouth shut.

"Thank you," he replied, with a quick smile. "So, Riley, where did you live before you moved here?"

"In L.A. It's so different from here in Timber Creek."

"I should say. How do you like living in the boonies of Colorado?"

"It's okay. Kinda hard to find things to do sometimes. I went to the opening of Happy Shack. That was kinda cool."

Cole's brow wrinkled. "What's Happy Shack?"

Angela jumped into the conversation. "It's a new place in town. They have ice cream, video games, and a pool table."

Riley nodded. "They have about ten flavors of ice cream, and the video games were free today. I hung out there all afternoon."

Mattie doubted that playing video games every day was a good habit for Riley to develop. "Who runs the place?"

"She said to call her Violet."

"I'll stop in and meet her when I can. Sounds like fun," she added, trying to disguise her real motivation of wanting to check things out.

"What's your dad's name, Riley?" Cole asked. "I don't think I've met him yet."

"Bret. Bret Flynn."

"What does he do?" Cole asked.

"He has a couple jobs now. He's working with the county road crew, and he tends bar in Hightower at the Hornet's Nest."

"Whoa, I bet that keeps him busy," Cole said.

"Yeah, he's not home very often." Riley looked down at her plate and used her fork to push around the last of her spaghetti. "He was around a lot more when we lived in L.A. Back then he stayed home to help my mom when she got sick. We both did."

"Gosh, I'm sorry your mom was sick," Cole said. Both Sophie and Angela were watching her with wide, sympathetic eyes.

Riley laid her fork on her plate. "Mom had cancer. She got treatment at first, but then . . . it just seemed like there was nothing more the doctors could do. She died in October."

Sophie made a quiet sound of sympathy while Angela narrowed her eyes against welling tears.

"I'm sorry to hear that," Cole murmured.

"Our mom lives in Denver," Sophie chimed in, as if that counted for something.

Riley nodded at her, and Mattie realized that in the minds of kids, maybe it did.

"After Mom died, Dad seemed in a hurry to move out here. I don't know why he picked Timber Creek. It seemed like we had a lot more money back in L.A., and he didn't have to work as much."

That statement tweaked Mattie's attention. Whenever anyone mentioned a lot of money, her mind shot straight to the drug trade. Occupational hazard. "What did your dad do in L.A.?"

Riley averted her eyes. "I don't know really. Something to do with business. Like selling and trading on eBay, but not that. Just something like it."

Her answer didn't satisfy Mattie's curiosity, but she decided to let it go. "I'd better take you home soon, Riley. You girls have school tomorrow. Maybe we should help Mrs. Gibbs clean up and get ready to leave."

"Oh, come now. I can clean up the kitchen me own self." The housekeeper's Irish brogue colored her words. She glanced at Sophie whose face was etched with disappointment. "Why don't you all go to the clinic to see the new coop and those chickens before you leave?"

Sophie jumped from her chair, gathering Riley's dishes with her own to carry to the sink. "There's three of them. Chicken Little is the smallest one, and there's Tootie and Buck. We thought Buck was a boy, but it looks like he's a girl. Dad and I built their chicken house." She looked at her sister. "You'll come with us, won't you, Angie?"

"Sure."

His eyes twinkling, Cole sent Mattie a quick smile.

"Thank you for dinner," Riley told Mrs. Gibbs as she helped clear the table.

"Why, sure. I hope you'll come back and eat with us again some time."

"Let's all go," Cole said. "Those chickens are probably inside on their roosts, but we'll take a couple of flashlights so Riley can see them."

Although the body up on the ridge had surfaced in her mind several times throughout the evening, it felt good to have something wholesome like caring for animals to focus on for a while. Mattie cleared her dishes and joined the others, reveling in the sense that she had become a solid part of this group—this family—that she loved.

★

## Early Monday Morning

Mattie startled awake. Drenched in sweat, she sat straight up in bed and her heart raced as she glanced toward the window. It was cracked open an inch, allowing a breeze to flow gently into the room, chilling her damp skin. Allowing escape.

Robo raised his head, ears pricked, immediately awake and alert.

"It's okay, buddy. Just a nightmare. You can go back to sleep."

He continued to stare at her, vigilant. She had no doubt that he would protect her from this enemy if he could.

A quick glance at the clock told her it was 4:16 AM. With a pang of regret, she remembered that she'd forgotten to return Willie's girlfriend's call. She couldn't call Tamara in the middle of the night, so she switched on her nightstand lamp and reached for her dream journal.

She'd been haunted with nightmares for months. Her counselor had prescribed using a dream journal to capture the details of the night terrors when they occurred, so that she could analyze them later during the light of day.

After picking up journal and pen, she plumped pillows behind her back, opened the journal in her lap, and began to write.

Familiar with this routine, Robo relaxed down on his cushion.

This nightmare had been so vivid, it was easy to recall and record. She'd dreamed about that poor corpse they'd found on the ridge, but in her dream she'd watched the man burn, surrounded and consumed by flames.

Police officers were often exposed to horrific sights, and this one was right up there at the top of the list. It might take a while before she could put these images away where they wouldn't come out to haunt her.

She recorded the details in her journal diligently, hoping that writing them down would help move them out of her head. She paused, her heart beating hard against the wall of her chest, her jaw clenched. Ever tuned-in to her emotions, Robo opened his eyes again and watched.

She drew a deep breath and tried to relax on the exhalation like Rainbow had taught her.

She thought for a few minutes, chewing on the end of her pen, but finally decided to give up. It was now a few minutes past five o'clock and time for her to get out of bed. She needed to pack supplies and make it to the station by six. She also needed to call Mama T to tell her that she might not be able to bring Riley over later, but she'd still try to make it on Tuesday to meet Doreen. Mama T would be awake by five thirty, so it wouldn't be too early to call before work.

Yet, even as she made plans and headed for the shower, she couldn't shake the feeling that the nightmare about the burning corpse felt so real. It felt like she'd been there in the mountains, watching it happen.

# ELEVEN

**Monday**

On her way to work, Mattie's cell phone rang, and caller ID told her it was another call from Willie's girlfriend. She was glad to get this chance to connect before she headed into the mountains for the day, and she swiped to take the call. "This is Mattie."

"Mattie, hi." The caller's voice held a note of relief. "This is Tamara Bennett, your brother's girlfriend?"

"Yes, Tamara, hello. I got home too late last night to call you. I was out of cell phone range most of the day yesterday."

"Oh . . . um . . . have you heard from Will lately?"

That was a strange question. Perhaps Tamara didn't know that she and Willie called each other about once a week. "I talked to him a little over a week ago I guess."

"Oh." Disappointment colored the word. "I'm worried about him. I haven't seen him since last Wednesday."

This wasn't what she expected to hear. Mattie squinted her eyes as she pulled into the station parking lot, noticing she was the last one on the team to arrive. An unfamiliar van sat parked among the staff vehicles. "He lives with you, right?"

"That's right, but he didn't come home Wednesday night and hasn't come back since."

"Has he ever done this before?"

"Never. I can always count on him to pick up my son, Elliott, at after-school care on Wednesdays, but he didn't show."

"And you tried reaching him at work?"

"They haven't heard from him either."

Mattie didn't know what to think. She wanted to give her brother the benefit of the doubt, but the fact remained that he was an addict, and once an addict, always etcetera. "Has he started using again?"

Tamara released an audible breath. "That's just it. Not that I know of, but he's been acting strange lately. Secretive. And he'd been going out after dinner to meet an old friend, or at least that's what he said."

Bingo. Old friends could spell danger to someone with a drug addiction. "I can see why you're worried. I'm sorry, Tamara, but I have to say it sounds like he might have fallen off the wagon."

After a long pause, Tamara spoke again, this time sounding close to tears. "I thought he was more dedicated than that to staying clean. I didn't see it coming. I filed a missing person report, but the police don't seem to be taking it seriously. I guess because of his history."

The loved ones were sometimes the last to believe there was a problem. But still this was Willie they were talking about. She wanted to believe in him, too. Besides, Tamara sounded like a nice person, and she seemed to trust that he was on the right track. "How can I help, Tamara?"

She paused. "Can you contact the police out here, tell them this is your brother that's missing? Maybe they would take it more seriously hearing the concern come from another police officer."

"I'd be happy to. Can you text me the phone number for the police department you're dealing with? And did they give you a case number on the missing person report?"

"They did. I'll text that, too. And, thank you, Mattie."

"Of course. I'm glad you contacted me. If I hear from him, I'll let you know."

"I'd appreciate that."

Mattie ended the call, and soon heard her phone ping with the text message from Tamara. She guessed she shouldn't be surprised at this turn of events, but she couldn't help but feel disappointed in her brother.

She unloaded Robo, grabbed her two backpacks, and entered the station, going first to clock in and then heading for her office. Since Rainbow's shift didn't start until seven, Sam Corns still manned the front desk, his shiny bald head lowered over a manual that he was reading.

Mattie used the information from Tamara to call the Hollywood police station. The dispatcher told her that a Detective Hastings had been assigned to her brother's case, but he hadn't checked in yet. He forwarded her call to voice messaging, and Mattie spoke to the recorder, stating her law enforcement title along with her concerns and her relationship to the missing person. She left her cell phone number and asked for a call if anything turned up during the day, stating she'd be out of cell phone range but would look for his message by evening. Maybe that would at least spur some action. It wasn't much, but it was all she could do at the moment.

She found the others in the briefing room, Stella and the sheriff seated at a front table along with a man that she assumed was the CBI agent from Denver. He stood when she entered, meeting her gaze with strong brown eyes that were so dark they were almost black. Though he was of medium height, his posture projected the illusion of someone taller. Built solid and muscular, he was probably a force to be reckoned with in a wrestling match, and his dark hair was cut close to his head.

His eyes flicked downward to take in Robo, but then moved right back up to lock onto hers in a way that indicated a propensity for keen observation. That, coupled with the hardened planes of his face, almost put Mattie off, but the instant he smiled, his entire set of features softened.

The sheriff was quick to stand and make introductions. "Good morning, Deputy Cobb. This is Special Agent Rick Lawson of the CBI. He'll be helping us with our investigation."

Mattie shook hands, not a bit surprised by the firmness of the man's grip. "We're going to need your expertise. Our victim's body is badly damaged."

"So I hear." Rick's intense, dark eyes moved to include the others. "I also hear that you've found some depressions in the area that warrant investigation."

"We did."

"Good eye. Did your dog hit on them?"

"No, but he's not cadaver trained."

His brow lifted slightly. "I heard he found your victim."

"True, but he was working from a scent article. He's trained for search and rescue, and he's real good at it."

"Well, I'm taking a portable, ground-penetrating radar unit up, so we can take a look with that after we excavate your victim."

Mattie nodded. "I'll be going to scout out the back of the ridge this morning, but Deputy Brody is already up at the crime scene. He can show you the area we're talking about."

"Sounds good."

"Have a seat," McCoy said, gesturing toward the food on the table. "My wife sent fruit Danish and we have fresh coffee."

Mattie had already eaten breakfast but still helped herself, knowing that anything that came from Mrs. McCoy's kitchen would be delicious.

Stella refilled her coffee cup. "The Byers County lab has sent tissue samples from the victim's foot to a forensics lab in Denver. They'll expedite searching for our victim through CODIS and the National DNA Index System. If we're lucky enough for him to be in the database, we'll have a match soon."

CODIS, the Combined DNA Index System operated by the FBI, contained DNA profiles taken from crime scenes and from offenders who'd been arrested for or convicted of violent crimes such as rape or homicide. If this victim had been connected with such a crime anytime since the 1990s, he'd most likely be in the system. NDIS, or the National DNA Index System, provided for identifying missing persons and the unidentified. The search could also be broadened to include a DNA family match, which made the two databases even more effective.

McCoy cleared his throat, as if brushing away morning cobwebs. "We have horses arriving here soon. We'll have two set up with pack saddles to pack in your gear," he told Rick.

"That should do it."

"Have you packed into a crime scene on horseback before?" Stella asked.

"Many times. It's not too unusual to find bodies in remote places here in Colorado."

Sam Corns rapped on the door and then peered inside. "Cole Walker and the rest of the cavalry are here."

"Send them in," McCoy said. "We'll fortify with coffee and then load up so we can get on our way."

★

*This second trip up the mountain doesn't seem nearly as scary,* Mattie thought, relaxing in the saddle atop Mountaineer as she followed Stella and Honey upslope beneath the pines. Today she could even register the pine scent that saturated the forest, a scent she loved. Perhaps her nightmare had put everything into perspective—nothing in this reality could outdo the terror she'd felt in that dream.

Ed Lovejoy rode along with them, and he, Cole, and Mattie planned to split off from the other investigators halfway up the trail to go to the backside of the ridge. Mattie felt torn about not returning to the gravesite with the rest of the party, but she and Robo had searched as much of the surrounding area as they could yesterday and found nothing. Although the chance seemed remote that their victim's killer might be the same person who killed the ram, it seemed important to find the spot where the shots came from, in case the shooter had left behind evidence that could be associated with their victim's case. Besides, the gravesite excavation required a skill set different from hers and Robo's. There would be little she could do to be of help there.

Within the hour, they came to the trail's fork, and it took only moments for the party to get sorted out. Soon Mattie found herself riding up a new trail, this one steeper and rockier than the other.

Lovejoy took the lead and Cole the rear as they ascended, while Robo trotted out in front. Once, when they faced a particularly steep grade, Mattie heard Cole speak softly behind her. "Remember to lean forward when you go uphill."

She tried to do what he said, but could feel her back stiffen when Mountaineer lurched and scrambled to climb, his hooves churning. She ended up clinging to the saddle horn like she'd done the day before.

The decades-old forest fire had not reached the backside of the ridge, so the trees grew dense along this narrow and seldom used access. She loved the mountains but the overhanging evergreens triggered her claustrophobia. Her sweaty palms grew slippery on the leather saddle horn, and she had to focus on slowing her breath. After what seemed like eons, the trail broke onto a granite slab that ran close to the top of the ridge. She breathed a sigh of relief as the space opened up and she could see again.

Lovejoy pointed to the top of a rise layered with rose-colored shale, too risky to reach on horseback. "We're probably near the opposite side from where the ram and the herd were yesterday. We might have to scout the top on foot."

"Let's tie up here where the horses have some shade," Cole said. "And where I can change into hiking boots."

"Well, shee-ite, Doc. Did you bring me a pair?"

"Sorry, Ed. I guess you're on your own."

With a good-natured grimace, Lovejoy spat a brown stream of tobacco and went to tie his horse.

Once on the ground, Mattie felt back in her element. She offered Robo a drink of water from his collapsible bowl, and he lapped for a long time. When he'd finished, she put the collar that he wore for evidence detection on him and told him he was going to work. He waved his tail and gazed into her eyes, telling her he understood although his typical excitement seemed dampened by the amount of energy it had taken to reach this elevation.

When Cole arose, stamping his rugged boots as if to test the tread, Mattie finished up with Robo and put her water supply away in her backpack. Then she gave her dog the command reserved for evidence detection, "Seek," which shifted him into sniffing mode.

Mattie had expanded Robo's skills by training him to find newly spent casings and shotgun shells, the ammo commonly used around Timber Creek. Even though her dog wasn't formally trained in explosives detection, she felt confident that he could scent gunpowder when she needed him to.

Cole and Lovejoy fell in behind while Mattie and Robo struck off toward the top of the ridge. She picked her way through boulders, sometimes leaning forward to get a handhold. Nose to the ground, Robo quartered the area in front of her, covering about twice the distance she did, while she kept a sharp eye out and scanned the same area visually.

Robo breached the top first and posed there against the skyline waiting for her. When she reached him, she could see that Lovejoy's estimation of their location had been spot-on. From this pinnacle, the ridge fell away, offering her a clear view of the meadow below, filled with the brilliant red of the fireweed, as well as a panorama of the burned area and dozens of miles of rolling evergreen forest. About a hundred yards downhill, she spotted the ram's carcass.

Cole came up beside her and handed her the binoculars. She focused and swept the sights along the ridgeline and below, and then pointed to an overlook about fifty yards away. "It looks like we could follow the ridge along the top, and then go downslope on that ledge. From there, we could pick our way through the boulders to get to the ram."

Heaving for breath, Lovejoy finally made his way up to join them.

Cole was scoping the area. "I think you're right, Mattie."

"I'll do a modified grid search on the ridgeline and see if Robo can find evidence that the shooter was here. Then we'll take it from there." Again, Mattie gave Robo the command to seek and followed him as closely as she could.

A tangle of slippery shale, rocks of all sizes, and huge boulders cluttered the topside of the ridge. She teetered from one rock to another, finding foothold after foothold, as she painstakingly searched the rugged terrain. Robo tiptoed easily ahead of her, searching with his nose.

After about fifty yards of careful examination, her dog came to the overlook that she'd spied through the binoculars. He poked his nose into a pile of rocks at the top part of the ledge, and then sat and turned his stare toward Mattie.

No mistaking that look. He'd found something.

"Good boy," Mattie praised him, thumping his side while she hugged him close to her leg. "What have you got?"

After she carefully removed the top layer of shale, something gold winked at her from between the remaining rocks. There it was. A brass casing from a spent bullet. Long enough to fit a hunting rifle.

This casing would most likely match the rifle that shot the ram. And there was a possibility, although remote, that it might be connected in some way to their human victim.

Mattie photographed the casing with her cell phone before taking an evidence bag from her utility belt. After turning the bag inside out, she scooped up the casing without touching it, enclosed it, and sealed it away. She could read .270 Winchester stamped on the end of the brass.

"Good job, Robo," she said, stroking his head as he gazed up at her. Then she looked at Cole. "I have no idea if this casing is related to the death of our victim, but if it is, we've just found our first piece of evidence."

# TWELVE

It had proven impossible to find boot prints on the rocky ledge that angled down toward the ram carcass. Cole followed Mattie and the sure-footed Robo as they made for the sheep's body, while Lovejoy waited for them up above. Even though this was his jurisdiction, the wildlife manager seemed willing to have them take over the investigation, and under the circumstances, it felt like the right thing to do. Mattie and Robo were more efficient and could photograph whatever was necessary without Ed having to risk his life.

Reaching the dead ram took only about five minutes. As they approached the carcass, the memory of the magnificent animal twisted Cole's gut. Only yesterday, this ram had been on top of his world, in charge of his harem. The ewes were still hanging around farther down the ridge, and he was relieved that they hadn't scattered to parts unknown when their leader was shot. Without wasting time, a younger male with a lesser horn curl appeared to have moved in on the old ram's territory.

Before Robo could get too close to the ram's body, Mattie called him and told him to wait. Decomposition was well underway, and the odor intensified as they drew near.

"Let's get some pictures," Mattie said.

While she photographed the site, Cole made his way toward the ram's front end. "Something bothers me about you finding that casing, Mattie."

"What's that?"

"A real hunter always picks up his brass, doesn't want to leave an environmental footprint."

"This shell was down in some rocks. Maybe he looked for it but couldn't find it."

"That's possible. But how hard is it to swipe away some shale?"

Mattie nodded, looking like she was taking that in and conceding the point as she squatted and snapped a few photos of the ledge and ridge above her.

Cole moved closer. "If you're done with pictures of the ram, I'll try to retrieve the slug."

"Go ahead."

Cole put on latex gloves and removed a bowie knife with a seven-inch blade from a sheath he wore on his belt.

"Do you think the shooter knew we were in the area?" Mattie asked.

"I think we could assume that. Why else would he disappear so quickly?"

Cole examined the entry wound on the ram's side. "Looks like a heart shot, which tells me the guy knew what he was doing. Odd for a hunter who leaves his casings behind."

Mattie shook her head, obviously pondering it.

Cole faced the job at hand. On normal terrain, he would use the animal's stiffened legs to roll it so that he could search for an exit wound, but if he rolled this ram, he would send it tumbling downhill and possibly set off a rockslide in the process. He decided to go into the chest cavity and search for the slug through the place of entry, counting on it not being a through-and-through wound.

He sliced upward between the ribs, carved through the cartilage at the spine, and sliced back down. Once he cut the rib away from its support, he removed it and inserted his hand into the space it left behind, feeling for the bullet. Within minutes, he located the projectile, withdrew it from the ram's chest, and delivered it into an evidence bag that Mattie held ready.

"Ballistics can tell if this slug and the brass that Robo found match." She appeared to be thinking aloud. "This has to be someone who knew his way around and could navigate this terrain. Maybe a local?"

"Makes sense." He stripped off his gloves, turned them inside out, and disposed of them in a ziplock bag that he would carry out.

Mattie turned upslope and scanned the area. She pointed to an outcropping about halfway up. "That looks like a place where someone could hide and not be seen from down below."

Robo fell in beside Mattie as they climbed toward the top. At the backside of the outcropping, she stopped, squatted, and searched the ground. Smudged boot prints.

Realization sunk in, raising the hair at the back of Cole's neck. He turned and searched the terrain below to confirm his suspicion. Yesterday, while he and Mattie climbed the hillside, someone had been perched up here hidden behind these boulders, armed with a hunting rifle, and quite likely watching them through the scope.

★

When they returned to the crime scene, a great transformation had taken place. Orange and blue domed tents had sprung up overnight, looking like huge colorful mushrooms sprouting among the evergreens. Several members of the sheriff's posse were tending a campfire and cooking a meal for the workers.

After tying their horses beside the others, Ed Lovejoy went to help out at the campfire while Mattie and Cole made their way up the trail to the shallow grave. Exhumation of the gravesite was well under way. Mattie stopped at a distance where she could watch the forensic team do their work but still stay out of their way.

Wearing a soiled white coverall and latex gloves, one of the human recovery team members knelt beside the pit, digging carefully with a hand trowel while his teammates used framed screens to sift through the dirt. He'd already dug a trench about eighteen inches wide and twelve inches deep most of the way around the body. Rick Lawson, Stella, Brody, and Sheriff McCoy stood a few feet away, watching.

Brody came over. "That's a forensic anthropologist heading up the recovery. From the size and shape of the corpse, he believes this victim is a man, although his features have been burned beyond recognition."

The information confirmed her first impression. Mattie briefed Brody on what she'd found, as well as Cole's belief that a true hunter wouldn't leave behind his brass. "I wish we'd gone after him yesterday. Maybe we could have caught him."

He appeared to mull over what he'd heard. "We were out of daylight and short staffed. Maybe the ram's death has nothing to do with our victim here. We'll have to see if we recover any lead during the autopsy."

Mattie had already had the same thought. A bullet recovered from the body could be analyzed by ballistics to see if it matched the same type of casing that Robo found.

Brody moved closer to the gravesite, while Mattie remained standing beside Cole. The recovery team had begun to remove the soil on top of the body, painstakingly separating dirt from charred wood. When they uncovered the victim's remaining foot, she could see that the charred boot matched the one that Bruno found.

Bit by bit, they uncovered the victim's remains. As they worked their way downward, continuing to trench below the level of the victim's back, Mattie moved forward to get a better view while Cole stayed where he was.

Gradually, it became apparent that the body had been placed directly in the dirt at the bottom of a pit. Whoever had tried to burn this victim had neglected to line the pit first with wood. Could the attempt to burn the victim have been an afterthought, or the work of somebody not used to the outdoors? Out here in the open, one could never burn a body completely without building a pyre of sorts and establishing a wicking effect from below. Even then, the temperature would likely never reach the intensity needed to burn away bone.

Stella must have been thinking along the same lines. "It looks like there's no wood under the body. Is that right?" she asked Lawson.

"That's right. The backside of the remains should be relatively intact. I can already see evidence of clothing that's spared. Denim pants, a light blue shirt. Dentition should be somewhat preserved. The tongue actually protects the teeth."

Mattie glanced at the blackened tongue that bulged from the victim's mouth and then looked away. It was hard to imagine how anyone could damage another person in this way.

Once they uncovered the body, Lawson turned to one of his teammates. "Let's go ahead and get the board in place."

They positioned a stretcher directly beside the burned corpse and spread open a body bag on it.

"We'll need to roll the remains," Lawson said.

With deft movements that demonstrated a great deal of experience, they positioned the body on its side at the edge of the stretcher.

Lawson was squatting behind the corpse. "There's a tattoo here at the base of the neck. It says 'Tamara and Elliott Forever' inside a heart. Looks like we might have a first name now. Elliott. At least the tattoo is clear enough for identification purposes on a missing persons database."

An oily wave of darkness washed through Mattie. Tamara and Elliott. She felt herself sway as the implications of those words hit her.

Cole stepped up beside her and took hold of her forearm. "Are you okay?"

She shook her head slightly as her eyes zeroed in on the body's damaged face. She'd been unable to let her gaze linger there before, but now she tried to distinguish its features.

*Willie?*

Stella approached. "What is it, Mattie?"

While Mattie locked eyes with Stella, Robo edged in closer, his warmth a comfort against her leg. "My brother has been missing since Wednesday. His girlfriend is Tamara and her son is Elliott."

Stella's eyes widened and then went to the corpse. Bile rose in Mattie's throat, and she turned away, lurching back toward the stream. Robo stayed beside her while Cole followed. She made it across the stream and into some bushes before heaving.

"Here, Robo," she heard Cole say as he held back her dog. Then she felt his warm hand on her shoulder, offering some sense of stability in a world turned upside down.

# THIRTEEN

Battling a quiver deep in her gut, Mattie sat on a log beside the campfire and sipped from her water supply. Stella hunkered down in front of her, staring at her with eyes that probed her depths, while Cole stood a few feet away, worry lines etched on his face.

Stella spoke, her voice quiet but intense. "Tell me what you know about your brother."

"Very little. He lives in Hollywood and works as a car mechanic." *Poor Willie.* She wished she knew him better.

"Fits with the boots."

*Steel-toed work boots.* "I suppose so."

"What's his full name?"

Mattie focused to retrieve Willie's middle name from memories stored when she was only six years old. "William James Cobb, if I remember right."

"What's his history?"

"Well . . . I only know recent."

"Recent might be what counts."

Mattie hated to divulge some of what she knew, but it was important and possibly relevant information. "He spent some time in a drug rehab center within the last year. Met a woman who worked there named Tamara and when he got out, he moved in with her and her son Elliott. He was trying to stay clean and hold down a job that he told me he liked."

"It would be a huge coincidence if this was someone else with that tattoo, Mattie. You know that, don't you?"

Mattie nodded agreement, glancing at Cole. He tilted his head to the side with an expression that signaled his dismay, his eyes filled with sympathy. It made her own tears well, so she quickly looked away.

"Why do you think he's turned up here outside of Timber Creek?" Stella asked.

"Wouldn't have happened of his own free will. He said he never wanted to come back to Timber Creek. Too many bad memories."

This time, it was Stella who glanced at Cole. "Do you mind if Mattie and I speak privately for a few minutes, Dr. Walker?"

"Of course not." Cole looked at Mattie before turning to leave. "Let me know if you need anything. I'll be over with the horses."

Stella knew almost as much about Mattie's past as she did—the childhood abuse at the hands of her father, Willie's regret that he couldn't protect his little sister from their father's advances, and their mother's abandonment. Now Mattie could see the detective's mind churning to find connections. "Could your past relate to his homicide?"

Mattie shook her head. "I don't know. I don't see how."

"But he's here, Mattie. He's not back in Hollywood where he belongs."

She shifted her mind away from Willie's damaged face and struggled to focus on finding connections. "Tamara told me this morning that lately he'd been acting different. Secretive. I assumed he'd started using again."

"Toxicology tests should be possible with his body being partially preserved. We'll be able to find that out."

"Did the forensic anthropologist estimate when he was killed?"

"Said it was hard to tell. Three or four days—as early as last Friday."

Mattie tried to recall more of her discussion with Tamara. "She said Willie was going out a lot in the evenings, like he was meeting someone."

"We need to find out more about that."

"I don't think she knows anything."

"I'll talk to someone at his job site." Stella stared into the middle distance for a few moments, thinking. "There has to be a link to Timber Creek that surfaced in William's life recently. When did you talk to him last?"

"It was the weekend before last. Saturday evening, ten days past. We talked about meeting each other in Vegas." A lump rose in Mattie's throat, and she struggled to suppress her tears.

"Did he mention meeting up with friends or anything that could explain his secretive behavior?"

"Not a thing. And from what Tamara said, I gathered that the change in his behavior was more recent than that."

"Your father is deceased. Could your mother be the reason that William returned to Timber Creek?"

*My mother?* The thought of her mother coming to Timber Creek squeezed her heart. "I don't know. I suppose anything's possible, but if she's in the area, I know nothing about it."

"Okay. We need to get down where we can make some phone calls. First, we need to talk to Tamara and gather more information, make a positive ID with the tattoo and go from there. Sheriff McCoy and Brody have this site covered. Do you want to go back to the office with me?"

Part of Mattie wanted to stay with Willie, show him respect by standing guard over his remains. But the larger part of her knew that she needed to be the one to speak with his girlfriend, show him respect by taking care of the one he obviously loved. "I'll go with you. We'll call Tamara together."

"Sounds good. Let's see if that man of yours will take us back down the mountain on those horses he's so fond of."

*

Mattie drove Stella and Robo back to the station in the K-9 unit, all the while trying to thrust the image of her brother's charred body out of her mind. They arrived a few minutes before six in the evening, and Rainbow was still on duty at the dispatcher's desk. She greeted Mattie and Stella with her typical enthusiasm, but backed off right away when she saw the look on their faces. Mattie nodded at her, signaling that they would talk later, and followed Stella into the detective's private office. After Robo came inside behind her, she closed the door, at the same time pulling her cell phone from her pocket.

"Here's Tamara's number." She rattled it off as she slumped into a chair beside Stella's desk. Robo circled once and, heaving a sigh, plopped down at her side. He'd had a long day with more than an enough exercise to tire him out.

Stella began to dial. "I'll introduce myself to her first."

After concentrating on listening for a few moments, Stella spoke. "Hello, is this Tamara Bennett?" After a pause, Stella continued. "This Detective Stella LoSasso from the Timber Creek County Sheriff's Department. I'm here with William Cobb's sister, Deputy Mattie Cobb. Are you able to speak with us for a few minutes?" Another pause. "Just one moment, let me put you on speaker phone."

Mattie spoke to let Tamara know she'd joined them on the line. "Hello, Tamara, this is Mattie."

Tamara's voice held a sharp edge of concern. "Mattie, what is it? What's going on?"

Stella nodded at Mattie to take the lead.

"We're calling to ask you some questions about Willie," Mattie said. She paused to take a deep breath, trying to loosen the tightness in her chest. "Does he have any tattoos on his back?"

"He has several. Why? Why are you asking?"

"How about at the base of his neck?"

"He has a heart with some ivy leaves entwined on the edges. Inside, it says 'Tamara and Elliott Forever'." Tamara's breath caught. "He said it would show his dedication to his new family." She had begun to cry, and Mattie hesitated, tears stinging her own eyes.

Stella jumped in, so that Mattie wouldn't have to say the next words. "Ms. Bennett, we've located a person who has a tattoo that matches that description. He was found in the mountains west of our town here in Colorado, and it's highly likely that he's your friend William. I'm very sorry to have to tell you that he was found dead."

Now Tamara's sobbing could be heard plainly, and Mattie squeezed her eyes shut to hold her grief in check. She wished she'd been able to meet this woman who'd shared Willie's life and had encouraged him to start over. She wished she could be in the same room with her instead of hundreds of miles apart. She wished . . . well, she wished everything had been different.

*Why did I wait to reconnect with my brother? Now it's too late.*

Tamara controlled her sobs enough to speak. "I knew it. I've had a terrible feeling that something bad happened to him."

Stella reached for paper and pen. "We need to find out more about William, and it's important that we get started with our investigation right away. Do you feel up to answering questions now, or should I give you a few minutes?"

"How did he die? Where did you find him?" Tamara asked.

The details were too grisly to share at this point. Mattie tried to reach out across the miles. "We're trying to find out how he died, Tamara. There'll be an autopsy very soon. He was found in the mountains west of Timber Creek."

"He hated Timber Creek."

"I know. Why do you think he was out here?"

A pause, and then Tamara answered, her voice strained. "He wouldn't go there. It wasn't like him to disappear. He never would have left Elliott stranded after school without calling me to cover for him. He must've been taken. I thought that from the very beginning."

"What do you mean by taken?" Stella asked.

"Taken against his will."

"Why would you think that?"

"Because he turned his back on some old friends from a rough crowd. You know, when he got out of rehab."

Stella gazed at Mattie for a few beats, a furrow between her eyebrows. She began writing on her pad. "Were any of these people from Timber Creek?"

"I don't think so. But I don't know really."

Stella showed Mattie what she'd written: *How do rough crowd in California and body here in Timber Creek connect???*

Mattie shrugged. "Tamara, can you give us the names of any of these people?"

Tamara heaved a breath, apparently pausing to think. "I know some street names. Ziggy the Fish, Shark, Popeye. Maybe the police here could help identify the gang these guys are in."

Stella was nodding while she recorded the names. "I think so, too. Do you have a case number on William's missing person report?"

"I have it," Mattie said. "That and the detective's name who was assigned to the case."

Stella acknowledged Mattie with a nod and moved on with another question for Tamara. "Where did William work?"

When she answered, Stella recorded the name and phone number of the business.

Mattie couldn't shake the thought that Willie's killer must have connected with him sometime in the past ten days. Everything had been fine when they talked—it had to be something since then. "You told me this morning that Willie's behavior changed recently. Can you pinpoint when that happened?"

Tamara sniffled. "I guess I first noticed it a week ago Sunday night. That was the night he made an excuse to leave home instead of watching movies with me and Elliott."

"What did he say?"

"That he had to go into work. I said, 'On a Sunday night?' And he said that they had a back load of work to do on Monday, and the boss wanted to get an early start."

"Did you call to check to see if he was actually there?"

"That's part of the whole rehab thing, see? I don't check up on him, at least not yet. If I want to be able to trust him, I have to act like I trust him until he shows me I can't."

Sounded a bit convoluted, but Mattie thought she understood the concept. "What happened after Sunday night?"

"Nothing on Monday, although he seemed more nervous than usual. But on Tuesday, he said he was going to have dinner with a friend. I asked him who the friend was, and he said it was an old friend of the family's."

Mattie's radar lit up. "Was this friend from Timber Creek?"

"I didn't get that. When I asked for details, William shut me down. That's what I meant by secretive. He wouldn't even look at me. Just said he had to go out and meet this guy, and that he might be out late. I was asleep when he got home, and it looked like he spent the rest of the night on the couch."

Mattie wondered if her mother was the one who'd shown up in Willie's life. "Did he say he was meeting a man or a woman?"

"A man. But who knows?"

"Did you talk about it Wednesday morning?"

"It was a rush. I'd stayed up late, so I was tired and overslept, and William looked really stressed out. I had to get Elliott ready and take him to school. I thought we'd talk about it that night. But then . . ." Tamara's voice broke and dissolved into sobs.

Mattie finished Tamara's thought for her. "Then he disappeared."

"Yeah."

Mattie felt herself choke up again. With a glance, she threw the lead back to Stella.

"Other than his old street gang, can you think of anyone else who might have harmed William?" Stella asked.

"Not anyone in our lives now."

*That's the problem,* Mattie thought. *This has to be connected to Timber Creek.*

"I want to see him," Tamara said. "If I come out there, can I see him?"

Mattie flinched and didn't know what to say.

"Do you have someone near you who can stay with you this evening?" Stella asked.

"My sister. I'll call her."

Stella avoided a direct answer. "Let me find out some details about the time of the autopsy and call you back later."

Mattie knew that Stella wanted Tamara to have a support person in place before sharing the grim details of William's condition.

Stella provided her own contact information and finished up the call. After disconnecting, she leaned back in her chair and stared at Mattie. "What are you thinking?"

Mattie gave her head a slight shake, trying to jiggle her thoughts into some kind of order. "We've got to find the connection between California and Timber Creek. I'm wondering if our mother showed up or something, but that doesn't make any sense. And this person that he met with last Sunday? It couldn't have been a friend of the family. Our family didn't have any friends."

"I think he said that to avoid the truth, whatever it is."

"Probably."

"I'll call his place of employment and see if the detective out there can help us work the local angle. Then I'll check back with Tamara and make sure her sister's with her. I need to let her know why it's not a good idea for her to rush out here to view his remains." Stella studied Mattie with a critical eye. "Why don't you finish up here and go home and get some sleep? You look about done in."

"I need to help you with these leads, or at least make that next call to Tamara."

"You've done all that you need to for today. Who knows what tomorrow will bring? Go home and get some rest while you can."

Stella was picking up the phone while Mattie woke up Robo and led him out of the office, closing the door quietly behind them.

Turning, she spied Rainbow striding across the lobby, a frown of concern etched on her face. "What happened, Mattie?" she asked as she approached.

Mattie knew she couldn't avoid telling her friend about the latest development in this case. Noticing that they were the only ones in the lobby, Mattie swallowed the lump in her throat and told her that they'd discovered the identity of their latest victim—her own brother.

The expression of dismay on her friend's face was almost her undoing. She made an excuse that she needed to complete her paperwork and clock out, and then escaped to the staff office. She needed to be alone to think through the details and try to remember anything from her past that she had forgotten.

Anything that might help solve her brother's murder.

# FOURTEEN

All through dinner, Cole worried about Mattie. He'd asked her to phone him when she left work, but she hadn't yet called. He'd also sent a couple of texts but received no response. He was afraid that her brother's death might make her withdraw from him the way she had after last Christmas, something he wanted to avoid.

When they'd finished eating, he told Mrs. Gibbs and his daughters about Mattie's brother. He hated having to do it, but they needed to know, and after everything that had happened this past year the kids were becoming experts at handling bad news. They talked it over for a long while, mostly about their concerns for Mattie, and then Angela left to go upstairs to do homework.

He had just finished getting Sophie started on hers at the kitchen table when his cell phone jingled in his pocket. Mattie? He checked caller ID and was disappointed to see a number he didn't recognize.

He answered it. "Timber Creek Veterinary Clinic. This is Dr. Walker."

A male voice came from the receiver. "Hi, I'm Bret Flynn. I have a horse with a cut on his hind leg. Looks like it needs stitches."

*Bret Flynn. Must be Riley's dad.* "Hi, Bret. Can you bring him in or do I need to come to your place?"

"I can trailer him in."

Cole gave him directions to the clinic and arranged to meet him in ten minutes. After disconnecting the call, he turned to his housekeeper who was wiping the kitchen countertops. "I've got an emergency at the clinic, Mrs. Gibbs. Can you do homework supervision until I get back?"

"Why, sure. I'll have my coffee here with Miss Sophie."

Sophie tipped her head up from the papers spread out in front of her. "When I finish this, Dad, I'll make a card for Mattie."

He placed his hand on her small shoulder. "She'll like that, Little Bit."

She bent over her worksheets and put pencil to paper, a look of concentration on her face. Cole gave her a quick hug and said goodbye before rushing off to open up the clinic. When he heard the rattle of truck and trailer coming down the lane, he rolled back the double door to open up the equine treatment room. Flynn parked close, exited his truck, and went to the back of the trailer to unload his horse.

Of average height with a broad chest and shoulders, Bret Flynn had the same dark eyes and hair as his daughter. He wore his hair long, almost to his shoulders, and gray strands intermingled with the brown. He looked to be in his fifties, older than Cole had expected. Flynn led a blaze-faced sorrel gelding toward the clinic, the horse limping on his bandaged left hind leg.

Cole unlatched the gate on the stocks—a metal stanchion designed to hold a horse still while being worked on. "Bring him on in here," he called.

The sorrel's shod hooves clopped in an uneven gait on the concrete floor of the treatment room as he entered the stocks without a fuss, letting Cole swing the side panel shut to secure him within the rectangular space. After settling the latch at the rear, he introduced himself to Flynn and received a firm handshake in return.

"I met Riley last night," Cole said. "She ate dinner with us."

"Thanks for that." Flynn made a slight grimace as he met Cole's gaze. "I was out later than I thought I'd be. She mentioned that she was over here, and she had a good time."

Cole gestured toward the sorrel's bandaged leg. "Did this happen yesterday?"

"Yeah, I had to work today so this was the earliest I could bring him in."

Cole placed his palm on the sorrel's stifle and slid it downward toward the hock as he squatted, moving slowly and letting the horse know where he was to avoid spooking him. The nicely wrapped bandage had been affixed with vet tape.

"What happened to him?"

"Scraped it on a rock."

Cole thought of the rocky trail he'd been on that day. Cuts of this type happened on trail rides. A shod hoof could slip from a rock, which in turn caught the lower leg with a sharp edge and scraped it. That's why he always packed a first aid kit; it looked like Flynn had been prepared, too. "Where did you go?"

"West of town. Scouting out some places to hunt this fall."

The mention of hunting made him think of the dead ram. "What do you hunt?"

"I haven't hunted much lately. We moved here from California, and I didn't have horses out there. Used to hunt deer here in Colorado when I was a kid, so I'm happy to get back to this way of life again."

"You grew up around here?"

"On the western slope near Palisade. My parents had an orchard there."

"Great peaches come from that part of the state."

"We grew peaches, pears, and apples when I was growing up."

Cole had removed the bandage by this time and was inspecting the laceration. Ointment and gauze covered what looked like a skin tear. "You did a good job with first aid. The cut looks superficial, although he's favoring that leg more than I'd expect."

"We were up pretty high when it happened. I hated to make him walk all the way down, but I couldn't carry him." Flynn lifted a corner of his mouth in a crooked smile.

"He's probably just sore then, maybe bruised. I'll clean this wound real good and suture it. We'll keep an eye on the lameness. He'll probably heal up okay." Cole stood, moving to fill a stainless steel bucket with warm water and to retrieve a bottle of iodine cleanser. He grabbed some cotton, squatted back down beside the sorrel, and began to scrub the leg gently.

"I was up around Redstone Ridge today," Cole said. "Were you anywhere near that area?"

"I was north of there, near Lowell Pass."

A trail that angled north and west outside of Timber Creek, not anywhere close to the area where the ram had been killed.

Cole remembered what he'd learned about the family from Riley last night. "Your daughter told us about you losing your wife. I'm sorry about that."

Flynn nodded, averting his eyes. "We're learning to deal with it. Takes a while."

"It surely does." He didn't feel comfortable sharing his own story, so he left it at that and went back to the business at hand. "This looks clean and I don't think we'll have any trouble closing it."

After blocking the area with a local anesthetic, Cole began the process of suturing the wound, keeping the conversation light. Grief was a private thing and not always something to be exposed to new acquaintances, and he thought he'd let the man keep his to himself.

Thinking about grief led his mind back to Mattie. When he finished up here, he would try to reach her again.

★

As Mattie and Robo left the station, her phone signaled an incoming text from Riley that said, "R u home. I'm at happy shack. Can I come over?"

Mattie sent a quick reply: "Stay put. I'm coming to get you."

While she'd been in her office completing her paperwork, Mattie had forced herself to reboot from being the victim's relative so she could switch back into cop mode. Sure, Willie's death hurt like hell, but the only thing she could do about it now was to find his killer. And that was something she vowed to do.

Past experience had taught her that work typically filled the

emptiness inside. And two things she needed to get done this evening were to find an after school place for Riley to hang out and
check out this Happy Shack ice cream parlor to make sure it was a
wholesome place. As always, drugs were her main concern. Timber
Creek had purchased Robo for their sheriff's department to reduce
drug traffic through their community. If there was someone out
there hoping to score a sale with minors in her town, she wanted to
be on the front line preventing it.

After loading Robo into his compartment, Mattie drove to
Main Street. The ice cream place had taken over a small clapboard
building near the grocery store. The owner had spruced up the front
with plywood cutouts of tulips spray painted with hues of rose, yellow, and purple as well as cutouts of ice cream cones topped with
chocolate, strawberry, and vanilla flavors. A handwritten board
labeled HAPPY SHACK leaned against the building by the door.

The sun had set and the atmosphere was taking on a chill for
the night. Mattie decided to leave Robo in the car for the few minutes this would take.

She navigated her way through the wooden flowers and ice
cream cones while she peeked inside through the windows. The few
video game machines that she'd heard so much about lined the back
wall of the open room while tables clustered in the middle. An old-
fashioned soda counter sat near the right wall, complete with fili-
greed stools. Riley—the only customer—perched on one of them.

She appeared to be deep in conversation with the woman on
the far side of the counter, but she swiveled her chair around and
greeted Mattie with a huge grin when she entered the store.

"I got your text," Riley said. "I'm so glad you're home! Thanks
for coming to get me."

The girl's enthusiastic greeting helped sooth her grieving soul.
"Sure. I'm glad I was able to."

The woman across the counter looked like a lady who spent
quite a bit of time in front of a mirror. She had lovely, purple-
colored eyes, probably enhanced with tinted contacts. She wore her
blond hair swept up into a cascade of curls that tumbled to her

shoulders, and her smooth skin and reddened lips were covered with makeup artfully applied. The whole effect was one of an attractive lady entering middle age but holding on to her youth for dear life. To Mattie, she was a perfect example of where less could have been more.

Mattie extended her hand and introduced herself.

"My name's Violet. Violet Carter," the lady said, offering Mattie a firm squeeze with the ends of her fingers and a smile that revealed pretty, white teeth. "I'm so glad to meet you. Riley says you're a friend of hers and you teach a class at the school. Sort of a Just Say No class."

"That's all correct." Mattie slipped a smile toward Riley before focusing back on Violet. The name matched her eyes, perhaps part of the overall plan. "Welcome to town. I hear you opened your business just this past weekend."

"We're so happy to be here. I've always dreamed of owning a business in a small town like this. And here we are."

Mattie leaned a hip against a stool and an elbow on the counter. "What brought you to Timber Creek?"

"Actually, it was my husband's idea to live in a small town. He wanted a place where he could fish and hunt, and I wanted a place where I could run a business that might make a difference in kids' lives. So Timber Creek looked like a place to try."

"You're interested in helping out kids?"

"Always. I ran a day care before. We had a houseful of children all the time. The little ones are too hard for me to keep up with anymore, so I thought an after school hangout might be the ticket. Especially in a town where it looks like there aren't too many places for the kids to spend time together and just have fun."

"Do you have children of your own?"

"Oh, my yes. I have three, but they're all grown and out living lives of their own. They don't have much time for their mama anymore." Riley was rotating the stool she sat on back and forth, and Violet reached to pat one of her hands that were braced against the counter. "It does my heart good to get to spend time with a girl like Riley. We hit it off the minute we met."

The door opened, and Violet's face lit as she glanced behind Mattie to see who had entered. "Darling, you're back," she said, her voice filled with pleasure. "Did you catch anything?"

Mattie turned to see a man who had iron-gray hair peppered with black. He was built wide and solid, like a fireplug. He gave her a keen once over before turning his attention back to Violet.

"I caught four brookies and a rainbow. Prettiest trout you've ever seen. Dinner tonight?" He walked behind the counter and gave Violet a quick kiss on the lips before turning his attention to Mattie and Riley. He offered his hand to Mattie first. "I'm John Carter, Violet's other half."

Mattie shook hands. "Deputy Mattie Cobb, and this is Riley."

"Pleased to meet you." John turned back to Violet. "I got home early and had time to put the horses away for the evening. Then I grabbed my tools and came over to hang that sign for you."

"Aren't you just the sweetest thing?" Violet was all smiles for her husband.

The mention of horses had caught Mattie's attention. "Were you out riding today, Mr. Carter?"

"Sure was. I couldn't wait to get back in the saddle. It's been years since I've had a good horse."

"Where did you ride?"

"I went out east of town in those open meadows where the creek runs through. There's some good fishing in Timber Creek."

Mattie nodded agreement. "This is a nice business you have here. Will you be working behind the counter, too?"

"Maybe on occasion, but I'm mostly just the handyman." He looked at his wife, returning her smile.

Violet cuddled up to him, taking hold of his upper arm and squeezing it to her bosom. "And I do appreciate my strong-armed carpenter. He did all the work inside here, including building this counter for me."

To Mattie, the woman's theatrics were a little over the top, but her husband seemed to be eating it up, gazing at her with nothing short of adoration.

"Anything to make you happy, my dear," he said. "I'd better get this done, so we can go home for the evening. Are you about ready to close up shop?"

"I might as well. All the kids have headed home, everyone but Riley. And Deputy Cobb is taking her home now, too."

John looked at Mattie. "Your daughter?"

"My friend," she said, glancing at Riley. The girl seemed focused on rubbing away a smudge on the countertop.

"I thought you looked too young for a daughter her age."

Mattie shrugged. "Moms and daughters come in all ages."

"Riley's mom died several months ago," Violet said, her words casting a shadow across the girl's face.

"I'm sorry to hear that, young lady," John said, pausing for a moment. "Well, you're welcome in here anytime. Violet will look after you. She loves kids."

Red blossomed on Riley's cheeks, and she murmured something that could be taken for a thank you.

Mattie decided to end the girl's discomfort by ending the conversation. "We'd better be going. It's nice to meet you both."

They said their goodbyes and went out to the car. Robo scrambled to the front of the cage to greet them.

"Hey, Robo," Riley said, reaching through the steel mesh to pet him. "How ya doin'?"

He answered by leaning in for an ear scratch.

"What do you think of this place?" Mattie asked, truly wanting Riley's opinion.

"It's fun. After the other kids left, Violet let me play one of the games for free."

"That was nice of her." Mattie thought the couple had been almost too sweet, but otherwise, the ice cream parlor had felt like any mom-and-pop establishment you might run across in any small town. "Where's your dad?"

"I don't know. I thought he'd be home by now, but he hasn't answered my text."

"Do you want dinner?" Riley seemed to be a bottomless pit, and Mattie didn't want to go home alone tonight.

"Sure!"

"Let's swing by the Pizza Palace and grab something. I want to tell you about a lady named Teresa Lovato who might have an after-school job for you. And if you're interested, I could take you by after dinner to meet her."

"All right. But Violet said she might have a job for me."

"That's great. Maybe you could find a way to do both."

Looking satisfied, Riley leaned back into her seat.

Mattie decided she would tell Mama T about Willie's death tonight, though she would spare her the details. She couldn't bear the thought of bringing that kind of horror into the good woman's world.

★

By the time Mattie drove up to park in front of her yard, her house was as dark as her spirits. She twisted the key to turn off her vehicle, reclined her seat slightly, and settled in, listening to the clicks coming from the front end as the engine cooled. She couldn't bear entering her empty house, and she needed a few minutes.

The evening had held one bright spot—the time she'd spent in Mama T's upstairs dormer room playing a board game with Riley and the kids. Afterwards, Riley had suggested that she read the kids a bedtime story, and Mattie sneaked away to find her foster mother downstairs in the kitchen. She wanted to tell Mama T about Willie before she heard about it on the Timber Creek grapevine.

At first her foster mother had been stunned by the news. "He can't be dead. You were going to see each other in just a few weeks."

Then she'd wept softly while Mattie fought to remain dry-eyed. She'd been afraid that if she broke down, she wouldn't be able to stop crying, and she still had to drive Riley home. Upon their departure, Mama had once again reminded Mattie to come over to meet Doreen the next day.

Mattie rubbed the knots at the base of her neck. It seemed to mean a great deal to Mama T for her two foster daughters to meet, so she needed to try to get back to town early enough to make it happen.

Robo came to the front of his compartment and rattled the gate with his nose. He must've been wondering why they were sitting here doing nothing. She popped open the latch, and he jumped through to stand on the passenger seat, training his gaze on the front porch, his next destination.

Mattie stroked the soft fur between his ears. From inside her chest pocket, her cell phone signaled an incoming text, and she took it out to check. The message was from Cole, asking her to call as soon as she could—it didn't matter what time.

He'd sent three texts and had made one missed phone call, but she couldn't bring herself to dial him. She felt emotionally and physically exhausted and the last thing she wanted to do tonight was blubber out her misery on the phone. She sent a text that said she was tied up in a meeting, and she would call him in the morning.

Robo pushed his nose under her arm and jiggled it, and then stared at her when she began stroking his fur again.

"You want me to pay attention to you, huh?" Mattie put her face against his and hugged him close. "Let's go inside and get ready for bed."

*Tomorrow will be a big day*, she thought as she exited her vehicle, Robo bailing out behind her. *We've got to find something that will lead us to Willie's killer.*

Using the last bit of energy she had left, she climbed the porch steps and used her key to let herself into her dark and lonely home.

# FIFTEEN

## Tuesday

Mattie joined Sheriff McCoy at the front table in the briefing room, while Robo settled on the floor underneath. Scheduled to observe Willie's autopsy, Stella had left for Denver before dawn. Brody and Agent Lawson were still up at the gravesite.

The sheriff was pouring coffee from an insulated carafe. "Coffee, Deputy?"

Mattie reached for the cup he was handing her. "Have you heard from Brody this morning?"

"He called in at six. They plan to excavate one of the depressions that you spotted when you were on the ridge. Their radar revealed dense objects, some elongated, some round. Lawson suspects the presence of skeletonized remains."

"In just the one spot?"

"In all three actually."

That hit Mattie hard. What were they dealing with here?

"They'll work on the one where the images appear closer to the surface. They'll know what they've got sometime today," McCoy said.

"I want to take Robo and search that area for anything that could be evidence."

"Garrett Hartman is on call to transport today. Cole can't manage another day off."

Cole had called while Mattie was in the shower and left her that message. He'd also said that Mountaineer had been designated for her use only, and that Garrett would pick him up whenever she needed him.

Mattie sipped her black coffee. She needed the caffeine, since she'd slept poorly again last night. "When shall we go?"

"Garrett can be ready in a couple of hours."

"I will be, too."

"I plan to go up as well. I want you to organize supplies and pack some extra evidence bags. I've got business I need to tie up before I leave." He studied her for a moment. "How are you holding up?"

Mattie looked him in the eye. "It's been rough. But I'm determined to find out who killed my brother."

Sheriff McCoy examined her face, apparently thinking. "Since you're related to the victim, there might be a time when we'll have to take you off the case. You realize that, don't you?"

"At this stage, we need Robo's nose."

"Agreed. But any evidence you find could be considered inadmissible in court. I want Deputy Brody to be with you every step of the way while you search today. If Robo hits on something, back off and let Brody retrieve it."

"That makes sense. We can work with that."

"Last evening, Stella reached Detective Hastings in the Hollywood Bureau. He's going to follow up on who might have made contact recently with your brother. He recognized the street names of William's old friends, and he plans to question them today."

Mattie nodded acknowledgment, though Stella had called her last night and given her the same information.

McCoy continued. "She also reached William's employer, Mr. Joseph Quintana. Mr. Quintana said William left for lunch on Wednesday and never returned. Although not showing up for work was unusual for William, Mr. Quintana didn't suspect foul play at that time. Apparently mechanics come and go at his shop, and he thought William would come back sooner or later to see if he still had a job."

"Has he talked to Detective Hastings?"

McCoy nodded. "Mr. Quintana says that he called on Friday to report William missing, and to give a character reference of sorts for him. Hastings indicated that he followed up with him on Saturday and again with Ms. Bennett, but found no further leads. His plan was to talk to some of his informants on the street. He said that he believed William had started using again and hoped he could get wind of his whereabouts."

She'd believed the exact same thing. Poor Willie. She should have given him the benefit of the doubt.

"Detective LoSasso has the impression that Detective Hastings is well motivated, and he will be diligent in following through with his end of the case."

Mattie remained noncommittal. The fact that it took her brother's death for anyone to take his disappearance as anything more than an addict falling off the wagon gave her a hollow feeling, but she had nothing she could say. She'd been guilty of doubting him herself.

"Is there anything more we need to discuss?" McCoy asked, pushing his chair back from the table.

"Not at the moment. I'll pack supplies. I also need to make a few phone calls."

"Let's get to work then."

On her way back to her office, she noticed the local bail bondsman passing through the lobby to leave. His presence reminded her of the cowboys from the fight at the Watering Hole on Saturday night. She knew they'd been held overnight to sober up but had been released on Sunday morning after posting bond. She hadn't had time to take a look at Garcia's report on the charges, but she suddenly remembered that the truck they'd been driving had borne California plates.

Robo circled and then flopped down on his dog bed beside her desk, heaving a sigh. He looked up at her as if to ask what they were waiting for. He'd become accustomed to starting the mornings with a trek in the mountains.

She logged onto her computer and pulled up the arrest reports from the weekend, focusing in on the mug shot of the guy who'd landed the head butt on her chest. Full name: Gibson "Gib" Galloway. Residence: Durango, Colorado. Former Residence: Bakersfield, California. Age: Thirty-five. Three prior arrests and one conviction in California for domestic violence.

*Must like to pick on women.*

She scanned the report. Apparently he and his buddies were going through town headed home to Durango from a rodeo in Kansas. They stopped at the Watering Hole, got drunk, he got into a fight with his girlfriend . . . and Mattie knew the rest of the story.

Looked like the group had been in Kansas prior to Saturday, and being from California didn't mean they'd been involved with Willie. Bakersfield wasn't that close to Hollywood, and California's population was huge. Something to keep in mind, but right now, she needed to return Cole's call.

Cole answered after the first ring. "Mattie."

"Sorry I couldn't call back last night, but it was too late when I got home. And this morning I was in the shower." At least her last excuse was true.

"You can call me anytime of the day or night, Mattie. How are you doing this morning?"

"I'm all right."

Cole paused. "Were you able to sleep?"

"Some."

Mattie realized that she was withholding her true feelings and he knew it, but she could at least show her gratitude. "Thanks for arranging for me to use Mountaineer today."

"I wish I could go with you, but things are piling up. I need today to catch up."

"Of course. Your patients need you."

"I wanted to tell you I met Riley's dad. His horse had a leg injury that he said happened on a mountain trail. The wound was consistent with a tear from a sharp rock, and it made me think of the trail we were on when we went to investigate the ram."

"Was he on that same trail?"

"He said he wasn't. He said he was over near Lowell Pass searching for a place to hunt next fall."

"All right, I'll keep that in mind. I need to meet him and talk to him about Riley."

"How so?"

"She's at loose ends most days after school, and I'm trying to make arrangements for her to have a job or at least a place to go. I figure he should be in on the plan."

"He seems like he's still dealing with his wife's death and spending a lot of time out in nature while he does it."

"Maybe he should consider taking his daughter with him." Mattie realized that she might not have a right to make that judgment, but she couldn't keep from saying it.

"I could make a place for her here at the clinic a couple afternoons if that would help. She could clean stalls and cages."

That sounded like a perfect opportunity. Being at Cole's clinic a couple days combined with a couple days at Mama T's could take care of a large part of Riley's after school time. A day or two at Happy Shack didn't seem like too much either. All in all, these options could work to keep the teen busy. "That would be great, Cole. I'll talk to her about it. Thank you."

"Anytime." Cole paused, and Mattie was about to end the conversation when he changed the subject. "I have to admit I'm worried about you. I know that discovering your brother's remains like we did was a terrible shock."

Mattie's throat constricted. "It was. I'm dealing with it."

"It's a lot to deal with." He paused, apparently organizing his words. "I told Mrs. Gibbs and the girls about it last night. They all send their love and Sophie has made you a card."

"That's sweet." Mattie's eyes welled, and she blinked back the tears. "How is Angie coping with what happened?"

"I think she's handling it so far. We talked last night, and she seemed more concerned about you than about herself. She wants to talk to you. Actually, we all do. How about coming over for dinner?"

"I'm getting ready to go back up to the site, and I don't know when I'll come down. If I make it back early enough, I already have a commitment this evening with Mama T."

"Maybe tomorrow?"

"I'll call you in the morning to let you know."

"Okay. And if you find you can drop by this evening, even for a short time, we'd all like to see you." Cole paused before he added. "I'd like to see you tonight even if it's late. Will you call me when you're free?"

Mattie didn't know why she hesitated to agree. Perhaps it was years of licking her own wounds that made it uncomfortable to even think about letting someone else in on her grief. "I'll try to, Cole. It's hard for me to predict how this day is going to go, but I'll check in with you if I can."

"Don't worry if it gets late. I'll keep my cell phone with me tonight."

Mattie wrapped it up and ended the call. Cole's compassionate tone made the pain in her heart swell, and she took a moment to restrain her sadness.

Robo lay on his cushion, his eyes pinned on her every move. She'd learned from experience that her emotions went straight to her dog, and she knelt beside him to rub his fur. "It'll be all right, buddy. We'll be all right."

As she continued to pet him, she hoped that time would prove her words to be true. Because right at this moment, she didn't know how this was all going to resolve. *Who brought Willie back to Timber Creek to kill him? And why?*

★

Mattie decided to grab a moment to see if she could find Bret Flynn at home before he left for work with the county road crew. She hurried outside with Robo trotting beside her. After loading him up, she drove west of town where Riley lived on a small acreage that contained an old log cabin and a newly constructed horse barn with an attached corral.

The early morning sun slanted in, its rays casting long shadows to the west of the upright hayrack in the middle of the corral. Two horses, a sorrel with a bandaged hind leg and a bay with a coat so dark and rich that the sun's rays glinted off it, browsed at their feed in a lazy way, indicating they'd already eaten their fill.

Mattie pulled up to the house and parked. "You're going to wait here," she said to Robo, hating to see his look of disappointment. "You'll get to go on a long run soon."

Mattie followed a stone pathway through a yard left in natural buffalo grass. She stepped up onto a concrete porch and knocked on the door.

Riley opened it. "Hey, Mattie. What are you doing here?"

"I came to talk to your dad. Is he still home?"

Riley turned and looked behind her, but due to the dim light inside the house, Mattie couldn't see beyond the screen door.

A man with longish brown hair streaked with gray and dark eyes that resembled Riley's materialized beside the girl. "I'm Riley's dad."

Mattie introduced herself. "Could I speak with you for a few minutes?"

"All right." He opened the screen door and stepped out onto the porch.

"I met Riley at the high school. Has she mentioned me to you?"

"Can't say that she has."

"She comes by my house occasionally after I get off work, and we have dinner together once in a while."

"I'll tell her to quit bothering you."

"Oh, no, I'm not complaining, and she's not a bother. I'm just telling you about it because she seems at loose ends after school and into the evening. I've had some ideas about how I might be able to help out, and I thought we should talk."

He raised one brow. "And you're involved because?"

"Riley and I have struck up a friendship. I'd like to make sure she has things to occupy her time while you're at work."

"Has she gotten into any kind of trouble?"

"Not at all, but I hope to keep her busy so it stays that way. I've found two after school jobs so far that she might be interested in, one helping with child care in a foster home and another at Dr. Walker's vet clinic."

"Dr. Walker? What would she do there?"

"Clean cages and stalls. It would be just a few hours twice a week."

He reached behind him to grasp the screen doorknob and partially opened the door. "I've really got to go or I'll be late for work, but I guess it's all right with me if she wants to do it. I'll be at work though, and I can't drive her out there."

"She'd have to ride her bike as long as weather allows. I'm sure Dr. Walker would let her cancel otherwise. Before you leave though, I thought I'd see if you had ideas for someone who could stay with Riley when you're working late at night or at least someone she could contact if she had concerns or whatever. You know, just someone to stay in touch with."

He frowned. "Riley is old enough to take care of herself. She doesn't need a babysitter."

"I misspoke. I should have said someone she can contact if she gets lonely. I think it's hard on her to be alone night after night."

Irritation showed in his frown. "I'll talk to Riley, but she's a big girl now and she's used to fending for herself. I don't think you need to be concerned, and if she's not in any trouble, it certainly doesn't look like you need to be involved."

Mattie realized she must have offended him and tried to explain. "Part of my job in Timber Creek is prevention oriented. We don't have many programs for kids or places for them to hang out. Until she gets connected with a group of friends, I'll keep an eye out for her. You know, kind of an 'it takes a village' philosophy when it comes to raising kids. And she's welcome to spend time with me if she wants to. It's just that I'm also often at work."

"I'm sure it's not as bad as you imagine it to be. She has a home she can come to, and I'll make sure that she does. Now, I really have to go." He stepped inside and closed the door, leaving Mattie hanging on the doorstep.

Walking back down the stone path to her SUV, she regretted that their conversation had turned south. She lacked experience in this type of parental contact, and she hoped it wouldn't result in negative consequences for Riley. But she had a sick feeling in the pit of her stomach that it would.

# SIXTEEN

Garrett Hartman led the way up the trail to Willie's gravesite with Mattie riding behind him and Sheriff McCoy bringing up the rear. Mattie found riding the steadfast Mountaineer less frightening each day, and though her body felt more relaxed in the saddle, her thoughts continued to chase around in her head.

Her mind flitted between images of Willie as a child beaten by their dad, and of him as a burned corpse, combining to create a sharp twist in her gut. Since she had no good memories in between to fall back on, she told herself that Willie had found happiness at the end of his life with Tamara and Elliott. He'd found a family, and that was the most comforting thought she could come up with.

When they arrived at the suspected gravesites at the edge of the meadow, things had changed. Yellow tape surrounded the area, taking in not only the three depressions that Mattie had spotted, but also a large area encircling them. The excavation team had assembled along with their tools.

They began to dig carefully, at first using shovels and then hand trowels. Rick Lawson watched over the process, at times on his knees with the rest of the crew.

At one point, the team leader gave further direction to the others. "Evidence of fire. Screen that out and save it."

Chunks of blackened coal or burned wood started appearing in the dirt, which in turn went into a bucket. Its contents were then poured onto a screen and the black chunks were separated and saved inside another bucket. They worked together to uncover a channel around the center where they expected to find bones.

Mattie watched with horrified fascination as she realized that this gravesite might present with the same MO as Willie's. A burning pit, first filled with a body and then filled with fire.

"Careful. Here's what could be the skull," the forensic anthropologist said. "Let's leave it in place and clear around it."

Using a brush and gloved fingers, he worked his way around the degraded bone, tinged gray from charcoal exposure. He slowly revealed the round frontal bone, the empty eye sockets, and finally the maxilla and gaped open jaw, both still holding teeth.

He held it up, inspecting it carefully. "This skull belonged to a child."

In a split second, an image of a burning boy surrounded by flames flashed into Mattie's mind.

Clenching her teeth, she turned and headed toward the volunteer's campsite, taking Robo with her.

★

Less than a half hour later, Brody joined Mattie by the campfire. She'd poured herself coffee from a pot that hung from a rod above the fire, and she huddled over the cup, warming her hands. As she gazed at the glowing embers and listened to the wood snap, she'd shut down her thoughts about unearthing a child's bones. Instead, she was thinking about the rough terrain around Willie's gravesite and the crevice beyond the waterfall that she and Brody had been unable to search.

Brody bent to grab an empty cup and tipped the pot to fill it. "We've got a full skeleton. Can't specify age until they get the remains to the lab, but they're thinking around six years old. Some clothing remnants—zippers from a jacket and pants, some buttons probably from a shirt, partially burned rubber from the soles of tennis shoes. They've moved on to another grave now."

Empty inside, Mattie nodded and took another sip of the bitter liquid.

Brody stared into the campfire as he sipped his coffee. "Why a dead child?"

Mattie shrugged, unable to speculate. She changed the subject. "You know that stream we crossed up by my brother's gravesite? You know how it flows into that gorge we couldn't get down into?"

"Yeah."

"Well, the stream is fairly small now, but don't you think there are times that it swells when runoff flows through there?"

Brody lowered his cup. "Yep, from snowmelt and rain. Could get a large head of water rolling if there's a downpour."

"Let's go search it, Brody. Let's follow the stream and see if we can find anything that might have washed downhill. It's rugged, but it looks like a place where trash might collect."

"All right. We're not needed to excavate those graves, so we might as well make ourselves useful."

"Do we have some rope we could take with us? It's going to be hard getting down into that ravine."

Brody nodded and then drained his cup before leaving to retrieve the rope. He came back carrying what looked like a curled lasso hanging from his shoulder. Mattie emptied her cup by tossing the remaining coffee aside.

Robo trotted out in front as they hiked the short distance uphill toward Willie's gravesite, but Mattie called him back and told him to heel as they drew near. When they reached the stream, she asked Robo to take a drink.

The ravine ran downhill, perpendicular to the trail. Although somewhat shallow at this point, it dropped off quickly into a deep, rocky crevice that they'd searched around earlier.

She pointed to some huge granite boulders at the top of the falls. "I guess we'll have to climb down there."

"I'll go look for the best way."

Mattie prepared Robo by exchanging his everyday collar for the blue one that he wore specifically for evidence detection and then led him to where the stream tumbled off the ledge, splashing over boulders until it landed about twenty-five feet below. From there, the ravine looked rugged, filled with current bushes, evergreen trees, willows, and deadfall, but Mattie thought Robo could search places that she couldn't.

Brody was busy at the top of the falls, tying the rope to a pine tree. "You can use the rope to let yourself down. Then I can lower Robo."

As long as she had support from the rope, Mattie thought she could manage the footholds offered by rocks on the way down.

"I have a full-body vest that I'll put on him." She secured the vest by centering its mesh panel beneath Robo's belly and buckling its straps over his back. To test it, she gripped the straps and lifted him a few inches off the ground, making sure the vest supported his weight throughout his entire length. "Slip the rope through these rings here on top."

"Is he going to fight this?"

"He shouldn't. He's done this many times in practice. He knows what to do."

After getting Robo rigged out, Mattie turned and tested the rope. She grabbed onto it and leaned back with most of her weight, pulling the knot tight against the thick tree trunk. Where the knot scraped the bark it released the sweet, pungent scent of pine, and sap stained the rope.

Mattie went to the edge of the boulders. "I'll go ahead now. Robo, stay."

She hated that his brow puckered in a worried expression, but she didn't want him bailing off the ledge to come after her. She grasped the rope firmly in both hands. Backing cautiously, she looked downward for her first foothold, feeling her world tilt as the rocky bottom of the ravine came into focus. She shifted her gaze from far to near, focusing instead on taking one step at a time.

The stream splashed in a fall beside her, creating a rushing noise and slippery stones. Going hand over hand along the rope and placing her feet carefully into footholds, Mattie glanced up to see Robo peering down at her, his mouth open in a nervous pant, pink tongue highlighted against black muzzle. Her boot slipped off a rock, jamming her knee against a boulder, and pain wrenched her attention back to her feet.

Step-by-step, the rope pinching at her palms, she eased her way down until, finally, she felt the firm earth at the base of the falls. "Okay," she shouted, releasing the rope. "Send Robo."

Brody tugged the rope back up to the ledge. Grateful that her dog had enough experience working around Brody that he wouldn't be frightened, Mattie waited the few minutes it took to secure the rope. Brody led Robo to the edge of the falls.

Her partner really looked worried now.

"It's okay, boy. You're going to come down here." She tapped the rocky wall.

Brody lifted Robo by his chest and carefully lowered him over the edge. He hung there for a brief moment, his body limp and his legs splayed, while Brody adjusted the rope and began lowering him slowly. Mattie spoke soothing words and held up her arms, locking onto Robo's gaze and sending him confidence with her eyes.

He landed in her arms without incident, and she held onto him, providing support as his feet came into contact with the ground. She hugged him and told him what a good boy he was, and in a split second his expression changed from worry to pure joy. The same response bubbled up inside her. As he took on every challenge that was asked of him, her brave dog was a huge source of both joy and pride. He always made her feel better.

Mattie untied the rope and looked up to see Brody peering down at her. "Your turn," she told him.

She led Robo out of the way so that Brody could descend. While he made his way down, she removed Robo's vest, leaving his collar in place. It took only a minute for Brody's long legs to navigate the cliff.

Mattie finished up with Robo. "Let's do what we can to search along this streambed. We'll go down one side and come back up on the other."

After Mattie told Robo to seek, he put his nose to the ground and squeezed through a tangle of willows, heading downhill. The solid rock walls gave her the sensation of pressing in from both sides. She ignored it and fought through the foliage, staying as close to Robo as she could, parting branches and inching forward. The clutter of branches and boulders made for slow passage, and Robo soon ranged out in front, outdistancing her.

After about fifty yards of pushing through timber, her shirt drenched with sweat despite the crisp air, she lost all sight of her dog. When the ground evened out, she thought about calling him back, but then spotted him sitting at the base of a pile of deadfall on the stream's bank where it looped out and slowed, creating a natural catchment.

He'd apparently been watching for her, and made eye contact as soon as she came into view. He'd dug a shallow pit in the mash of dead leaves, twigs, and branches that he now put his mouth into, touched something, and then looked back into her eyes. His signal for evidence detection.

"What did you find?"

She rushed to join him and knelt, hugging him close with one arm while she reached to probe near the hole that he'd made. Metal glinted through the dead leaves.

Brody came up behind her. "What's he got?"

His presence reminded her of the sheriff's instruction. "Sheriff McCoy told me that you need to recover any evidence that Robo finds up here."

"Yeah, I know."

Evidently McCoy had given Brody the same instructions. She pulled out her cell phone. "Let me take a photo."

She snapped shots at different angles and then moved aside, pulling Robo along with her.

Brody squatted and began scooping aside the dried leafy deposit with one hand while Mattie videoed the process. It didn't take long to uncover Robo's find.

It was a handgun—a semi-automatic pistol. Black and caked

with dirt, ugly and deadly-looking. Fingers trembling from a rush of adrenaline, Mattie snapped several photos of it in place.

"Looks like a .357 Magnum," Brody said. "Desert Eagle from back in the early eighties."

Brody knew his guns, and he was probably right about the age of this one. From its condition, she would guess it had lain here in the ravine for a long time. But why would it be here, only yards away from Willie's gravesite? A coincidence? And who had disposed of it in the first place?

# SEVENTEEN

The deadfall yielded a cache of debris that included plastic bags, food wrappers, Styrofoam cups, and the like. Mattie and Brody bagged it all and then searched a little farther down before heading back up on the other side of the stream. They found nothing more.

Sheriff McCoy and Rick Lawson were still at the gravesites in the meadow when Mattie and Brody returned, and the excavation team had made progress. Two more skeletons with clothing remnants had been unearthed, both adults, and both had been burned. Three body bags were laid out side-by-side, waiting for helicopter pickup.

Brody handed the paper bag containing the gun to the sheriff.

"What's this?" McCoy said, looking into the bag.

"Desert Eagle, .357 Magnum," Brody said. "Robo found it in the ravine at the upper gravesite."

McCoy offered the bag to Lawson, who peered into it before focusing on Mattie. "This gun was manufactured back in the eighties. We can't say exactly how long ago those bodies were buried, but it could have been around then. There are signs of projectile penetration on both adult skulls, and we've got lead inside one of them. We'll have to see if that slug came from this handgun."

Mattie glanced down at Robo, and he gazed back at her as if waiting for her to tell him what his next job would be. Her limbs were heavy from exhaustion, her clothing covered with sweat, dirt, and mud, but the pride she felt for her dog's accomplishments made it all worth it.

"The team is going to stay here tonight and look for sign of more graves, but I'm heading back down to the sheriff's station," Lawson said. "I'll clean this gun and see if I can get a serial number off it. Then I'll put it through the ATF National Tracing Center. We can probably find out who purchased it originally and maybe trace it to its final owner."

"How long will that take?" Mattie asked.

"I might get results within twenty-four hours."

That came as a surprise. Having Lawson on their team had its benefits.

McCoy told Mattie that she should return to Timber Creek in the next party as well. She started back to where the horses were tied, and Brody came along with her. He looked as dirty and beat as she did. "Do you need a break to go back to town?" she asked him.

"Nah. We've got a shower rigged up with a solar heated bag of water, and the sheriff brought me up a clean set of clothes."

"Is there anything you need me to do when I get to the station? Anyone you need me to call?"

"Nope. I'm good." Brody gave her a look that told her she needed to back off. He wasn't a touchy-feely sort of guy, and he usually kept his private business to himself.

Mattie remained silent for the rest of the way, saying goodbye when they reached the camp. She found Garrett saddling up Mountaineer at the rope picket line where they'd tied the horses. Grateful to be transported downhill on horseback instead of having to use her own two legs, she squatted beside Robo and hugged him close while she waited.

"Are you about ready to go?" Garrett asked.

"We are. The others will be here soon."

The craggy planes of the rancher's face were etched with concern. "You look beat. Wait here while I get the others rounded up."

He returned shortly with a cup of coffee and then left again. His gesture touched her, and she fought back that hollow feeling inside as she thought of Willie, of her family. They hadn't taken care of each other the way they should.

Garrett returned with the rest of the party. After mounting up, she looked down at Robo, wishing he could ride home, too, but he trotted alongside her as the horses moved out, perfectly happy with going on his own.

This time, Mattie relaxed completely in the saddle, bracing herself and leaning back automatically on the steeper grades and then swaying with Mountaineer's steps on the flat. The sun set and the forest took on the muted light of dusk, making her sleepy. Robo seemed content with staying close. Her phone beeped with messages as they came back into range for cell phone service.

When they arrived at the parking lot, she thanked Garrett and loaded up Robo, giving him some water before climbing into the driver's seat and checking her voicemail. The first message was from Mama T, and it soothed Mattie's spirit just to hear her voice. "Don't forget to come over this evening, *mijita*. Doreen is here and she's anxious to meet you."

She wondered if her foster mom called Doreen 'my little daughter' as well.

The second message was from Cole. "Hi, Mattie. We're thinking of you today." There was a long pause. "I know this has to be tough on you and . . . I hope we can at least talk tonight. Call me when you get a chance, okay? No matter how late. Well, bye."

Sounded like it was tough on Cole, too. She would call him after she carried through with her commitment to Mama T. She sent him a message saying she would phone as soon as she was free.

There was also a text from Riley. "Hey Mattie. Dad says I can't come to your house anymore. Sorry if I was a bother. I still want the job with the kids. When can I start?"

*For Pete's sake*, Mattie thought, quickly sending a reply. "You're not a bother! You can come over anytime. I'll check with Mama T and get back to you."

She yawned as she settled in behind the wheel for the short drive to town. As if contagious, Robo joined her in a squeaky yawn, his pink tongue curling, and then he circled on his cushion and plopped down with a sigh. When she checked him in the rearview mirror, it looked like he'd fallen asleep within seconds.

Robo slept all the way into town. She tried to check in with

Stella as she drove, but there was no answer, so she left a message for her to call back.

After a shower and a change of clothes, Mattie left Robo asleep on his dog bed and drove the short distance to Mama T's house. Mama T had left the front porch light on for her, but she slipped around to the side door that led into the kitchen where she knew the two women would be cooking, visiting, or both. After tapping on the door, she opened it and was greeted by a wonderful, spicy aroma that could come only from her foster mother's stove.

Mama T and Doreen sat at the table wrapping tamales, her mama's special recipe and one that Mattie had helped with many a time. They both looked up with smiles, and she could tell by the expression on Mama T's face that she was in her element—cooking with someone she loved.

Her mama gave her a long hug, and Mattie could feel the concern and sympathy flowing from her heart. Mama T leaned away, still holding her by the arms, and fixed her with intense scrutiny. "I'm happy to see you, *mijita*. How are you?"

Mattie's eyes prickled with tears. "I'll be all right."

Mama T squeezed her upper arms before releasing her and taking her hand. "You're here now. I told Doreen I knew you would come, and we must keep busy while we wait. The time goes faster, right? Come, meet your sister."

Doreen had stood, holding back while Mattie and Mama T greeted each other, but now she approached, opening her arms for an embrace. As Mattie leaned forward to accept the hug, she caught a whiff of lavender infused into the woman's long, black hair. Her foster sister was dressed in a flowing, vanilla-colored tunic over black trousers, and she came across as strong and sturdy. She had a broad, round face with soft, pleasant features and kind, dark eyes. She appeared to be of mixed race, perhaps Hispanic and Caucasian like Mattie.

"I am so very sorry about your brother," Doreen said. "Come, sit at the table. Can I get you something to eat or drink?"

Mattie realized that she was starving. "I haven't had much to eat today, and Mama T's kitchen smells amazing. But you don't have to get it for me, I can help myself."

"Sit down at the table," Mama T said, bustling over to the cupboard to grab a plate and then heading for the stove. She opened one of the pots, revealing the tops of cornhusk-covered tamales wedged upright inside for steaming. She served up three of them, set the plate in front of Mattie, and then went back to the stove to dish up a bowl of green chili. She also grabbed a jar of homemade tomatillo salsa and plopped both dishes down beside the plate. "Now, what to drink? Iced tea?"

Mattie stayed out of her foster mom's way and helped herself to cutlery and napkins from the cafeteria-style containers that always sat on the table. "Iced tea would be great."

Doreen had settled back into her seat and taken up a cornhusk to open wide on the cutting board she was using. She placed a spoonful of viscous cornmeal into the middle of the husk and spread it into a thin rectangle, followed by a dollop of seasoned, chopped beef. She then folded one side over and rolled the tamale so that the cornmeal encircled the meat, after which she enclosed it by wrapping each side of the cornhusk over and folding up a flap at the bottom. She placed the finished tamale open end up into a pot, ready for steaming.

Mattie found it soothing to watch the familiar process performed by Doreen's flying fingers, and realized with some surprise that this felt like home. Even though these women weren't related to her by blood, she still felt like she was among family.

Her first bite of Mama T's spicy chili confirmed her feeling. Comfort food.

"Do you have any idea who killed your brother?"

Doreen's words threw up a wall between them; Mattie might feel like she was home, but that didn't mean she would share information about Willie's case. "Nothing I can talk about."

Mama T placed her warm hand on her shoulder, and it steadied her. She realized she'd come across as abrupt, and she put her own hand up to cover her mama's.

Doreen's gaze conveyed sympathy. "I'm sorry. We should talk about other things."

As she went back to wrapping tamales, Doreen told Mattie how she'd grown up in Timber Creek but left after high school, how she'd driven an old beat up Chevy wherever her heart and her savings would take her and had ended up in New Mexico, and how she'd married a man who was a farmer and had been later blessed with two children, a boy and a girl.

Mattie felt the knots in her shoulders release, and her appetite returned as she listened. She finished her plate and stood to take her dish to the sink, a rule established for all of Mama T's children.

"Mama T said you were looking for your biological mother," Doreen said.

"My brother and I had talked about it."

"I have to say again that I'm so, so sorry about your brother." Doreen's eyes brimmed, and her sorrow appeared genuine. "But maybe you can carry on by yourself and find your mom. If I can help in any way, please tell me. What's her name?"

"Ramona Cobb."

"Ramona—such a pretty name."

Mattie thought so, too. Her phone vibrated in her pocket, and she reached for it to check caller ID—Stella. "Excuse me for a minute. I've got to take this call."

She rose from her chair, stepped outside the kitchen door as she answered the phone, and leaned up against the white stucco wall of the house. "Hi, Stella. You back in town?"

"Just about. Are you home?"

"I'm at my foster mom's, a few blocks away."

"Can you meet me at your house in a few minutes?"

"Sure."

She knew that Stella had information she wanted to share privately, and the thought gave her a chill. Stella was coming back from Willie's autopsy. What had she learned?

Mattie returned to the kitchen, remembering she needed to confirm a start date for Riley. She mentioned it to Mama T, they agreed on Thursday after school, and then Mattie turned to Doreen to say goodbye.

Doreen clasped her in a warm hug and murmured, "I hope to see you tomorrow for dinner, my sister." The sentiment made Mattie's eyes fill, and she turned away so that her emotion wouldn't show. Though Doreen's words were meant to be kind, they came as a reminder that the one who could truly call her "sister" was now gone.

As she drove the few blocks to her home, she realized that her emotions were raw, which she attributed to being exhausted. The circumstances of Willie's death and the physical demands of the last two days had taken their toll. And now, the foreboding associated with the information that Stella might be bringing weighed heavily on her.

When she pulled up in front of her house, she felt relieved that she'd left on the porch light. That bit of brightness seemed to give her an inordinate amount of comfort. She sent a text to Riley, telling her when she could start work with the kids, before she unlocked the door and let herself inside. Robo's *woof* came from the bedroom followed by the ticking sound of his toenails as he scrambled out of bed to greet her, yawning as he trotted across the room. She sank to her knees and opened her arms, clasping his warm, furry body to her heart and holding him. He swiped a wet kiss against her cheek.

"Did you have a good sleep? Hmm?" She dodged his tongue as he revved up for a serious face licking. "Stop that now." She grasped the ruff at the back of his neck and gave it a gentle shake, an imitation of the way a mother dog disciplines her pup. Although Mattie allowed a small amount of licking now and then, it was always important with Robo to remind him of who was alpha in their two-member pack. She'd been taught this at academy and time had proven that consistency kept him from testing her boundaries, as these high-drive male dogs were prone to do.

"Do you want to go outside? Come on, let's take a break."

After letting Robo outside in the backyard, she heard the doorbell ring. Stepping back into the kitchen, she hurried through to the living room to open the front door for Stella. The detective's eyes were red-rimmed and bloodshot from strain, and Mattie could tell that she wasn't the only one running on empty.

Stella came inside, shucking her jacket and kicking off her loafers before making a beeline for the kitchen. "You got a beer in here for me?"

"Sure."

"You want one?"

"No, thanks." Although she kept a supply on hand for Stella, Mattie avoided alcohol after learning the hard way that she didn't handle it well. She drank an occasional beer, but the last thing she wanted was to end up being a drunk like her father.

She opened the back door for Robo, and he trotted inside, rushing to greet their guest. Stella gave him a playful ear rub. "Look at you, all full of pep. I see running up and down the mountain hasn't interfered with your mojo."

"He'll be ready to go again by tomorrow."

"I can see that." Examining Mattie's face, Stella popped the cap off her beer. "And how are you doing?"

"I'm okay."

"I'm afraid I've got some bad news from the autopsy that I need to share with you."

"I thought that might be the case."

They settled on opposite ends of the couch—Stella with her legs stretched out and feet on the coffee table, Mattie with both legs bent, hugging her knees. Robo leaned against the couch beside Mattie, his head against her hip as if aware that she needed him.

Stella finished a few swallows of her drink, apparently fortifying herself. They'd been in this position before, and they'd learned there was no need to soften the blow with each other. "The medical examiner found soot in William's trachea."

Even though Mattie suspected bad news of some kind, the words hit her hard. "Meaning he was alive when he was set on fire."

"Yes."

Curling into herself, Mattie put her forehead on her knees and closed her eyes. Robo nosed her side, and she rested one hand on his head.

"I'm sorry, Mattie. Damn it all anyway."

Her eyes were blurry with unshed tears when she looked at Stella, but there was nothing she could dredge up to say.

"The ME confirmed ligature marks on his legs and multiple marks at the back of his neck. Although his wrists were too damaged by fire to tell, it appears that he'd been bound prior to death, and he was possibly strangled more than once. That's speculation of course, but . . . that's what the evidence points to. There are some marks on his back that look like cigarette burns. No sign of bullets or being shot."

Willie had been tortured. Mattie buried her face against her knees, unable to respond.

"I hate having to tell you this." Stella sighed. "We sent blood tests for drugs and other substances to the lab. We'll have results in a few days."

Drawing a deep breath, Mattie focused on Robo's upturned face. He was staring at her as if trying to determine why she was upset. She stroked his ears. "Thank you for telling me this tonight, before I have to hear it in the meeting tomorrow."

"Well, that's the other thing. Sheriff McCoy sent the message that you can sit this one out if you want to. I can meet with you separately."

Mattie shook her head. "That won't be necessary. I'll be at the meeting in the morning. What time will it be?"

"Seven o'clock. Rick Lawson will be there, too."

With her eyes still fixed on Robo, Mattie nodded. She owed it to Willie to do whatever she could to bring his killer to justice, and she would stay on the job no matter what.

# EIGHTEEN

After Stella left, Mattie wasn't sure what to do with herself. Thoughts of Willie's last hours on earth chased through her mind like demons, taunting her. There was only one thing she could do to roust out of this state, and that was to run. Even though her legs felt rubbery with fatigue, she had to stay on the move to escape the torment of her thoughts.

She changed into sweats and running shoes, dodging Robo as she went back to the living room. He gamboled in front of her, his mouth wide in a happy grin, alternating between leaping about and play posing. "Yes, we're going for a run."

His nails skittered on the hardwood floor as he whirled to retrieve the leash that was hanging by the front door. Before she could snap it on his collar, the doorbell rang, sending him back to the door to bark.

"Robo, it's me." Cole's voice.

With mixed feelings, Mattie shushed Robo and clipped his leash to his collar. She was in such turmoil, she wasn't sure she could deal with another person, even someone she loved. Or maybe especially someone she loved. She opened the door.

Cole wore a sheepish expression. "Sorry to drop in on you like this, but I happened to be in the neighborhood and saw you were home."

Mattie lived on a quiet street that led to nowhere, and she doubted that Cole just happened to drive by. Nevertheless, she felt glad to see him. And from the way Robo was acting the fool by pressing his body against Cole's legs, he must be glad to see him, too.

"I should have called you after I got home from Mama T's house, but it's been just one thing after another," she said.

"I had to see you tonight."

He was still standing on the porch. Since he was dressed in jeans, western shirt, and boots, Mattie guessed she would need to postpone her run for a few minutes instead of inviting him to join her. She opened the door wide. "Do you want to come in?"

He hesitated. "Were you about to go somewhere?"

"I thought I'd go for a run."

He looked surprised. "Weren't you up at Redstone Ridge today?"

She nodded, bending down to settle Robo beside her with a touch. "Sometimes I just need to run. You know, before I can turn in at night. It relaxes me."

"I would've thought you'd had enough exercise for the day."

She felt an overwhelming urge to confide in him, to share her sorrow with someone she could trust, someone who would be sympathetic. "I got some bad news tonight."

Without saying a word, he stepped inside, away from the spotlight on the well-lit porch, and took her in his arms. The tension that had quivered inside her like a bowstring eased somewhat as Mattie allowed herself to lean against Cole's broad chest. She clenched her teeth to hold back tears.

He spoke in a soft voice. "Do you want to talk about it?"

"I think so." The walls of her home felt like they were closing in on her, and she needed to escape into the outdoors. "But I don't want to sit in here right now."

He paused, still holding her close. "Would you like to take a drive?"

It sounded like a solution for her tired body. "That sounds good."

He squeezed her before letting go. "Robo can come too."

Mattie locked the front door behind her and Cole led the way to his truck, going to the passenger side to open the rear door. Robo hopped into the back seat and Mattie unclipped his leash. After Cole moved the passenger seat back into position, Mattie settled in while he went around to the driver's side.

The truck's diesel engine roared to life, and Cole headed toward the highway, turning left to go north out of town toward his place. The motion of the truck calmed her as he drove past his house and on another half mile, signaling left at the turnoff to Lookout Mountain.

She knew where they were going, and as they entered the thin stand of pine that covered the hillside, she rolled down her window to take in the scent of the forest. This wasn't really a mountain, but rather a hill that rose up on the north side of town, with a road that wound up the backside leading all the way to the top. Once there, they could take in a view of the entire town and beyond into the surrounding meadows. During the day, that is. Tonight, the view would be different.

The sound of Robo's yawn came from the back, making Cole glance in the rearview mirror before catching Mattie's eye. "A drive always puts the kids to sleep."

She acknowledged his humor with a thin smile and turned away to look out at the shadowy evergreens. A quarter moon cast a weak glow, allowing the stars to pop. It looked like every star in the sky shimmered, and though Mattie seldom thought about life after death, she wondered about it now. Was Willie in some heavenly place where he no longer felt pain and the stresses of life? Or was death the end of everything? Oblivion, nothingness?

They reached the end of the road, and Cole pulled over to park at the lookout. The streetlights of Timber Creek lit up the east side of town, while the windows of homes on the west side glowed warmly.

"I hear they're going to put streetlights on the west side of town," she said. That seemed like a safe topic. "It's a good thing for families with kids out after sundown, but I think I'll miss the darkness."

"Why is that?"

Mattie hadn't given any thought about why; she'd merely been musing aloud. "I guess I like the privacy. Maybe it feels more cozy."

Cole didn't comment as he shut down the engine and turned off the headlights. Then he leaned back, and Mattie knew he was waiting for her to speak first. Robo circled and lay down on the back seat.

"Stella came by with results of Willie's autopsy." She glanced at him, but he was looking out the windshield at the lights of Timber Creek. "There was evidence that he'd been tortured and then set on fire while he was still alive."

"Good God, Mattie!" He looked at her now, shadows overlaying his face so that she couldn't see his eyes. He reached out to grasp her hand and she held on, not realizing her fingers were so cold until he'd clasped them within the warmth of his.

"They've sent blood tests to the lab to see if he'd started using again, and to look for other substances. I guess that will be back in a few days."

"I think it hardly matters if he'd started using again. Your brother was murdered, that's what matters. I think that's where the focus should be, not on whether he might've brought this on himself." Cole waved his hand in frustration. "That's not . . . you know what I mean."

"I know. But if he was back into drugs, we might get a lead out of California, someone he used to be associated with. Or even a new connection. A lot will depend on what the detective in L.A. can turn up. See if any of his old gang had connections to Timber Creek."

He began chafing her fingers between his two hands. "You're cold. Do you want me to turn on the heater?"

"No, it's only my hands that are cold, and now they're warming up." She slipped her free hand under her leg for warmth, thinking about the other thing that plagued her. "I wish I could go back in time and meet with Willie as soon as he contacted me last fall."

"Life can be full of regrets if you focus on them. We make decisions for whatever reasons we have in the moment, not because we have some superhuman vision of what will happen in the future."

She'd pulled away from her brother after he apologized to her for not keeping their father from molesting her, memories she'd suppressed until then. Although she didn't blame Willie for their father's actions, she'd had to withdraw from him to deal with the tumult he'd set off with his one phone call. It had taken time and counseling to sort out exactly how she felt toward both him and her mother, something she had to determine before she could tackle the prospect of reuniting with either of them.

Her past was something she felt ashamed of, and she'd never shared all the details with Cole. She couldn't explain to him now how complicated it had all been.

"I know I can't focus on the regret, but it still slips into my mind, you know."

"I know."

They sat in silence for a few moments while Mattie decided what to say next. "I want justice for Willie. I want to find something that will pull this case together, but most of what we've found so far seems related to something else, not him."

"Like the slug and casing we found with the dead ram. But we have to wonder if the ram's death is related to William's death in some way. Why would someone take that shot when all of us were up there in the area? I still think the shooter might have been trying to pull us away from the area around the gravesite."

But there was more he hadn't heard about. "Today they excavated three graves in the depressions we saw from the ridge. Old graves, with skeletonized remains."

"Good grief. I thought that could be the case, although I didn't want to believe it. Not here, not so close to home."

"One was a child."

Cole's breath released in a huff, the news evidently leaving him speechless. He stared out the windshield. Finally, he spoke. "Can they tell how many years ago those bodies were buried?"

"Not with pinpoint accuracy. But Robo found a handgun, a

Desert Eagle .357 Magnum that was manufactured in the eighties. Agent Lawson thinks the gun might be the weapon used. There was lead inside one skull, and ballistics can tell if it matches up with the pistol."

Cole tapped the steering wheel with his index finger. "Did this gun have anything to do with William's death?"

"We found it in the ravine by his gravesite, but it looks like it's been exposed to the elements for years. So probably not." She struggled to speak normally despite the tightness in her throat. "Besides, there were no bullets found in his body."

Cole continued to hold her hand as he studied her. "The way he died is a horrible thing, Mattie. Are you going to be all right?"

She turned away from him to look out her window, struggling to control the urge to weep. The console between the bucket seats acted as a barrier, but Cole scooted as close as he could and reached to place his arm around her shoulders. He drew her gently against his chest. The comfort of his embrace tipped the balance, and Mattie couldn't hold her tears back any longer. She buried her face against him and sobbed, while he stroked her hair and murmured his sympathy.

When she quieted, Cole shifted slightly, still holding her close, and then offered her his handkerchief. She tried to pull away, but Cole adjusted his arm so that she could face front and he continued to hold her, pressing his lips against her hair. Spent, she leaned against his shoulder and wiped her eyes and wet cheeks with his bandana.

"How can I help?" Cole asked.

She squeezed shut her eyelids and fought the temptation to withdraw, her fallback move. "It helps to talk."

"I'm listening."

"When we were kids," she said, "Willie and I spent a lot of time together. Most of the attention we got from our dad was abusive, and our mom seemed preoccupied. She loved us, but she didn't play with us like you do with your kids. We were on our own."

She fought the rising of her sorrow as she gathered her thoughts.

"After Willie called me last October, I've been working with a counselor to deal with repressed memories from my childhood. Willie remembered more about what happened to me than I do."

A shiver forced Mattie to stop and catch her breath before continuing. "Now he's gone. I wasted all that time, and he's gone."

"Maybe you don't have to remember everything. Maybe what's important is the here and now."

Mattie wasn't sure he fully understood the complexity of the situation, but she appreciated his comment.

Cole continued to speak. "Your brother is gone, but you're not alone, Mattie. Your foster mother, the people you work with, the kids and me, even Mrs. Gibbs—we all care about you. You've got us."

She was nodding her agreement even as he finished talking. "I'll remember that. Thanks for reminding me."

Her cell phone signaled a text message coming in, and she moved away from him, straightening in her seat so that she could take her phone from her pocket to check it. "It's from Riley. Her dad's working at the bar tonight and she wants to come over."

Cole held his watch up to the moonlight. "It's after ten. Kind of late for that, isn't it?"

"Probably, but I need to talk to her about a job helping Mama T." She began to text a reply. "I'll tell her to stay home, and that I'll call her in about ten minutes."

"She can start work at my place any day. How about tomorrow?"

"I'll let her know. I really appreciate this, Cole."

"We can use the help."

"I supposed I'd better go home now," Mattie said, although she wasn't sure that she wanted to leave him for the silence of her house.

"All right." He leaned forward to press a tender kiss on her lips that made her want to cry again. Then he gave her a keen look as he started the truck and shifted it into reverse. "Will you call me tomorrow?"

"Okay. After work."

"I won't let you forget."

# NINETEEN

## Wednesday

Cole slept poorly and awoke before sunrise, haunted by images of William's gravesite, something he would most likely never forget. Poor Mattie. Those images would be with her forever, too.

On Lookout Mountain last night, he'd recognized again that there were things that Mattie didn't want to share with him. Which was okay—he didn't need for her to, unless it was something she wanted. But now he worried that there were terrible things in her past, things so horrible that she'd repressed the memory of them, and that was a whole different ballgame. How could he help her heal from those past experiences and gain happiness in her present life?

Unable to fall back asleep, he decided to go to the clinic to check on his patients, two dogs that he'd spayed yesterday afternoon. He showered and dressed quickly and then jogged the short distance up the lane, unlocked the front door, and let himself in. Turning on lights as he made his way back to the kennel room, he was gratified to see that both dogs were awake from the anesthesia and resting in their cages. He splashed a small amount of water into their bowls, which were elevated on the cage doors so the dogs could reach the water but not harm themselves by falling in before fully conscious. Both roused themselves and were steady on their feet when they stood to lap the water. They would be ready to discharge to their homes this morning.

A bit later, the door opened, and his office assistant, Tess Murphy, sang out her usual melodic greeting. "Hi, hi."

"In here," he called to her.

Tess came through the lobby and joined him in the treatment room. Some might have thought her spiky red hair was still mussed from sleep, but that was just the way she wore it. "You're here early," she said.

"What time is it?" Cole glanced at the clock—shortly after seven. "Oh gosh, I lost track. I'd better run to the house to say goodbye to the kids before they leave for school. When's our first client?"

Tess went back to the lobby to check the schedule. "Eight o'clock," she called through the opening between the lobby and treatment room.

"Then I'd better hustle."

As he sprinted toward home, he thought of Mattie. He'd hated leaving her alone last night. He decided to send her a text to tell her he was thinking about her. And he would make sure that he got to see her tonight, even if he had to show up again on her doorstep.

★

When Mattie received Cole's text, she and Robo were already at the station. She'd helped Stella rearrange the furniture in the briefing room so they could set up the boards for their investigations. Now, instead of just one board for Willie's case, they had added another board for the three skeletons that had been found.

Stella had enlarged a photo of Willie that she'd received from Tamara, and she'd taped it to the top of his board. He looked handsome and untroubled as he leaned over a car engine, his hands reaching for some part inside and a smile on his lips that touched off a twinkle in his dark eyes. He had a mop of brunette hair the same color as Mattie's. Seeing the photo nearly broke her heart.

McCoy entered the room, followed by Agent Rick Lawson who held a sheaf of papers and a tablet in his hand. Brody was still at the gravesites on Redstone Ridge, and his absence felt strange.

They each took a seat. Robo had been watching Mattie work from a spot near the wall, but when she sat, he padded over, circled twice, and lay down beside her chair. He heaved a sigh of contentment, and she stroked his head. Not everyone was fortunate enough to have their best friend accompany them to work every day.

McCoy gave Stella a nod. "Go ahead and take the lead. The rest of us will jump in as we go."

Stella had already recorded autopsy results on Willie's board, and the others had discussed them the evening before. Much to Mattie's relief, it wasn't necessary to rehash those details. Instead, Stella opened with the current agenda. "Let's discuss information from the three gravesites that were excavated yesterday."

Lawson spread his papers in front of him. "From the degree of degradation of the skeletonized remains, these three appear to have been burned and buried at around the same time. We're estimating between twenty to thirty years ago.

"The two adult skeletons are male, as is the skeleton of the child. Measurement of the child's femur puts him in the six- to seven-year-old range. It's harder to estimate the ages of the adults, but best guess is older than twenty-one and younger than forty."

Stella pulled out salient bits of information and recorded them on the board as Lawson spoke. He paused to let her catch up, glancing down at his papers before resuming.

"There's evidence of projectile penetration in both adult skulls. One skull has both entry and exit wounds while the other has only an entry wound. As you know, we found a slug inside this second skull, which we've sent to ballistics to compare to the Desert Eagle pistol. There was evidence of blunt force trauma at the back of the child's skull, severe enough to be ruled cause of death."

Mattie suppressed a shiver. Her muscles were tight enough to spring, and she exhaled slowly, trying to force herself to relax. Robo raised his head, and she put her hand on it to settle them both.

Lawson continued. "These three graves appear to have been used first as burning pits before the sites were covered with dirt, which is the same MO discovered at the William Cobb gravesite. Of course, we don't know for sure, but the proximity of the location combined with the identical MO leads us to believe the two crime scenes are probably linked, despite the gap of years between them."

During the pause that followed, Stella began recording evidence on the skeletons' board. "I'm going to list the Desert Eagle pistol that Robo found here," she said as she wrote. "I'll put a question mark beside it since we don't know yet if the slug matches the gun. When should we have those results?"

"Sometime today," Lawson said. "And I was able to get a serial number off that pistol. I started a search for registration through the ATF National Tracing Center. If we're lucky, we could get a hit off that as early as today, too."

"Results today would be excellent." Stella finished recording and looked at Lawson. "Anything else?"

"Teeth were pretty much intact. It's not much to go on for ID, but my team is researching missing persons from the time period. You can imagine the numbers they're up against. All of this is going to take some time."

McCoy leaned forward. "What are the chances that these three were affiliated with each other, or even related?"

"We're searching for a missing father and son, or two related men and a boy who went missing at the same time. If we turn up a relationship of some kind, it will certainly make the identification easier."

"That would indeed be fortunate," McCoy said. "Anything else to add, Agent?"

"That's all for now."

Stella walked over to Willie's board and used her marking pen to point to a column labeled CALIFORNIA PERSONS OF INTEREST as she spoke. "Let's move on and discuss our first crime scene. Detective Hastings from the Hollywood Detective Bureau interviewed past associates of Mr. Cobb's, and he's convinced that they can contribute nothing of value to our case. They haven't been in touch with our victim for well over six months. With Mr. Cobb, I should say."

Stella glanced at Mattie before continuing. "I've interviewed

William's girlfriend, Tamara Bennett, and I've spoken with his employer, Mr. Joseph Quintana. So far, I've uncovered nothing new."

Mattie noticed that Lawson had begun to squirm in his chair, as if growing more and more uncomfortable. When Stella paused, he jumped in with what was bothering him.

"I'm not sure that Deputy Cobb should be a part of this investigation," he said.

McCoy straightened. "Deputy Cobb and Robo have uncovered a large part if not all of our evidence. I don't think she should be eliminated from the team at this point."

Lawson sent a sidelong glance in Mattie's direction. "I'm bringing in cadaver dogs to search for more gravesites at our crime scene today. If we need a dog for another purpose, I can bring one in from the state."

"Robo is not just any dog, and he and Mattie aren't your typical K-9 team," Stella said with some heat.

Mattie felt like she should speak up and try to diffuse Stella's temper. "I appreciate your concern, Agent Lawson, but I believe I still need to be involved in this investigation, and I can remain objective. You can speak freely in front of me."

Lawson turned to McCoy, appealing for a decision.

"We'll leave the team as it is for now," McCoy said, his tone indicating he was done with the subject. "What did you want to say, Agent?"

Lawson's lips thinned as he clamped them shut. He looked down at his papers before speaking. "Both Tamara Bennett and Deputy Cobb believe that William wouldn't have come to Timber Creek of his own free will. If that is indeed true, it would lead us to believe that he was abducted and brought here before he was killed. But I'm not sure that makes sense."

"We don't have a motive for him coming by himself from California either," Stella said.

"This is awkward with you present, Deputy." Lawson gave Mattie a pointed look before turning away. "This is pure speculation. Timber Creek has had a drug problem in the past twelve months with a couple of large busts. Maybe Mr. Cobb had become involved with the drug trade. Maybe he was running drugs through town."

Stella turned to the board to record his theory. "Any comments?"

Mattie hated to consider this possibility, but she was determined to project a neutral attitude. "We need to follow up on that idea. If William hasn't been back in touch with his old gang, are there new contacts he made lately? Did he meet someone when he was in rehab that he connected with?"

The tension in the room eased somewhat as they all paused to think.

"Any other ideas regarding motive?" Stella jiggled the marker in her hand.

McCoy broke the silence that followed her question. "If there aren't other ideas about motive right now, let's discuss whether or not we believe the ram shooting is linked to Mr. Cobb's homicide."

Mattie summarized her discussion with Cole. "Someone shot the ram while we were investigating the gravesite. We think this shooter was *not* a local hunter for a couple of reasons. One, the shooter didn't pick up his brass, which most hunters do. And two, the shooter didn't go down to the ram to harvest meat or a trophy; instead, he hid and watched us from the upper part of the ridge."

"So we can speculate that the shooter was trying to draw you away from the gravesite?" McCoy asked.

"Dr. Walker and I both think so."

"We should receive word today on whether or not the casing Robo found and the slug from the ram carcass match." Stella started a new column on the board. "Who might have been up in that area on Sunday? Any ideas on who might have shot that ram?"

Mattie hated to bring up Riley's father, but she felt like she had to. "Dr. Walker sewed up a horse that got cut on a mountain trail last Sunday. The owner is from California and new to town. His name's Bret Flynn. He told Cole that he was on a different trail, but one of us should talk to him about it. Check out his hunting rifle to see what kind of ammo it uses."

"We should also look at Tucker York," McCoy said. He explained for Lawson's benefit. "He's the Wildlife Department supervisor out of Denver. The day Dr. Walker found William's partial remains, York insisted on going up to the area by himself. He was at the meadow alone for hours before the rest of us could get up there."

Stella turned to McCoy with a bemused expression. "What about Ed Lovejoy?"

"He wasn't available to shoot the ram," Mattie said. "He was riding down the trail with you that afternoon."

"He started out with us, but then he split off about halfway down, saying he wanted to scout elk in the lower meadow and get a head count."

McCoy nodded. "Put him on the list. We need to talk to him."

*Ed Lovejoy*, Mattie thought. *I've known him for years.* Hard to believe the local wildlife manager would have anything to do with Willie's death, much less shoot a ram out of season. But it was also strange that he'd split off from the party on Sunday afternoon.

"Any others?" Stella asked.

"This might be nothing," Mattie said, "but I'm thinking of that California connection. Gibson Galloway, the man we arrested Saturday night for disorderly conduct. He's from Bakersfield, and I think he deserves some investigation. We released him Sunday morning, and I remember that there were rifles racked in the back window of his truck. All of his weapons should be listed on the arrest report. He and his buddies had a trailer full of horses and ample time to ride up to the Ridge."

"Any of this could lead to nothing, but we won't know until we look into it," Stella said. "What else do we have?"

Mattie put her elbows on the table and leaned on them to help steady her emotion. She fought to project an air of detachment. "We found horseshoe and cowboy boot prints up at the crime scene. I know they were too washed-out to get a clear casting, but the boot measurement indicates a male, which suggests at least one man accompanied William to the crime scene, probably on horseback."

"And when horses are involved, so are trucks and trailers,"

McCoy said. "I'll put a notice in the newspaper asking for tips regarding a rig spotted at the trailhead parking lot. During what time period, Agent Lawson?"

"That crime scene couldn't have been more than four days old. Let's say Thursday through Sunday."

"We'll see if we can turn up any tips," McCoy said.

Mattie hoped they could uncover pivotal information soon. She was sure that Willie had been brought to Timber Creek against his will. But for the life of her, she had no idea why.

The silence deepened until McCoy broke it. "Agent Lawson, you're headed back up to the crime scene. Our team will get started investigating these leads."

"Good luck, and we'll check back in later today," Lawson said.

Relieved that she was still part of the investigation, Mattie pushed back her chair, ready to get started.

# TWENTY

Mattie and Stella decided to hit Colorado Parks and Wildlife first and were driving there in Mattie's SUV with Robo in the back. They hoped to catch Ed Lovejoy in his office—it was early enough that he probably hadn't yet left for the field.

Stella turned in the passenger seat to appraise Mattie. "What did you think of Lawson's suggestion to take you off the case?"

"He was just doing his job, expressing his opinion. I didn't take it personally like you did."

Stella wrinkled her nose. "I guess I did a little bit."

"I appreciate the support. So does Robo." Mattie directed the conversation to the upcoming interview. "How do you want to handle Lovejoy?"

"How well do you know him?"

"He's lived here for years. He does a good job, and he's never caused any trouble. We don't even have a parking ticket on him."

"Then let's go into it easy," Stella said. "Save the confrontational stuff for the end. Watch his body language, see what we think."

Pleased to see Lovejoy's green truck parked in front of the tan stucco building with brown trim and a metal roof, Mattie pulled up and parked beside it. "I could take the lead if you want, start with his opinion of the search we did together Monday morning."

"Take it away."

Mattie turned to look at Robo. As usual, he stood, eager and ready to go. "You're going to stay here," she told him, and he sat, ears pricked, apparently willing to wait.

At the front desk, Mattie asked for Lovejoy, and she and Stella were directed back to his office. They approached the open doorway and spotted Lovejoy seated behind a desk piled high with paper, manuals, and books. He was writing on a notepad, his forehead wrinkled in concentration. Mattie tapped on the doorjamb.

Lovejoy looked up and his face lit. He leaned forward to pick up a coffee can from his desk, pulled off the plastic lid and spat a stream of tobacco juice into it. "Mattie!" he said when his mouth was clear enough to talk. "To what do I owe the pleasure?"

"Geez, Ed. Do you chew that stuff all the time?"

His cheeks bunched as he tried to grin around the wad of snuff behind his bottom lip. "It'll kill what ails ya."

"I sincerely hope that it doesn't kill *you* someday." Mattie gestured toward Stella. "You know Detective LoSasso, right?"

"Call me Stella," the detective said as she offered a handshake.

Lovejoy stood to shake her hand and then scurried from his office, returning with two folding chairs. Mattie and Stella sat them in front of his desk while he went around to his own seat.

"Where are you with your investigation of the ram shooting, Ed?" Mattie asked.

"I'm filling out the paperwork this morning. All I've got so far is what you've given me—date, time, the .270 Winchester casing found at the top of the ridge, and the slug Doc Walker retrieved from the carcass. When will you find out if that casing and the slug match?"

"Possibly today. What do you plan to do next?"

"I'll file the report, keep my eyes and ears open, see if I can dig up any leads on the shooter."

"What are your thoughts about the type of rifle used to fire that bullet?" Mattie asked.

Lovejoy leaned back, making the chair's spring creak in complaint. "Well, we know it's a bolt-action rifle, but that's about all I can say. That .270 is a good round, accurate at long distances. From what Cole said, the guy made a clean heart shot. He knew what he was doing."

Mattie nodded. "You have any locals in mind who could make that shot? Poachers you've busted in the past?"

"Not really. Poachers are usually going after the meat, and they're looking for deer or elk. This was different."

"It certainly was," Mattie said. "Do you have any ties to California, Ed? Relatives or business?"

"Nah, but it seems like every other person moving into Colorado these days is from California." His discouraged expression reflected his opinion about this trend. "Even my own boss is from there."

That scored a hit with Mattie. "Oh yeah, are you talking about Tucker York?"

"Yep. When that job opened up, the powers that be hired him from out of state."

"How long ago was that?"

"Oh, I don't know." Lovejoy scratched the blond stubble on his chin. "I'd say a little over a year ago."

"Where in California was he from?"

"I think somewhere north of L.A. I don't know for sure."

Mattie thought she'd exhausted the subject with Lovejoy, but had gained valuable new information to flesh out when they interviewed York. She sent a glance toward Stella to signal that she could take the lead.

Stella took the interview a new direction. "How familiar are you with that backside of the ridge, Ed, where you all went yesterday morning?"

"We've been scouting that ridge for a couple years now to make sure there's enough feed. That herd has grown beyond the feed supply, which forces us to relocate some of them."

"Do you ever kill some of the animals or open up an additional season to reduce the herd?"

Lovejoy frowned as he shook his head. "It's not done that way, and especially not with mountain sheep. A set number of hunting permits are allowed each season to protect the state's sheep population."

"Have you ever seen anyone up there, scouting the sheep when you are?" Stella asked.

"People don't go up that trail very often. I've run into only a handful of people during the past couple years, and I've never ticketed anyone up there for illegal activity."

"I noticed you carried a rifle with you on both days when we went up to the scene. Is that typical for you?"

"Almost always carry and seldom use." Lovejoy removed the coffee can lid so that he could spit again. "I carry for protection when I'm in the high country. You know, from cougar and bear. Occasionally, I have to put down an injured or sick animal, but that's rare."

"What type of rifle do you carry?"

"It's a Model 70 Winchester with pre-64 action," Lovejoy said, smiling proudly. "It's a beauty."

"Impressive. Does it shoot the .270 Winchester ammo?"

"It does."

"Is that what it has in it now?"

"Yep."

Despite Stella's probing questions, Mattie thought Lovejoy had maintained an even keel. She wondered if he was having to work at it.

"You split off from Sheriff McCoy and me when we were riding down to go back to Timber Creek on Sunday afternoon," Stella said. "Where did you go exactly?"

Lovejoy lowered one brow and squinted at her. "Now, you're not thinking I shot that ram, are you?"

"I'm covering my bases, Ed. I've gotta figure out where each of the players who were up on that mountain were at all times, from the moment the partial remains were found Sunday morning until now. You get that, don't you?"

Lovejoy frowned, apparently thinking for several seconds before looking at Mattie. "You know me, Mattie."

"I do."

"Am I the kind of guy who'd poach an animal out of season?" Not waiting for an answer, he continued. "I enforce the wildlife management rules and regulations, for cripes' sake."

"And Stella has a job to do. All we need from you is information."

His face showed his distaste as he looked back at Stella. "I rode north to the meadow down below Redstone Ridge. I didn't go anywhere near the trail that leads up to the backside. When I went up there yesterday, it was the first time I'd been there since last fall."

Stella nodded as if in encouragement. "Thank you, Ed. Did you see anyone in that lower meadow?"

"I did not. I counted elk." He shuffled through some papers and pulled one out to show her. "Do you want to see my report?"

Stella took the paper and scanned it. "Good. Just one more thing. May I take your rifle to have our lab test it to make sure it isn't a match to the casing that was found?"

"Shee-ite, Detective." Lovejoy stood abruptly, his chair shooting backwards. "What gives you the right to ask for it?"

"I think you know the answer to that question, Ed. I've got to rule things out as we go."

"I suppose I don't have much of a choice. If I don't give it up, you're going to think I'm a suspect." He gave Stella a disgusted look, raising his index finger for emphasis. "My rifle is not going to match that casing. And if there's any damage to that gun at all, even the tiniest little scratch, I'm going to hold you personally accountable."

Calm and composed, Stella stood. "I appreciate your cooperation, Ed. We'll get the gun back to you as soon as we can."

Lovejoy stormed out of the room, and Stella quirked a brow at Mattie before turning to follow him.

★

"That went well," Stella said as Mattie drove the Explorer away from the Wildlife Division building. "What's your take on Lovejoy?"

"We have to look at him. He's got horses, he's got the rig, and he's got the gun that might link to the ram. But he's got no motive that I can see, and he's not tied into California that we know of. I don't think he's our guy."

Mattie observed Lovejoy in the rearview mirror. He was still standing, arms crossed, glaring after them from the parking lot. He'd insisted on putting the rifle in the gun rack himself, checking to make sure it was well protected by its case.

"Either way, let's drop the gun off at the station," Stella said, "and I'll get a courier to run it to the ballistics lab. Then we'll look up Mr. Gibson Galloway in Hightower. Hope the address he gave us is actually real."

"I checked his arrest report for the rifles that were in the back of Galloway's truck," Mattie said. "He's got a Remington and a Winchester 70 Featherweight bolt-action rifle."

"Compatible with our ammo casing?"

"Both are."

At the station, Mattie gave Robo a pit stop while Stella ran the gun inside. They were back on the road within minutes. Apparently deep in thought, Stella pursed her lips and stared out the passenger window. Mattie brought the Explorer up to speed on the highway, setting a course through the hay meadows around Timber Creek toward the foothills that surrounded Hightower.

The silence in the car gave her mind freedom to revisit Willie's gravesite, leaving her despondent. There'd been no indication that Ed Lovejoy was connected to Willie. If ballistics proved that he didn't shoot the ram, it would eliminate him as a suspect, which would also eliminate that lead toward solving Willie's case. She hoped they could glean information from Gibson Galloway that would hold more promise.

# TWENTY-ONE

They reached the address that Galloway had given, and Mattie turned into a short lane that led to a ramshackle trailer house with faded blue and white siding. No trees or shrubs grew in the yard to block the view, and behind the trailer she could see an old pole barn and a corral shored up with various types of boards and wire. The same pickup that she'd first seen in front of the Watering Hole was now parked beside the tumbledown corral where four horses stood, listlessly swishing their tails.

Mattie shook off her depression and scanned the property. It was important to remain vigilant. "Shall we stop at the house or at the barn?"

As she spoke, a man came from the barn and headed for the corral carrying a bale of hay. Sunlight glinted off his bald head, and Mattie immediately recognized him.

"Looks like that's our guy," Stella said.

Mattie steered around the trailer house and parked alongside Galloway's pickup. "I think you should take the lead on this one. And leave the doors open in case I need to pop the cage to let Robo out." She was referring to the remote popper button she wore on her utility belt. It controlled the door into Robo's compartment, and she could release her partner with the press of a finger.

Stella nodded. "Good plan. You weren't exactly in this guy's good graces the last time you tangled with him."

Leaving both doors open, they exited the car while Galloway

kept a hostile eye on them. He tossed the hay to the horses, and then stood waiting for them at the fence, his hands on his hips as they approached. Mattie stayed back a few feet, positioning herself between Stella and the SUV.

"Good morning, Mr. Galloway," Stella said. "I hope you remember us. I'm Detective LoSasso and this is Deputy Cobb from the Timber Creek County Sheriff Department."

"I know who you are." He didn't offer a handshake, and Stella didn't push it by offering one herself.

"You were a bit under the influence when we met and possibly not yourself." Stella was giving him the benefit of the doubt, probably hoping to soften him up. "We need to speak with you and get some follow up information, if we could."

"What if I don't want to talk to you?"

"Then I'd have to wonder why not. I'm content to talk with you here today instead of taking you in for questioning, if you'll let me."

With a disgusted expression, Galloway turned his gaze from Stella to Robo, who remained standing at his window, staring back at the man. "What do you want?"

"Tell me why you were in Timber Creek Saturday night."

"I told you guys that once. Didn't anyone write it down?"

Stella offered a thin smile. "I need to confirm some things."

"We were driving through town on our way back home. We stopped to have some food."

"Driving from where?"

He shifted with impatience. "From Kansas."

"And what were you doing in Kansas?"

"We were at a rodeo."

Stella raised her palm slightly, as if encouraging him to open up. "Where exactly?"

"Dodge City."

"What was the name of the event?"

He paused. "We were at the Roundup."

Mattie retrieved a notebook from her pocket to jot down what he'd said. That fact would be easy enough to check.

"Were you participating in the rodeo?" Stella asked.

He glanced away and then back, narrowing his eyes. "We were entered, but we didn't make it on time to check in."

*And there goes his alibi.* Mattie's pulse quickened with that bit of information.

Stella paused for a moment. "Was there someone you met there or someone in the crowd who could confirm you were present?"

"My buddies can confirm it."

"Do you have receipts from your trip?"

"I don't keep receipts."

None of this would lead to establishing an alibi for the possible dates that Willie had been killed.

Stella switched direction of the interview. "You still have California plates on your truck. How long have you lived here in Hightower?"

"A few months."

"Where did you live in California?"

"Bakersfield. I told all this to the guy at the sheriff's station."

"Do you have any friends, family, or acquaintances in the Hollywood or Los Angeles area?"

He studied Stella, a perplexed look on his face. "No."

"Not anyone in that whole city, huh? Do you know or have you ever heard of a man named William Cobb?"

He gestured toward Mattie. "Any relation to her?"

"Just answer the question."

He ground his boot into the dirt, looking down at his feet. "No, I never heard of a William Cobb."

That looked like deceptive behavior, and Mattie wondered if he was telling the truth.

"Do you hunt wild game, Mr. Galloway?" Stella asked.

He pretended to startle at the change in subject, holding up his hand. "What's that got to do with anything? Oh I know, I know, just answer the question. I do like to hunt—deer and antelope—and I plan to this fall."

"What's your gun of choice for hunting?"

"I use my Remington."

"And the ammo?"

He threw her an impatient look. "I use a .300 Winchester Short Magnum."

*Not the same round used on the ram*, Mattie thought.

"One of the guns listed on your arrest report is a Winchester 70 rifle. Do you use it to hunt?" Stella asked.

"Not usually. It's a varmint gun. I want something with more power for big game."

"But you carry it with you."

He shrugged. "It was already in the truck."

"I appreciate your cooperation, Mr. Galloway. I need to know where you went last Sunday after you were released from the sheriff's station?"

"We came straight home, of course." He raised his hands slightly, palms up. "You and your people threw a wrench into our plans. Delayed us getting back."

Stella continued in a pleasant manner, refusing to rise to the bait despite Galloway's sour expression. "Just one more thing. What ammo do you use in your Winchester 70 rifle?"

He crossed his arms. "Why do you want to know?"

"Curiosity."

Mattie could tell that he was starting to shut down even a semblance of cooperation.

He took a step back. "Look, I've answered your questions, but I'm done with this now."

"Could I see your rifle, Mr. Galloway?" Stella asked.

"No, I'm done. If you come back, you'd better have a warrant. Because otherwise, I'm not letting you on my property." He turned and strode toward the barn.

"Sorry you feel that way, Mr. Galloway. We'll leave now," Stella said to his back.

They retreated to the Explorer.

Mattie felt more positive about this interview. Maybe it would lead somewhere. "No alibi for Willie's dates, deceptive behavior when you asked him about knowing Willie, and he seemed pretty sensitive about that Winchester."

"Maybe." Stella looked dubious. "Or maybe just fed up with me and my questions. I'll check out that rodeo in Dodge City for a start. We can't get a warrant yet, but if the casing doesn't match Lovejoy's Winchester, we might team up with the Wildlife Department and see if we can get our hands on Galloway's gun for testing."

Feeling like they'd made a tiny bit of progress, Mattie started the engine, turned onto the highway, and headed back toward Timber Creek.

Stella took out her cell phone. "I'll check in with Sheriff McCoy and see if he connected with Tucker York."

Mattie kept an eye on Robo in the rearview mirror while she listened to Stella's side of the conversation. At first, he was sitting up front staring out the windshield, but then he yawned, circled, and plopped onto his cushion, content to settle in for the ride.

Stella disconnected her call. "This is our lucky day. Tucker York is on his way down to Timber Creek from Denver, and he'll meet with us at the station this afternoon."

"Do you know if this was a scheduled trip? Why is he coming back to Timber Creek so soon?"

"Apparently he's concerned about the ram shooting, and he's touching base with Ed Lovejoy about it."

"You'd think he could've done that by phone."

Stella paused to consider it. "Do you think it's suspicious that he's coming back here for this?"

"Actually, I don't know what to think."

★

Back in her office, Mattie filled a water dish for Robo, settled him onto his cushion, and sat down at her computer. She took out her spiral notebook and flipped the pages to retrieve the name of the rodeo Galloway had mentioned. Stella would be doing the exact same thing, but Mattie didn't want to wait.

The search results listed the rodeo at the top, and by following the link she learned that it actually did exist, and had run from last Wednesday through Sunday. It was possible that Galloway had told the truth about attending it. That didn't clear him for the ram shooting, but it could give him an alibi for Willie's death if he could prove he'd been there.

She decided to leave it up to Stella, and turned a couple pages back in her notebook to find a phone number for Joseph Quintana, Willie's boss. She hoped that connecting with one of Willie's friends would uncover something useful. She used her own cell phone instead of a department line to make the call.

Someone with a gruff voice answered after the first ring. "Joe's Auto Repair."

"Could I speak to Joseph Quintana, please?"

"That's me."

"Mr. Quintana, this is Mattie Cobb. I'm William Cobb's sister."

The gruff tone immediately turned sympathetic. "Oh, Will's sister? I'm sorry for your loss. He was a good guy."

The detached facade she'd built up throughout the morning cracked around the edges, and she swallowed against a lump in her throat. "It's a comfort to know you thought well of him. So he was doing a good job working for you?"

"He knew his way around a car engine. We're going to miss him."

Mattie had already decided what her strategy would be, but a quiver in her voice that she couldn't control had not been part of it. "Mr. Quintana, I'm hoping to talk to one of William's friends, someone who knew him well. You see, we were separated as kids and had just recently found each other again. We didn't have a chance to get together in person before he was killed."

"Oh, man." His voice was filled with compassion. "That's awful. Let me see—Carlos might be the one you should talk to. But one problem, he only speaks Spanish."

"That's not a problem for me. I speak it, too."

"Let me get him on the phone."

Mattie waited, trying to regain her composure. She wanted a lead that would help her with the case, but at the same time, she feared that she might learn something about Willie that would be disappointing or even hurtful. What if he had returned to the drug scene? What if she found out something about him that was even worse?

"*Hola.*" The speaker's voice was of medium timbre, young, somewhat hesitant.

Mattie replied in Spanish. "Hi, my name is Mattie Cobb. Did Mr. Quintana tell you that I'm William Cobb's sister?"

"Yes."

"Great. It's Carlos, right?"

"Carlos Martinez."

"Thank you for talking to me." She repeated what she'd told his boss about her and William's history. "I was hoping I could get to know him a little better by talking to you. You were friends?"

"We worked together."

"Oh." She'd hoped for more than that. Disappointed, she soldiered on. "Did you have conversations with each other, talk about what was going on in his life, his family?"

"He said he had a sister who was a cop."

*Ah, maybe that's why he's being so distant,* she thought. She decided to stick to the truth. There was no reason to lie to this man, and perhaps being open would draw him out. "That's me. I'm trying to learn more about Willie's life to try to figure out what he was doing his last days."

"Okay."

Mattie paused, but he didn't volunteer more. "I talked to Tamara, Willie's girlfriend. Do you know her?"

"No."

"She said that last week, before he disappeared, Willie might have connected with someone from his past, an old friend of the family. Do you know anything about that?"

After several seconds, Carlos answered. "Maybe."

"What do you mean by maybe?"

"Will said that he got a call from someone he never knew existed before. It was making him feel crazy."

"Did he say why?"

"He said he should have known about this guy."

Mattie wondered what that could mean. *Someone Willie didn't know existed, but he should have.* Could this be the old friend of the family he'd mentioned? "He said guy? It was a man, not a woman?"

"*Si.* The man stopped by here, and Will went off with him in his car during his lunch break."

Adrenaline kicked in, giving her a rush. "What day was that?"

"Uh . . . I think last Tuesday."

"Did you see the man?"

"No, but I saw the car."

"What kind of car was it?"

"A silver Chevrolet Tahoe, recent year."

A mechanic would know. Mattie jotted it down in her notepad. "Did you notice the plates?"

"California. That's all."

"Did Will say anything when he got back? What did he look like? Mad, scared, shaken?"

"Oh, he was upset. Nervous. Said he hoped he could get rid of the guy. He was asking questions Will didn't know how to answer."

None of this sounded good. "Is there anything else you can tell me about this man? Something I could use to find him?"

"No. That's all I know."

Mattie wished she could be face-to-face with her informant. She couldn't tell if he was being truthful or withholding more information because he was afraid to get involved. "Carlos, I need to ask you something else about my brother, something important that could help us find his killer. Could he have gotten involved with drugs lately?"

"Your brother didn't even drink beer with us. He was proud of his new boy, Elliott. Will wanted to be the kind of man Elliot could look up to. He said if he was ever tempted to start using again, he wanted us to kick his butt."

Mattie closed her eyes and released a breath. That sounded like Willie. "Could he have started selling drugs or gotten involved with drug running?"

"He would have nothing to do with it. That's not the life he wanted."

"You've been a great help, Carlos. Thank you for taking the time to talk with me. Could I leave my number for you to call if you think of anything else? Or if this man in the Tahoe happens to come back."

He agreed, and Mattie gave him her cell phone number. After thanking him again, she disconnected the call and leaned back in her chair. She felt depleted and filled with emotion—sadness for Willie mixed with exhilaration that she might have unearthed information that could help with his case. After a few seconds she roused herself and hurried to go tell Stella what she'd learned.

# TWENTY-TWO

It was midafternoon, and while they waited for Tucker York to show up, Mattie and Stella retreated to the war room. Stella had just received the report from ballistics, and was scanning it for new information.

"Okay, here are the results on the casing that Robo found. The slug retrieved from the ram's carcass is a match to the casing. But Ed Lovejoy's rifle didn't fire it." Stella glanced up from the report to look at Mattie. "The striations on the casing that Robo found do not match those on a bullet the lab tech fired from Lovejoy's gun, indicating that this particular rifle didn't shoot the ram."

"I have to admit that I'm glad Ed is in the clear. I would've hated for our wildlife manager to be responsible for such a thing. Not to mention that it could implicate his involvement with Willie's death."

"Yeah, I know what you mean. But here's the big score." Stella paused as if for effect. "The Desert Eagle .357 Magnum is ninety-nine percent likely to be the gun that killed John Doe Number One, the man who had the slug inside his skull. Thanks to you and Robo, we have a murder weapon for that case. And get this. The entry wound on the skull of John Doe Number Two is the same size and shape. It's quite possible that the gun killed both of the adults."

Mattie should have felt elated, but didn't. "Blunt force trauma killed the child, John Doe Number Three. Any speculation about what instrument might have caused it?"

"Some sort of blunt object. Could be consistent with the butt of that Desert Eagle."

Mattie shuddered as she pictured two men and a child kneeling before their killer. She hoped the child had gone first and been spared the horror of watching the others die before him.

The door opened and Sheriff McCoy entered. Stella handed him the ballistics report while Mattie briefed him on her interview with Carlos Martinez. Then he announced his reason for coming to join them. "Tucker York is in the lobby, waiting for us to talk to him. I want all three of us to handle it. Deputy Cobb, you take the seat on the same side of the table as him, and we'll keep the tone friendly."

They went to the lobby to greet York, and after shaking the wildlife supervisor's hand, Mattie followed the others into the inter-rogation room. As they entered, McCoy was saying, "Sorry for the starkness of this room, but this is the only available space to talk privately. Could I get you something to drink? Coffee, a soft drink?"

"No thanks, I've had plenty of coffee today." York picked a chair across the table from McCoy and sat. Mattie followed suit, angling her chair toward his so that she could observe him comfortably.

"Thank you for coming in to talk with us," McCoy said. "We have somewhat of a shared investigation involving this ram killing."

"I'm not quite sure why your department has become so involved," York said. "And I'm definitely concerned that you have the local wildlife manager under suspicion. He's the last person you should be looking at."

"You can be assured that we agree," McCoy said, "but we're talking to everyone who was up at the crime scene on Sunday. Ed just happened to be carrying a rifle that day loaded with the same ammo as the slug that killed the ram. I can share with you that, right before we entered this room, I received a report that elimi-nated Ed's gun. We'll return it to him as soon as possible."

"That's good news. But tell me, Sheriff, why have you decided that investigation of this ram shooting is your responsibility?"

"We believe that someone shot him to draw us away from the crime scene."

Mattie noted that the sheriff wasn't mentioning that they also found evidence that someone hid at the top of the ridge that same day and watched the action below as she and Cole climbed to investigate.

"It seems far-fetched," York said, "but all right. That's why I'm down here again, by the way—to look into this incident. Especially when I heard that you confiscated Ed's rifle this morning."

"Not confiscated," Stella said. "Just checking it against evidence."

York raised a brow and slanted a look Stella's way. "So what do you need from me?"

"I'm talking to everyone who was up at Redstone Ridge on Sunday, from the time Dr. Walker found the partial remains until that night. I want to know where all the players were, what they observed, and whether or not they can lend information to our homicide investigation."

"I told you Sunday that I observed nothing out of the ordinary in the meadow and on the ridge when I rode up alone." A fleeting glimpse of impatience crossed York's face. "With the intent of keeping the area secure, I watched for anyone who might enter while I counted sheep and scoped the ridge. I don't know what else I can tell you."

Mattie thought that York had more than enough time to scope and count, considering how long he'd been alone in the area. She watched him closely for any sign of deception.

"We believe the ram's killer took his shot from the top of Redstone Ridge. In hindsight, can you recall noticing anything suspicious while you were observing that area?" Stella asked.

"No, but I didn't keep my binoculars trained on the top. I was scoping the entire ridge and focusing in on groups of sheep when they came into view."

"I see. And as you rode back down to the parking lot at the trailhead, what did you observe?"

"Not a thing out of the ordinary."

"Do you recall what time you got back to your truck that day?"

"I do exactly. It was 3:42, and I was late getting on the road to Denver."

Stella leaned an elbow casually on the table. "Oh yes, you had a meeting scheduled that night."

"I did, but it got cancelled. I received the text about halfway there. Just as well. I would've been about an hour late."

Mattie thought that bit of news was an interesting turn of events. So far, his story could've given him a nice alibi for the ram shooting, but the cancellation of the alleged meeting ruined it.

Stella propped her chin on her fist. "At least you didn't have to keep rushing. What did you do instead?"

"Just ask your questions, Detective. I know where you're headed." York squinted at Stella. "I drove straight home to unload my horse. Since I'd left Denver before sunrise to drive down to Timber Creek, it had been a long day. I arrived at seven forty PM and no one can vouch for that. I live alone."

"All right, Mr. York. Thank you for your cooperation. Any gasoline receipts, food, or other purchases to show where you were?"

"I filled up with gas in Timber Creek prior to driving west to the Ridge trailhead with Ed. I made no stops on the way home. But as you must know, my rig was gone by the time the rest of you got down from the ridge. That proves that I left prior to everyone else that day."

"Yes, Mr. York," Stella said. "We are indeed aware of that fact."

But Mattie and Stella both knew that more than one trailhead led to the backside of Redstone Ridge. York could have easily moved his rig to a different parking lot and ridden back up.

Stella continued her questions. "What kind of rifle did you carry that day?"

York settled back in his chair and crossed his arms. "A Weatherby bolt-action with Winchester Short Magnum ammo. It's in my truck right now if you want to take a look at it."

"I'd like to see it," McCoy said in a pleasant conversational tone. "We'll take a look after we're done here. Anything else, Detective?"

"I understand you moved to Denver from California. Is that correct?"

"I worked in the California state wildlife department for five years prior to this job."

"Which city did you live in?"

"I lived in the suburbs of Sacramento. There are several wildlife preserves in that area. Why is this important?"

"Did you have friends or family in the L.A. area?"

"I know many people from L.A." York leaned back in his chair and narrowed his eyes at Stella, as if to say he was growing impatient with her line of questioning.

"Do you know a man named William Cobb from the Hollywood area?"

"Cobb." He paused as if thinking and then looked at Mattie. "That's your name, isn't it?"

As she nodded, Mattie had to wonder if he was putting on an act. "It is."

"Is he related to you?" Then when Mattie offered only a thin smile, he said to Stella, "I guess it's a common enough name. No, I've never met or heard of a man named William Cobb before."

"You're sure?"

"Completely."

"All right then. I think that's all for now." As she stood, Stella offered a handshake, which York returned with a stony expression. "I appreciate your time and your willingness to be so forthcoming, Mr. York."

Mattie trailed along as the others went outside to see York's rifle. The sheriff handled the gun like an expert, taking a peek at the ammo while he was at it. While York drove away, the three of them huddled at the entryway and watched him go.

"Smooth, well thought out delivery of the fact that he had no alibi," Stella said.

"Do you buy it?" Mattie asked.

"I usually don't buy anything on the first pass," Stella said, but a car pulling into the parking lot ended the discussion. "It's Agent Lawson. Let's see if they found anything else up at Redstone today."

His face smudged with sweat and dirt, Lawson exited his car, rummaged in the back seat for his pack, and walked over to join them. He looked tired.

"Nothing," he said as he approached. "No more gravesites found around the edges of the meadow. The team was still searching when I left. They'll spend the night and search the area up above by William's grave in the morning."

"We have updates when you're ready," McCoy said, opening the door into the station for the rest of them to pass through.

"Let me clean up and check my computer. I might have updates, too."

"We'll be in the briefing room."

Mattie told the others she should check on Robo, and she split off to go to her office. He had awakened, left his cushion where she'd told him to stay, and was waiting for her by the door. His greeting was so exuberant one would have thought she'd been gone forever.

Always glad to see him, she was even more so today when she needed his love for comfort. She ruffled his fur on both sides of his neck while he danced on his hind paws. "I thought I told you to stay on your bed."

He whirled and jumped on his cushion, shoulders down in a play pose.

"Now you're all revved up and ready to go. Come on, I'll take you outside for a break, but then we've got more work to do."

When Robo finished his short romp, Mattie told him to heel and went back inside, going through the lobby to join Stella and McCoy in the war room. Mattie sat and settled Robo beside her. Lawson entered the room, carrying his laptop, and he joined her at the table. He'd washed the dirt from his face but still looked weary.

Stella reviewed the case. She asked Mattie to present the findings from her interview with Carlos Martinez, and when she did, Lawson nodded but didn't comment. His computer appeared to be holding his attention as he opened it and began to scroll.

"The ATF has a hit on the Desert Eagle," Lawson said, typing the keyboard, evidently retrieving the report. When he paused to read the screen, his brow lifted with surprise. He looked up from the computer screen and cleared his throat. "The last date of sale on the gun was thirty years ago, purchased new from a gun shop in San Diego by a man named Harold Cobb."

Mattie felt as if she were falling, and her stomach flipped. Her father was the last registered owner of a gun she'd found near her brother's grave? How could that be? She wondered if she'd heard right.

Lawson frowned as he turned his head to make eye contact with her. "Any relation to you, Deputy Cobb?"

Her mouth had gone dry, and it was all she could do to form words—words that articulated a relationship she hated to admit. "He was my father."

# TWENTY-THREE

Silence reigned while Mattie waged war with her emotions. All eyes were on her, even Robo's. Shock and dismay triumphed over her ability to remain detached. Her eyes prickled, and she knew her cop face was beginning to crumble. She leaned over to pet Robo, bowing her head to hide her weakness from the others.

Lawson turned his chair to face her, and its scrape against the linoleum resounded in the silent room. "*Was* your father? Is he deceased?"

"Yes." Mattie forced in a deep breath as she remained hunched over Robo.

"Is that definite?" Lawson sounded like he doubted her.

McCoy cleared his throat. "I confirmed it myself. He died twenty-four years ago."

"Was he living here at the time?"

"Harold Cobb was a resident of Timber Creek," McCoy said, "but he died while incarcerated at the Colorado State Penitentiary in Canon City."

Mattie used the few moments when their attention shifted away from her to realign the features of her face. She lifted her chin to meet Lawson's gaze, confident that she could remain expressionless. "My father was convicted of domestic violence and killed during a prison fight. He died when I was six years old."

"How long had he lived in Timber Creek?" Lawson asked.

"Harold and Ramona Cobb lived here for approximately four

years prior to his arrest," McCoy said. "He had no prior record at the time."

The fact that McCoy could relay her father's history from memory stunned her. He'd been a young deputy when he'd responded to her call for help the night her father tried to kill her mother. It was a long time ago and he'd seen countless arrests since then.

Lawson was observing McCoy with narrowed eyes. "This is too much, Sheriff. Deputy Cobb's brother is a victim in our first case, and now her father's a firm suspect for the murders of our three victims in the second case. I insist we take her off this investigation."

Stella leaned forward and fastened Lawson with a heated gaze. "Do you realize that our deputy is the source of the major points of evidence we have in this case? I insist she stays."

A sinking sensation gripped Mattie's belly. Lawson was right. Both cases had crossed over the line and become too personal. Even she couldn't deny it.

Though it hurt to surrender, she felt forced to. "He's right, Stella. The gun registration implicating my father makes a difference, because it designates me as family times two. These two cases are now linked by MO, location, and family relationship. No court would accept anything I discovered as fact."

Stella turned her glare on Mattie, but she could tell underneath that anger lay helplessness in the face of the inevitable, a helplessness Mattie shared.

"Detective LoSasso, you will act as family liaison to Deputy Cobb," McCoy said, sounding resigned. "You'll share appropriate details with her as well as bring any information that might come her way back to us. Deputy Cobb, you'll cease investigating both cases."

"Understood," Mattie said. She needed to get her hands on her computer to search for any information about her father that she could find.

Lawson might have read her mind. "Thank you, Deputy. I'll be following up with a thorough search of your father's history, trying to find any known associates who might be involved with your brother's homicide. We need to remove you from the investigative process, but we'll still keep you in the loop."

"Appreciated." Mattie stood, her movement as abrupt as her reply, determined to leave the room before someone told her to. Robo jumped up to follow, and she'd never been more grateful for his championship.

★

During the last hour of her shift, Mattie uncovered nothing new about Harold Cobb. His case had been archived, but she could pull up a mug shot, the record of his arrest, disposition of his charges, and his date of death.

She studied the photo. She'd seen it before, and it had lost its ability to move her. Harold Cobb was Caucasian with pale skin, lank brown hair, and a scruffy dark beard. She tried to see her own features and even Willie's in his likeness, but she couldn't. She'd never seen a picture of her mother, but both she and her brother had inherited the Hispanic features of their maternal ancestry.

She glanced at the clock and decided to finish her paperwork. She'd promised Mama T that she would come to dinner to say goodbye to Doreen, and it was important to stand by her word. First, she would drop Robo off at her house.

Several hours later, Mattie returned home from dinner at Mama T's, tired but in a calmer state of mind than when she'd left work. She leaned back in her seat, studying the front of her house by the glow of the porch light and thinking about her evening.

Being with her foster family had lifted her spirits more than she'd thought possible. She'd surprised herself by discovering that she actually enjoyed visiting with Doreen. Much to Mama T's delight, the two of them had entertained their foster mother by telling stories about their memories from growing up in her home, and Mattie had found relief from the turmoil of her own life during her time with the two women.

Her phone signaled a text from Riley, asking if she had time to talk. At the same time, Robo's face popped into the picture window of her house, paws braced against the sill, his nose pressed against the windowpane.

Mattie texted back: I'll call you in ten minutes after I take care of Robo.

While she went toward the porch, she remembered that she needed to call Cole, too. When he'd texted earlier in the evening, she'd promised him a call after she got home.

She unlocked the front door, turning off the porch light as she entered. Robo greeted her but then made a beeline for the kitchen and scratched on the back door. "Do you need to go out?"

She opened the door to the backyard. Robo charged onto the porch and leaped off, growling a low-pitched warning in his chest. He rushed around the corner of the house into the side yard that led to the gate. *Must be a rabbit or something on that side of the house,* Mattie thought and started after him.

A loud *pfft*, similar to air escaping from a hydraulic valve, came from somewhere in the darkness.

Robo yelped.

Mattie dashed around the corner of the house. A shadow that could only be Robo lunged against the chain link in an awkward leap, bouncing off the fencing. She called to him, and he stumbled toward her, taking a few steps before falling.

Her heart pounded in her throat. *Was that a pellet gun? Kids? Did he get hit?*

She reached his side and sank to her knees. Robo tried to raise his head, but he collapsed, one paw stretched forward, his body limp.

It was too dark to see, so she ran her hands over his fur, searching for blood. She lifted him and slipped her hand down the far side of his body. It connected with a hard object stuck in his fur.

She pulled it loose, and held it up to catch the moonlight. A dart, like the kind used to tranquilize animals.

*Pfft!*

Something hit her square in the back, between her shoulders. Pain bit hard, and a burning sensation spread outward. *Another dart!*

She reached over her shoulder, but she couldn't touch it. She tried reaching below, and it glanced off her fingertips. She struggled for another inch, grasped it, and pulled it out.

Her arms grew slack; her hands shook. With a huge effort, she tossed the dart toward the tall grass at the edge of the house.

Her vision narrowed to a tunnel, and threads of thought dangled in her mind. Her Glock—locked away in her gun safe. Willie—with his disfigured face and blackened tongue. *Robo—is he still breathing?*

As she lost control of her body, she flopped down beside her dog. She struggled to press her face against his chest to see if she could detect his breath, a heartbeat.

A shape loomed over her, and she tried to focus her narrowing vision. Dark clothing, hood pulled tight, gas mask hiding his face. He nudged her with his foot.

And then, there was nothing but darkness.

# TWENTY-FOUR

Cole was waiting to hear from Mattie. After everyone else went to bed, he'd turned off the lights and was watching television in the darkened family room. When his phone jingled in his pocket, he fished it out, hoping the call would be from her.

Unknown number. Though tempted to push it through to voice mail, he soon changed his mind. A caller at this time of night probably had an emergency. He answered the phone.

The voice on the other end sounded panicky. "Dr. Walker, help! Come to Mattie's house."

"Who is this?"

"Riley. Something's wrong with Robo!"

Cole headed toward the garage. "Let me talk to Mattie."

"She's not here!"

"Where did she go?"

Riley began to sob. "She's not here! I don't know. She didn't answer the door. The front door was locked, but the yard gate was open. Mattie never leaves it open."

The garage door rumbled upward, and he jumped into the truck, turning the key in the ignition and jamming the gear-shift into reverse. "Take a breath, Riley. Stay calm. Tell me what's wrong with Robo."

"I think . . . I think he's dead. He's down in the yard, and his tongue, it's hanging out."

"Check to see if he's breathing."

"I can't tell. It's too dark."

Cole had sped halfway down his lane. "Put your ear to his chest, Riley. See if you can hear a heartbeat."

There was a pause on the line during which he hit the highway and turned toward town. He floored the gas pedal.

Riley spoke, her voice quivering with tension. "It's beating. He's barely breathing."

*But where's Mattie?* He tried to keep his voice calm. "I'm almost there. Leave him where he is. Don't move him."

He searched for ideas. Someone had tried to poison Robo last summer; maybe this was a repeat. "Have you called the police yet?"

"No, I called you first."

"Can you go to a neighbor's house or someplace that's well lit?"

"The neighbors all have their lights off. And I don't want to leave him."

"I'm almost there. Go ahead and pet him and talk to him, but stay on the line with me."

He'd powered the truck up to well over ninety during the mile of highway that led into town, but slowed as he hit the city limits. Pressing hard on the brakes, he screeched around the turn onto the street that would lead west to Mattie's house.

He could hear Riley talking to Robo in soothing tones; she'd evidently managed to get her panic under control.

"I'm a block away, Riley."

Her voice quivered. "He's still breathing, but he's not moving at all."

He reached Mattie's yard, pulled the truck onto the grass, and aimed its headlights toward the open gate, lighting up Riley's silhouette as she knelt beside the prostrate dog. "I'm here, Riley. I'm hanging up now."

As he gathered his stethoscope and a flashlight from the truck console, he disconnected the call and tapped 9-1-1. Dispatch at the sheriff's office answered.

"This is Cole Walker. There's an emergency at Deputy Mattie Cobb's house. Her dog Robo is down in the back yard, unresponsive, and Mattie isn't on the premises as far as we know. Send an officer right away and get the sheriff over here, too, as soon as possible."

He ended the call, sprinting toward the back yard to kneel next to Riley. "Good job, kiddo. Let me take a look."

Cole flipped on the flashlight and inserted the earpieces of his stethoscope, splaying the light over Robo's body as he placed the resonator on his chest. Heart rate was slow but strong, respirations shallow and intermittent. Limbs and torso were immobile, no muscular movement or fasciculation. No sign of vomiting or foaming at the mouth. He quickly palpated Robo's fur and entire body. No blood that he could see or feel.

He lifted an eyelid and shone the light, waved the light away and back—pupil constricted, pinpoint, no reflexive movement. He tapped Robo's eyelid. No eye blink.

This didn't look like poison. It looked like sedation, paralysis. Even though Robo's heartbeat remained strong, the lack of steady respiration concerned him. If his oxygen levels went too low, his heart could stop beating at any time.

*What am I dealing with here? Phenobarbital? Ketamine? How could someone get to a protection dog like this and sedate him?*

He thought of a dart gun—like the one Ed Lovejoy planned to use with the sheep. He rolled the limp dog into a sternal position, looking for a dart. Not seeing one, he swept the light around the grass. Nothing.

He placed one hand lightly on Robo's chest to monitor the pattern of his breathing.

Riley had begun to sob. "Is he going to be okay?"

"I don't know yet, but he's still alive, and we'll do what we can to keep him that way." A patrol car, overhead lights pulsing red and blue, pulled up beside his truck. Riley started to get up and go toward it. "Stay put, Riley. Let him come to us."

Cole didn't want there to be any confusion that would put the girl in danger. He shouted to the officer and waved him over. The deputy came running, hunkered down and on guard, hand on his holstered weapon.

"Is that you, Dr. Walker?"

"Yes. This is Riley, she's with me. We've got Robo here. He's unconscious. Neither one of us has been in the house. We don't know where Mattie is." He tried to be as succinct as possible. "I've got to get Robo to the clinic, and fast. He's having trouble breathing."

"I'll check the house," the officer said as he dashed away.

Even though his first impulse had been to follow and go look for Mattie, he knew that Robo took priority. *Mattie must be around somewhere. I can't let her dog die.*

The time between Robo's breaths had grown more prolonged. Cole shone his light on his mouth and checked his mucous membrane. Blanched. He pressed the gum with one finger and released. Poor capillary profusion and refill.

*Time to give him a boost.* He gave the flashlight to Riley. "Train the light on his chest for me, okay?"

He let Robo settle back on his side, positioned the dog's tongue in his mouth and closed his jaw, cupped his muzzle with his hands, and began mouth-to-nostril respirations. Cole could see his breath lift the dog's ribcage. He kept up a rhythm for several rounds, gratified to see Robo's chest rise with each one and then fall as he allowed him to exhale on his own.

Cole stayed focused on Robo but was acutely aware of the activity around him. Another car pulled up in the front yard, overheads flashing. The deputy who'd gone to search Mattie's house approached from the backyard, and relief washed through Cole when he heard McCoy's steady voice. "What's going on here, Deputy Garcia?"

Garcia summed up everything that Cole had told him earlier. "Mattie's not in the house, Sheriff. We don't know where she is."

"The lock on this gate has been broken," McCoy said.

Cole paused, monitoring Robo's ability to breathe on his own. The shallow, intermittent breath pattern returned. "I have to get Robo to the clinic, stat. I need to put him on a respirator."

"Was he poisoned?" McCoy asked.

"Tranquilized. Search this grassy area for a dart. I need to know what was used on him. If you find one, don't touch it with your bare hands. These drugs can be dangerous." As he spoke, Cole squatted and gathered the big dog up in his arms, clasping him by chest and haunches. Riley hurried to help. Straining, he stood, rearranged his grip on the limp dog, and headed for his truck. "Go open the back door of the truck, Riley."

Sheriff McCoy followed close behind. "What can I do to help?"

Cole groaned as he lifted Robo into the back seat. McCoy reached through to help him adjust him on his side. "Could you drive? I better not leave him back here alone." McCoy agreed and Cole climbed into the back of the cab, wedging between the front and back seats so he could lean over Robo.

McCoy shouted to Garcia that he was going to the vet clinic and that Deputy Johnson was on his way. Then he climbed into the driver's seat. Riley was standing back, her face white, her distress evident. Cole couldn't leave her alone in the yard like that. "Riley, do you want to come with me?"

"Yes!"

"Hop in front."

Even though McCoy made good time on the drive to the clinic, Cole had to deliver more respirations to Robo. Thank goodness the young dog had a healthy heart. It was still beating, but its increased rate told Cole that it was stressed. Riley gave McCoy directions to drive down the lane to the clinic's front door.

"The key is the silver one beside the truck key," Cole told him, throwing open the back door as soon as the sheriff parked. "I've got Robo. Go ahead and open the doors into the surgery room."

Relieved that his respiratory equipment was now seconds away, Cole hoisted Robo out of the back seat and carried him through the lobby into the surgery room. He laid him on the stainless steel surgical table and positioned him on his back. Grabbing a cannula, he opened Robo's limp jaw, positioned his tongue out of the way, and performed the intubation. Within seconds, he hooked up the oxygen, made sure that the knob for passing the sedative was set to off, and let the machine start sending life-giving air to Robo's lungs.

As he watched the dog's chest rise and fall in a regular pattern, he thought, *Okay, buddy, you're safe for now. But where is she? Where's Mattie?*

# TWENTY-FIVE

Cole didn't have time to waste. He'd bought a reprieve by using the respirator, but Robo was far from medically stable. He needed to know what drug had been injected into this dog and what he could do to reverse its action.

McCoy was on his cell phone. "Send Johnson over with it now. Tape off the yard. Avoid going in there until I can get back with Detective LoSasso."

After ending the call, McCoy turned to Cole. "Garcia found a dart in the grass by the house, and it's on its way here. I should get back to the scene, but do you need me to help you?"

"Riley can help until I get Tess to come in." Cole began securing Robo to the table with straps to keep him from falling off in case of seizures. "You can take my truck."

"I'll go back with Deputy Johnson after he brings the dart. What does Robo need?"

Cole listened to Robo's heartbeat and felt reassured that it was still steady and strong. "He's heavily sedated, either with a drug overdose or with something that suppresses his breathing. I have some anesthesia reversal drugs on hand, but I need to know what I'm dealing with to determine what to use."

McCoy glanced at the machine that was breathing for Robo. "Is he stable now?"

"For the moment. But I don't know how long that will last, whether there are side effects to what he's been given, or whether the drug's done any permanent damage to his brain or heart. The sooner we can get this state reversed, the better." He looked at Riley. "Can you stay beside him while I search for options?"

Although pale, the teen appeared to be back in control of her emotions. She stepped forward to follow through with what she'd been asked.

"Let me know if anything changes or if he starts to move, okay?" Cole said.

Riley nodded.

Cole called Tess, waking her from sleep, and she agreed to come as soon as possible. He hurried to the office to power up his laptop.

Johnson arrived with the dart, which had been sealed into a clear, plastic bag labeled "Biohazard." The sheriff turned the baggie to study the dart's front and back, and then laid it on the desk beside Cole's computer. "Cole, Deputy Johnson and I both have to go back to Mattie's house. I want to leave this dart with you, but I don't have a spare officer to stay and keep it within the departmental chain of custody. I want to swear you in as a Special Deputy."

Cole glanced up from his computer. "Now?"

"Right now. Do you accept the duty of maintaining this evidence and keeping it within your possession until it's returned to another law enforcement officer?"

"I do."

"You are officially appointed. Call me with an update when you can." And with that, McCoy and Johnson hurried out the front door.

"Is Robo still the same?" Cole called to Riley through the pass-through.

"Yes. He hasn't moved."

Cole picked up the bag and examined the dart. It was exactly like the ones used by the wildlife department: heavy gauge, one-and-a-quarter inch, steel needle; four inch plastic cylinder that contained the dosage; and an orange plastic, daisy-shaped flight stabilizer at the rear.

With the tranquilizer delivery system confirmed, now he

needed to figure out what drug had been in the cylinder. His first thought was BAM, the drug the wildlife department used to sedate wild animals. BAM was actually a combination of drugs, and they planned to use it on the mountain sheep in a few weeks. Unfortunately, though Cole had ordered the kits that contained the reversal agent, he hadn't received them yet.

He carried both laptop and dart into the surgery room where he could relieve Riley. He set them down on a countertop and tapped the drug reference words onto the keyboard. He quickly located an official site for BAM and opened the webpage.

Scanning through the information, he zeroed in on its effects. It worked quickly, provided low-level sedation for two to four hours, and was often the drug of choice because it allowed relaxed respirations—no "frozen chest."

Studying Robo, he processed the information. Frozen chest was a good description of this dog's condition, which meant that either a different drug had been used, or Robo had been given an overdose. *Which is it?*

"What can we do to help him?"

Riley was apparently growing impatient with doing nothing, but Cole wasn't ready to inject another drug into Robo's bloodstream just yet. He scrolled down to the section that talked about reversal of the drug. "I've got to do a little bit more research. Hang in there, kiddo."

BAM could be reversed with two different drugs, one of which Cole kept in his drug inventory for reversing horse sedation for surgery, but he didn't have the other drug on hand.

He took out his cell phone and dialed Ed Lovejoy. Using his shoulder to hold the phone to his ear, he began typing in more reference words, searching for opioid sedation for animals. No answer from Ed. Instead of leaving a message, Cole disconnected and redialed. A list of websites popped onto the screen, and he clicked a link to one of them.

"Come on," he muttered as he listened to the phone ring. No answer. He redialed.

He found an article that talked about an opioid called thiafent-anil oxalate, a drug he'd never used. He skimmed through the list of websites again and found one with the drug insert information; he clicked on it.

"What?" Ed Lovejoy's angry voice boomed from the receiver.

"Ed, this is Cole Walker. I've got an emergency and need your help."

"Gosh darn it. What time is it, Doc?"

He wasn't calling to deliver a time update. "Do you have any BAM kits on hand?"

"No. I thought you were supposed to order those."

"They're not in yet. You don't have any left over from another project?"

"No. If there are any left over, the state supervisor keeps those secured in his office."

*Tucker York*, Cole thought. At the same time, he scanned the drug insert that was displayed on his computer screen. "Have you ever used thiafentanil oxalate, Ed, brand name Thianil?"

"Not on anything I've worked on. You have to keep that stuff out of the human food chain."

"What do you know about it?" Cole had swept down to the "warnings" part of the insert. The drug could cause slow breathing and cyanosis, which accounted for Robo's blanched gums.

"It's dangerous stuff," Ed was saying. "You have to be trained to use that shit. And wear gloves and a mask when you do."

"And to reverse it?"

"I don't know. I hear that without reversal, coming out of that stuff can be ugly."

Cole became aware that Tess had arrived when the front door opened and banged shut. At the sudden noise, Robo's whole body jerked on the table, making Riley flinch and her eyes widen.

The Thianil insert label warned that the sedated animal might react to sudden noise. *Bingo! This has to be the drug!*

Robo's paws began to paddle against his restraints, in what looked like the onset of a seizure. Cole's window of time was closing. He had to make a decision. "Gotta go, Ed," he said before tapping the end button and plunking his phone down on the desk.

Tess came into the room, took one look at the situation, grabbed a stethoscope from the countertop, and placed its resonator on Robo's chest to monitor his heartbeat. Looking relieved that someone else could take over, Riley stepped back against the wall, hugging herself.

Cole skimmed to the "antidote" section—naltrexone hydrochloride. The drug he had in stock for equine surgeries. Now, the dosage—ten milligrams for each milligram of Thianil. He had no idea how much tranquilizer had been injected into Robo.

He hurried to the locked cabinet where he stored sedatives while he ran through a mental calculation, converting the amount used for an animal weighing as much as a horse to a lower dose suitable for this one-hundred-pound dog.

Tess called out Robo's heart rate. Too fast. He was going into tachycardia.

Cole drew the dosage into a syringe. "Intravenous," he said to Tess.

She grabbed one of Robo's front legs, holding it still. Cole grasped the foreleg and applied pressure to occlude the vein, relieved when he saw it plump up beneath the dog's short leg hair. He inserted the needle and pulled back on the plunger to make sure he was in the vein. Blood flowed into the syringe cylinder, and he injected half the dosage into Robo's bloodstream.

Holding his breath, he secured the syringe to Robo's leg with strips of medical tape in case he needed to inject more of the medicine into the vein. Now it was white-knuckle time—all he could do was wait and see if the antidote helped or made Robo's condition worse.

In the first quiet seconds of waiting, a nervous flutter began to ripple his gut. There'd been no time to take in the fact that Mattie had gone missing and what that might mean. But he knew her well enough to know one thing for certain—she only would have separated from this dog at gunpoint.

# TWENTY-SIX

Awareness crept into Mattie's consciousness, fading in and out. She floated, unable to see. Darkness. Swaying. She was dangling, head down. She struggled to lift her face so that she could see, but the messages sent by her brain failed to reach her muscles.

Nausea penetrated the inky oblivion. She was going to be sick. She struggled to right herself, but couldn't budge. She smelled horse—the deep, musky scent of hay and grain. Leather creaked. A shod hoof struck against a rock.

Gradually, it dawned on her that she was draped over a saddle on top of a horse. Its rolling gait made her gag. *Robo! Is he okay?* But her mind slipped away, back into the safety of not knowing.

★

Robo's paddling motions had quieted. Cole kept one eye on him while he dialed Sheriff McCoy. "Let's get a heart rate," he murmured to Tess.

McCoy answered. "What is it, Cole?"

"Have you located Mattie yet?"

"We haven't. We're searching for her. How is Robo?"

"I'm trying an antidote, but he's still unresponsive. Will you call me as soon as you know anything about Mattie?"

"I'll keep in touch to the extent that I can."

A wave of frustration hit him. "Keep me in the loop, Sheriff. Mattie's like family to us."

McCoy paused and then said he would call back later. Cole ended the call with a promise to do the same when he had news about changes in Robo.

As soon as he disconnected, Tess gave him details on Robo's heart rate and oxygen level. Oxygen was normal—the respirator was doing its job. Heart rate had slowed, a positive response. Cole tapped Robo's eyelid and was rewarded with a blink reflex, sluggish but better than nothing.

He pushed half of what was left of the dosage into Robo's vein.

"What's this about Mattie?" Tess asked, her face creased with concern.

Keeping watch over Robo, he filled her in on what he knew, which was precious little.

"Oh, dear," she murmured. "Mattie would never leave this dog alone like that."

Cole glanced at Riley. She sagged against the wall, shivering. He wondered how she'd come to be at Mattie's house and decided he would question her later.

He tapped Robo's eyelid again and got a healthy blink reflex. Robo began to gag and chew at the intubation tube, sending Cole into overdrive.

"He's coming around," he said to Tess, at the same time pushing the last of the antidote into Robo's vein. He grasped the syringe, jerked off the small piece of medical tape he'd used to secure it, and withdrew the needle from the vein.

Robo's chest heaved, indicating he was starting to breathe on his own. Cole unhooked the intubation tube from the respirator while Tess turned the knob to shut it off. The beautiful sound of strong and steady exhalations whooshed through the short tube that was still secure within Robo's trachea.

Moving fast, Cole deflated the cuff on the intubation tube, unwrapped the tape that held it in place, and withdrew the tube entirely. At this point Robo's eyes opened, and he started to struggle against the safety restraints. "Let's unstrap him."

They released the straps on both sides of the table. Gripping

Robo to keep him from falling, Cole skirted the surgical table to get behind the big dog. "Stay back," he warned Tess. "He could bite."

Robo wouldn't mean to, but his bite-reflex might be strong before he became fully aware of his surroundings. Risking a bite himself, he clasped Robo around the chest and transferred him to the floor in one smooth movement. Then he backed away to give the dog the room he needed to fully recover.

Robo flopped a couple of times before he could right himself. He paused for a few seconds, looking around to take in his surroundings, and then gave his head a mighty shake. Though Cole was tempted to kneel beside him, he stood back, waiting for Robo to adjust to his environment on his own.

In all his years of practice, he'd never been so relieved to watch a recovery. The antidote had worked exactly as it was supposed to, reversing the action of the opioid and restoring Robo's ability to breathe and move within minutes.

Robo anchored his front feet and pushed the top half of his body up to sit, resting for a brief moment before standing with a quick lurch. He shook his whole body, including his tail, his feet lifting from the floor in small hops. When he finished, he focused on Cole and offered a half tail wag before sweeping the room with his eyes. He trotted toward the exit, alternating between nose down to sniff the floor and nose up to sniff the air.

Cole felt certain he was searching for Mattie.

"Well, that was a miracle," Tess murmured.

"Is he going to be okay?" Riley asked, her voice thick with pent-up emotion.

Deciding it was safe to approach now, Cole went to Robo and bent to stroke him gently on his side. "Let's ask him," he answered in a quiet tone. "Are you going to be okay, buddy?"

Robo looked up at Cole, waved his tail a couple beats, and then focused his stare on the door, lifting one paw to scrape it in a request to be let outside.

Cole continued to pet him in long, firm, soothing strokes. "I think he's going to be fine, Riley. Thank goodness you found him when you did. He wouldn't have lasted on his own much longer. How did you happen to be there?"

Riley looked at Cole for a second before letting her gaze slide away. "Mattie told me to come over."

He'd been around teenage girls enough to know when one wasn't being as truthful as she should. He gave her his stern dad face. "Are you sure? She told you to come over this late at night?"

Color infused the girl's pale face. "Well, she said she'd call in ten minutes, but when she didn't, I tried to call her. She didn't answer, so I rode my bike over to her house."

Cole nodded, watching Robo and thinking this version sounded closer to the truth. Robo waited patiently beside him, willing the door to open with his eyes, and Cole bent to place his stethoscope against his chest to listen to the strong, steady heartbeat for a minute. He felt confident that the opioid had been neutralized and all of the dog's systems had returned to normal.

While he was listening to Robo's chest, another thought occurred to him. "Riley, I need to look at your cell phone logs. I need the time that Mattie texted you and the time that you called her. That will lock in the gap of time when Robo was sedated."

*And when Mattie went missing*, he thought. Dread washed through him as the inevitable conclusion hit. When Sophie went missing a month ago, he'd vowed he'd never let someone he loved get taken from him again. But he had a bad feeling that's what had just happened.

Riley looked embarrassed as she pulled her cell phone out of her pocket. "I might have called her more than once."

"Doesn't matter. Let me jot down the times." He reached for the phone, and Riley gave it over with reluctance. He imagined it held information that she considered private. "All I want to look at are your texts to Mattie and your call log."

When Cole went to the countertop for notepad and paper, Robo gave up on the door and trotted around the room, giving everything a cursory sniff. He whined, darting back to the door to paw at it before dashing around the room again.

Cole located the string of texts to and from Mattie. The last one from Mattie told Riley she would call in ten minutes, after she took care of Robo. He recorded the time the text had been sent— 10:10 PM. The call log showed five calls from Riley that Mattie didn't answer, one right after the other, starting at 10:30. A twenty minute gap of time.

As he dialed McCoy, he watched Robo search the premises for Mattie's scent, the dog acting more and more distressed.

The sheriff answered immediately, and there was an edge of anxiety in his typically calm voice. "Yes, Cole. Any news?"

"We reversed the drug. Robo's up and moving around."

"Thank goodness."

"Riley and Mattie had been texting this evening, and we can narrow down the time that Mattie stopped answering her phone." Cole couldn't bring himself to say the words "went missing." He explained the time gap between texts and calls.

"I'll get that information to the officers that are canvassing the neighborhood for anything suspicious. It helps to know an exact timeframe."

"Robo is already looking for Mattie here at the clinic. I'm going to bring him over, see what he can find."

"Are you sure he's healthy enough for that?"

"The antidote reversed the drug that was used on him, and he's back to normal. And Sheriff, if the same drug was used on Mattie, it won't be easy for her. We need to find her."

When Cole disconnected the call, he looked at Tess. "Do we have a box I can put that dart in? I need to make sure no one gets a needle stick and an accidental exposure."

"I'll find one." Tess headed for the back storage room.

"Where is your dad, Riley?"

"He's working in Hightower tonight. He won't get home until after two."

"That makes for a late night." He wondered if Riley would be safe at her house. All of sudden danger seemed to loom every- where, and he didn't want to leave her alone. "Do you want to sleep on the couch in our den? You could text your dad and let him know where you are."

"Can I go with you?" He shook his head, and she didn't argue. "Then I want to stay at your house. Could you call me if you find Mattie?"

He took a moment to enter her number into his contacts list. Tess came back with a box that would work, and he enclosed the dart inside. He thanked Tess for coming in to help and grabbed a short leash and a long, retractable one from off a hook by the exam room door. He clipped the short one onto Robo's collar.

As he locked the clinic door behind him, he wondered how someone could obtain the powerful drug that had been used on Robo. It was a schedule two opioid that couldn't be purchased without a doctor's or a veterinarian's prescription.

The niggling thought that the same drug might have been used on Mattie continued to poke at him, and now that he was no longer absorbed with Robo's care, it broke free to torment him full-blown. Ed Lovejoy's words sent a chill down his spine—*without reversal, recovery would be ugly.*

★

Red and blue lights strobed the walls of Mattie's house. Robo leaped from the back to the front passenger seat and stared out the windshield, ears forward, mouth open in a nervous pant. Cole pulled over to park across the street and gave Robo's head a few quick pats, wishing he were bringing him home to Mattie.

He grasped the end of Robo's leash and exited the truck, leading Robo out the driver's side with him. The dog darted toward the yard, hitting the end of the short leash and pausing to look up at Cole with an impatient expression. He was ready to go.

Sheriff McCoy met him at the edge of the crime scene tape that surrounded the premises. "That's a sight for sore eyes," he said, gesturing toward Robo.

"He's already searching for Mattie. I brought a long leash, and I think we should let him go to work."

The dim light revealed McCoy's frown. "We don't have a handler."

"You're not going to need one. He wants to do this on his own, so let's see where he takes us."

Stella came from the front door to join them, carrying a gallon-sized ziplock bag with a black T-shirt inside it. She handed it to Cole. "From Mattie's laundry basket."

They had all learned the basics from Mattie, including the need for a scent article worn recently by the missing person, not freshly laundered. Cole had practiced search and rescue techniques with his own dogs many times with the kids and even with Mattie, but he'd never worked the end of Robo's leash. Robo was Mattie's dog, a professional, and their bond was nothing to fool around with.

"I'm not sure he even needs this," Cole said, taking the scent article from Stella. "But we'll see."

Mattie would have changed out Robo's gear, but Cole didn't want to take the time, and truth be told, he didn't see the need. Robo looked charged up and ready. He led him to the back of the truck and unlatched the door on his mobile vet unit, took out a water bowl that he used for Bruno and Belle when they traveled with him, and splashed some water into it.

Robo didn't want the water, but Cole murmured encouragement to take a few laps. He switched to the retractable leash as he eyed Mattie's house. Robo had been found in the backyard, and that seemed like a good place to start.

Robo surged against the leash, but Cole kept him close, trying for a semblance of control, gently insisting that Robo pay attention to him. Once they reached the small concrete slab that made up the back porch, he opened the bag, lowered the scent article, and offered it to Robo. As suspected, the dog gave it only a brief sniff, dropped his nose to the porch, and started to search without needing to be cued. Cole gave the command to search more for the sake of routine rather than direction.

Cole let the leash play out to give Robo the freedom to go where he wanted. He leapt from the porch, skirted around the corner of the house, and ran directly to the spot where he'd been felled by the dart. He paused there briefly, sniffing the area, before heading out the side gate. Cole followed while Robo edged forward more slowly, nose quartering the ground, as if vacuuming up scent from the blades of grass.

At the south edge of the front lawn, Robo took a sharp turn into an empty lot beside Mattie's house. Stella and McCoy followed behind, throwing ahead beams from their powerful flashlights to light the way for Cole. Robo, depending on his sense of smell, didn't need it.

A short, springtime growth of weeds covered the lot. Robo sneezed as he burrowed his nose under the plants, seeking scent from where skin cells might have lodged in the fresh, moist vegetation. He moved his head back and forth in the green stuff, as though searching the cone of scent to narrow in on the trail rather than following a direct track.

*Mattie didn't tread this ground on her own two feet.* The pit, which had opened in his belly earlier, widened.

Robo advanced to a spot where the weeds were mashed down, indentations obviously made by a vehicle. Cole stayed away, letting the leash out to its full length, and allowed Robo to search the area on his own.

"Hold back," he said to the sheriff and Stella. "There was a vehicle parked here, and there might be prints."

Nose to the ground, Robo swept the area. While the sheriff kept his light trained on the smashed foliage, Stella shifted hers around the lot, illuminating a couple of abandoned car skeletons and a tumbledown wooden shed with its door hanging from a hinge, the darkened entryway gaping.

Robo went on the move again, headed out to the street. Not wanting to disturb evidence, Cole stayed off to the side about twenty feet from Robo, while he worked to keep the leash from catching in the weeds. Mattie would have allowed Robo to go on his own, knowing he would always come back to her, but Cole didn't have that kind of bond.

When Robo reached the street, Cole fell in behind him. The unpaved street that ran past Mattie's house consisted of hard-packed road base made from chipped rock and gravel. Robo trotted out fast, and Cole broke into a jog to keep up.

"We'll light your way from behind," McCoy called as he and Stella struck off to get his Jeep.

Cole jogged away from Mattie's house, heading south, with Robo leading the way. An engine rumbled to life behind him and headlights lit the road from his back. They turned east toward the highway, and now Robo trotted fast, panting and with his head up. Cole began to suspect that the German shepherd wasn't tracking a scent trail; he was merely looking for Mattie and following the route where she took him to exercise.

"Robo, wait."

Robo continued forward, stopping only when he hit the end of the leash. Cole held him as McCoy drove up and rolled down his window.

"I don't think he's following her scent at this point. I think he's just looking for her."

McCoy gazed down at Robo for a moment. "What do you suggest?"

"I'm going back to the house to see if we've missed something."

While the sheriff turned the jeep around, Cole told Robo to heel and began jogging back to Mattie's house. The ease with which Robo gave up his own route to come along told Cole that he'd been right—Robo hadn't been on a scent trail when he took to the road.

But maybe, just maybe, he'd been onto something when he'd gone to the abandoned lot next to Mattie's house. And maybe that would contain evidence that would lead to finding her soon.

# TWENTY-SEVEN

## After Midnight, Early Thursday Morning

Mattie heaved up the contents of her stomach. She moaned and tried to move away from the stench. Gradually she became aware that she was lying on her side on a cold slab of rock. Her muscles twitched in uncontrolled spasms, and her limbs wouldn't move when she told them to.

She fought to control her gag reflex and willed herself to lie still, allowing her muscle tremors to quiet into a suppressed quiver. She remembered the lurching gait of a horse and welcomed the cold, hard stone beneath her cheek.

*Robo!* An image popped into her sluggish mind—Robo stretched out, struggling to come back to her. *Is he all right? Where is he?*

*Where am I?*

From out of nowhere, a hand grabbed her hair and yanked her head back. A flashlight shone into her eyes, blinding her. Pain from her scalp jolted her whole body into spasm again.

"Can you talk yet?" The voice sounded eerie, mechanically distorted.

She tried to say yes, but her mouth wouldn't cooperate. She could produce only a kitten-like mewl.

The person pulled her away from the pool of vomit and dropped her. Her cheek slammed against rock, tiny, sharp pebbles gritting underneath. Brilliant pain flared inside her skull. His footsteps crunched on gravel as he walked away.

She tried to lie still so that her muscles would stop their violent shudder, but this time her anxiety had risen too high to reach a calm state. Her breath came in shallow pants as nausea climbed from her stomach into her throat. She fought against the pain in her head and struggled to slow her breathing, but it felt like her body and her brain were disconnected.

*I was darted, too.* Strange that her memories were coming back to her in bits and pieces. She remembered Robo clearly, but the memory of her own darting seemed dim and blurry. *Right before I went under.*

She focused hard on her memory of Robo. Was he breathing? Was he still alive? She didn't know the answers. She didn't think she'd had time to determine his condition, so trying to remember was useless.

Pain from thinking about her dog threatened to overwhelm her, so she shifted focus back to the breathing lessons that her friend Rainbow had taught her. Slow and steady—inhale . . . exhale. Her ribcage barely responded. Panting for breath was about the best she could do.

She needed to regain control. Though in her current state, under the influence of whatever drug this guy had used on her, she had no idea how she was going to accomplish getting the upper hand.

★

When Cole returned to the vacant lot next to Mattie's, it had been taped off, and headlights from one of the cruisers lit the area where the weeds were smashed.

McCoy parked his Jeep at the edge of the lot, and he and Stella got out.

"I had dispatch send a bulletin out statewide. Every officer in the state will be looking for her," McCoy said. "I've also called in the crime scene unit from Byers County. They should arrive shortly."

"I'm going to go see if I can turn up anything on the surveillance cameras out by the highway," Stella said before turning away to sprint to her car.

"Where are the cameras?" Cole asked McCoy.

"There's one at the feed store and one at the gas station, both installed in the last few weeks. We might be able to get a view of the highway off one of them."

"I have the dart secured in my truck. We need to get that to a lab as soon as possible to confirm if I'm on the right track about the drug that was used."

"We'll turn it over to the crime scene unit. You said that a reversal agent is required?"

"From what I've read, the drug shouldn't even be used without having a reversal agent on hand. Gloves and a mask should be used to avoid human exposure."

"Can it be deadly?"

"You saw Robo. Without the respirator, he would have died. But I don't know how large a dose he was given. It might have been a purposeful overdose."

"But what about death by accidental exposure?"

"The product insert warns about dizziness, nausea, respiratory problems, and unconsciousness. That's just from exposure. It's not meant to be used on humans."

"What is the drug's purpose?"

Cole explained how the drug was used for immobilizing wildlife that had to be transferred or processed for research studies.

"Who has access to it?" McCoy asked.

"It's an opioid dispensed by veterinary prescription only."

"Wildlife managers, then?"

Cole nodded. "I got some of my information from Ed Lovejoy. He said he'd heard of it but never used it."

"I need to talk to him."

"I woke him up. As far as I know, he's at his house. I'll take you there."

"I have the keys to Mattie's vehicle. Let's take it. Robo will be safer if he's secured in his compartment."

Cole hurried to the Explorer with Robo running out front. He loaded into the back as soon as Cole opened the hatch, clearly eager to be inside his own domain. McCoy took the driver's seat, and Cole gave him directions to Lovejoy's property, which was about a half mile outside of town beyond the high school.

McCoy gave Cole a sideways glance. "You should know that we ran Ed Lovejoy's gun against the casing and slug recovered from the ram site. Although the casing and slug are a match with each other, Lovejoy's gun was eliminated."

"All right."

Ed's place was dark when they pulled up.

"You're staying here," Cole told Robo, echoing what he'd heard Mattie say countless times. She always told Robo what was expected of him.

Robo sat and stared at him as Cole opened the door to leave.

They walked through what little remained of a yard. Tufts of grass and weeds sprouted here and there on what consisted mostly of hard packed soil in front of a white, boxy modular home with green trim.

McCoy stepped upon the wooden deck and thumped on the front door. When there was no answer, he pounded harder. A porch light came on and a voice shouted from within, "Hold on, damn it."

Wearing royal blue boxers, a T-shirt, and a serious scowl on his face, Ed opened the door. He adjusted the scowl somewhat when he took in the fact that the sheriff was his midnight caller. "What is it?"

"We've got a situation that I need to talk to you about. Can we come in?"

"I suppose so," Ed said, opening the door. "The place is a mess."

Cole followed McCoy inside and verified that Ed's statement about his home's condition had been spot on. They'd entered the kitchen area where every horizontal surface was covered with dirty dishes. He wondered if the beige linoleum on the floor had ever benefitted from a wet mop, and a cat's litter box in need of scooping sat against the wall next to the refrigerator. Dingy white undershorts and socks nested in a pile beneath the kitchen table where it appeared Ed had kicked them off.

They all stood inside the doorway in the kitchen. A brown tiger cat that weighed more than was healthy for her came into the living room from the hallway, crouched, and watched the newcomers from afar. If Cole remembered right, her name was Kit.

McCoy started the conversation. "We need information about this drug that was used on our police dog. What can you tell us?"

Ed glanced at Cole. "Was it BAM or Thianil?"

"Thianil."

"I don't know much about it. I've never worked with it." He repeated what he'd told Cole earlier on the phone.

"Do you know of anyone who's been killed by it?"

Ed shook his head. "We don't use it that I know of. I mean, maybe it could be used on cougars or coyotes, but not food animals."

"Who orders the drugs for your department?"

"We use a vet that's assigned to the project. Cole is handling the order for our next sheep project."

McCoy looked at Cole.

Cole nodded. "BAM kits—ordered but not in yet."

McCoy turned back to Ed. "Do you keep any of these drugs on hand?"

Ed gave the same answer he'd given to Cole, explaining how kits were stored at the state supervisory level.

"And that's Tucker York?"

It gratified Cole that the sheriff had come to the same conclusion he did. Tucker York would have access to the drugs.

"I need to contact him," McCoy said. "He was in town today. Do you know if he's still here?"

Hearing that Tucker York had been in Timber Creek concerned Cole. He didn't know that the supervisor had returned. Could he be the one who attacked Mattie?

"He left," Lovejoy replied. "Said he was headed to Grand Junction before going back to Denver."

"I need his cell phone number."

"Why do you need to talk to him? I don't think he can tell you anything more than I can."

McCoy fixed his stare on Ed, and his deep voice rumbled. "Darting a canine officer with a sedative is a serious offense, never mind that this drug might have been meant to kill. I plan to find the person who did it, and I'll follow every potential lead to get information."

Ed appeared reluctant, but he turned to cross through the living room, going toward the hallway. "It's in my phone. I'll go get it."

The cat leapt from where she crouched and scampered into the hallway in front of him.

The sheriff hadn't yet mentioned that Mattie was missing, and Cole guessed he had his reasons. He followed McCoy's lead and remained silent, noticing the worry lines etched on the sheriff's face as he studied his surroundings.

Ed returned, his cell phone in hand. He read off York's number while both McCoy and Cole plugged it into their phones.

McCoy's dark eyes burned as he fixed his stare on Ed. "Do you have a wildlife dart gun here on your premises?"

"Actually I do. I have an old one from a project a few years ago."

"Can I see it?"

"Geez, Sheriff. It's buried in the closet in my bedroom. I'll have to go back there now to get it." He sighed and turned, starting to lumber away as if the thirty feet he had to walk was a marathon.

McCoy spoke to Ed's retreating backside. "Do you have any darts?"

Ed stopped and turned. "I think so. Some old, used ones."

"Bring those, too. Show me whatever you've got. Actually, I'll come with you."

Ed made a noise that sounded like protest, but he threw up his hands in surrender and headed back toward his bedroom. Cole followed the sheriff, entering a room that looked like it had been struck by a tornado: clothing scattered everywhere, shotgun shells and bullets scattered on top of the dresser among other collectibles such as pocket knives and loose change.

Ed dug into the closet, tossing coats, sweatshirts, pants, down vests, and other clothing out onto the floor. Back in the nether region of the far corner, he found what he'd buried there—the dart gun and a bag full of darts, similar to the one found in Mattie's back yard, only these had plastic feathers on the ends instead of the daisy shape.

"Is there anything significant about how the dart is made? I've seen one with a flowerlike pattern on the end instead of these feathers," McCoy said.

"That end part just stabilizes the projectile. There's nothing special about it," Ed said.

"Have you ever used the other type in your department—the one with the daisy?"

"Sure. These are just the ones I happen to have."

McCoy nodded.

"Here's how the projector works," Ed said, as he demonstrated unlocking a lever-type bolt on the gun that resembled a smaller version of a rifle. He pointed to the opening used for ammo. "You load the dart in here, lock the bolt, pump it with this lever, aim, and fire."

"How loud is the report when it's shot?" McCoy asked.

"It's powered by a carbon dioxide cartridge instead of gunpowder. It sounds like an air gun or a kid's pellet gun."

McCoy withdrew a pair of latex gloves from his pocket. "I need to take these with me, Ed."

"All right. Can I ask why?"

"We suspect this type of equipment was used on our patrol dog. Even if this isn't the exact equipment, it will give us a better understanding of what the gun looks like and how it functions. We'll return it to you as soon as we're done with it."

"I haven't used it for years. We have newer projectors we'll be using on the sheep project, so I won't need it back right away."

McCoy seemed to be turning that over in his head as he put on a glove and picked up the gun. "Do you have those newer projectors here at your local office?"

"Nah. Tucker has them at his office."

"Who else is involved with this sheep project?"

"Oh, let's see. The southwest regional manager will be coming in, and we'll have several wildlife technicians and another district wildlife manager like myself. Probably at least one biologist will be on the team. Cole will be our vet."

"Do you have the names of these people?"

"Sure."

"Who has access to the darts and the guns?"

"Well, I suppose any of us might. I mean, the equipment isn't exactly kept locked up like the drugs are. Tucker stores the new equipment, but some of the older stuff could be anywhere."

"I'll need a list of names and phone numbers for the project team members."

A furrow appeared between Ed's eyebrows. "I can get that together for you when I go into the office in the morning."

"Sorry, Ed, but I need it now."

"Gol-durnit, Sheriff. I thought you were gonna say that."

"Get me everyone's home and cell phone numbers if you can. It's imperative that I start contacting these people tonight."

"Give me a few minutes to get dressed, and then I'll go." Ed grumbled under his breath as he bent to grab a pair of jeans off the floor, saying something about all this hoopla over a dang dog.

McCoy drilled the man with his eyes, his face set in a grim frown.

"I'll tell you something in confidence as a wildlife officer of the state," McCoy said. "This is about more than the attack on my K-9. My K-9 handler is missing and unaccounted for now, too."

Ed looked back at the sheriff, and the surprise in his eyes appeared genuine. "You mean Mattie?"

McCoy nodded, and Cole was glad that the seriousness of the matter had finally been emphasized.

"Geez, Sheriff." Ed stepped briskly into his pants, pulled them on, and grabbed a shirt. "Why didn't you tell me that in the first place? Let's go see what I can find out at the office."

# TWENTY-EIGHT

Pain danced along every nerve ending of Mattie's body, shooting from one extremity to another. Her head pounded, and shards of shale bit into her cheek.

She lay on her side, slack-jawed, taking slow breaths through her mouth. She could see nothing, but she heard the occasional shuffle of a small animal in the night and the footsteps of her captor as he came and went. Whenever he approached, she pretended to be unconscious.

In the air she could smell the scent of a horse, the smoke from a campfire, the pine of the forest, and the earthiness of the hard stone beneath her. When the man drew near, she caught the musky odor of his body along with some type of cologne. Was that a hint of cinnamon? She wracked her brain, trying to recall if she'd ever smelled that scent before on anyone.

After he left, she tried to wiggle her toes and this time felt a tiny sensation of them pressing against her boot leather. Now, fingers. Her head told them to flex, but they refused to budge.

At least her brain seemed to be thinking more clearly. Robo came into her mind. Her brave dog, willing to tear into someone to protect her, yet willing to do anything she asked of him. Tears sprang to her eyes.

She couldn't allow herself to think of Robo. It would be her weakness. And if there was one thing she knew, it was this—she needed to remain strong, because she was going to be in for the fight of her life.

★

After retrieving a list of the sheep project team members from Lovejoy, Cole rode shotgun as McCoy drove back toward Mattie's house. "Do you think Ed had anything to do with this?" Cole asked.

McCoy remained tight-lipped. "What's your opinion?"

Cole thought it over. Lovejoy's reactions, both when he'd called earlier and when he and the sheriff made him open his door, seemed genuine. "I don't think so."

"I tend to agree." McCoy's cell phone rang. He checked caller ID and connected the call via the SUV's hands-free system. "Yes, Detective. You're on speakerphone and Cole Walker is here with me."

"I've roused both owners of the surveillance cameras," Stella said. "I just finished with Moses Randall at the feed store. The view of the highway is blurry and distorted at best, but I could see the shape of what looks like a light colored sedan cruise past at 10:23 PM on the tape. It came from the south, which would be the direction from Mattie's house, headed north on Highway 12. There was one more vehicle that passed from the south four minutes later. It was a dark colored pickup truck."

"Can you ID the car or the truck?"

"Too distorted. Can't tell make or model. But I'm headed to the gas station. If either vehicle turned west at the intersection, and if we have a better picture, I'll be able to spot them in the same timeframe."

Sounded like a lot of ifs to Cole.

"Good work. Call if you get anything," McCoy said, signing off.

Cole thought of the two pickup trucks he'd spotted in the parking lot on the day he and the kids found the boot. "Tucker York drives a dark blue pickup truck."

McCoy swiped and tapped his phone. "I'll try his cell again."

Cole waited while the sheriff ended the call and redialed, repeating the process several more times. Finally, he left a message: "Mr. York, this is Sheriff McCoy of Timber Creek County. Call me back when you get this message."

"So he's not answering his phone," Cole said.

"Could be sound asleep. The phone could be turned off or in a different room."

Cole knew that to be true, but still felt a growing suspicion that the man could be involved. He was in a prime position for having access to the drug and the method used to tranquilize Robo. But, he reasoned, there was no known connection between York and Mattie or her brother.

They were nearing Mattie's house when McCoy spoke again. "What are we going to do about your involvement in this investigation, Cole? I deputized you to secure the chain of evidence on that dart, but you're still a civilian."

"A civilian trained in the use of firearms and who has worked with you on cases before. You know you can trust me to keep my mouth shut."

"Not worried about that."

"I'm the closest thing you have to a K-9 handler for Robo right now, and I've trained with Mattie before. You deputized me, Sheriff, and I'm staying on the case."

When he heard his name, Robo poked his nose through the heavy-gauge mesh that separated his compartment from the front. Cole reached through to stroke the top of his head, squaring off toward the driver's side of the vehicle. He wouldn't let Sheriff McCoy send him home now.

"It's not your responsibility, and I can't guarantee that we can keep you safe," McCoy said.

"I'm safer investigating with your team than I am out there on my own. And I *will* search for Mattie on my own. You know I'm not good at sitting at home waiting by the phone."

McCoy shot a glance his way. "Let's take this a step at a time. For now, you're still deputized, and you're still in. I'll inform you if I change my mind."

They pulled up in front of Mattie's house and found the Byers County van parked at the vacant lot. Additional lights had been set up in both the lot and Mattie's back yard.

"You know how Robo learned to do a scent lineup last month?" Cole asked. He'd been mulling over what Mattie had told him about teaching Robo to match a scent article to a lineup of people. It was a skill used more frequently in European countries, and one not necessarily given credence in American courts of law. However, it had proven valuable for Mattie to ferret out the owner of a piece of evidence.

McCoy murmured a sound of agreement.

"I want to take him to the backyard now and ask him to do a thorough sweep. I don't know if he'll find something that your officers couldn't, but he'll at least get his nose full of this person's scent. If he locks it into his memory, maybe he could identify the person later. You never know."

McCoy raised an eyebrow. "Go to it. I'll tell Johnson and Garcia what you're up to."

Cole fastened a leash on Robo's collar, making a stop at his truck to give McCoy the box that contained the dart. He also wanted to keep offering Robo water to help him metabolize any remaining effects of the drug. He followed McCoy to the backyard, leading Robo past the fence where the sheriff huddled with his deputies.

After going to the porch, Cole paused and gave Robo several firm pats on his side, hugging him against his leg the way he'd seen Mattie do time and time again. Robo tolerated the affection but didn't look into his eyes with the ecstatic pleasure he always shared with his girl. "Just doing the best I can, buddy," he murmured.

He remembered the command Mattie used for evidence detection. *Seek!* He tried to get Robo to search a grid. Directing the dog with gestures wasn't as easy as it looked when Mattie did it, but Robo put his nose to the ground and started quartering the yard in a two-foot swath. *Thank goodness*, Cole thought as he followed the shepherd.

Robo charged up and down the yard quickly until they approached the fence along the side yard. At that point, he slowed, thoroughly sniffing the ground. Cole could imagine him taking in all the scents he was collecting and cataloging them into his memory. About halfway down the fence line, Robo broke from the grid pattern and followed his nose to the area where Riley had found him down and unconscious.

"I think someone came at Mattie and Robo from along the fence here," Cole told McCoy, who was standing by observing the process. Cole gestured along the ground. "This appears to be a scent trail."

McCoy indicated that he understood.

Cole knew the information was anticlimactic, but he'd pinned his hopes on logging the guy's scent into Robo's unique data bank, which appeared to be a success. He finished up the search without any objects or visual evidence to show for it.

But he'd come up with another thought, which he shared with McCoy as they led Robo toward the front yard. "Mattie spent most of the evening with her foster mother, Teresa Lovato. She knows Mattie as well as anyone. I wonder if she'd have any idea who might have attacked her and Robo."

"Are you thinking this is someone from Mattie's personal life?"

"I'm just trying to cast a wide net. We know it's possible that someone associated with her past might have killed her brother. So it's possible the person who took her could've known her, too, or at least could've known who she is."

"I'll go with you. I need to inform Mrs. Lovato about what's happened."

After Cole loaded Robo into the K-9 unit, McCoy drove them to a white, stucco two-story on the west side of town, a home that Cole had never been to before. On their way, the sheriff had called Mattie's foster mother to warn her they were coming.

The porch light flicked on. As McCoy shut down the car's engine, the front door opened, revealing a Hispanic woman of short stature wrapped in a pink bathrobe. Cole followed the sheriff up the sidewalk, and as they approached, more detail became apparent; the woman's gray-streaked black hair was worn in a long side braid that trailed down her chest, her wrinkled face etched with concern.

"What's this about Mattie, Sheriff?" She extended her hand to draw the officer into her home. "I was asleep and not thinking too good, so tell me again."

Cole paused at the threshold while McCoy explained that Mattie was missing after an apparent attack on her dog. Though she didn't make a sound, tears began to stream down the lady's wrinkled cheeks while he spoke. When he finished filling her in, McCoy introduced Cole.

She extended her hand, and Cole grasped it in both of his. This lady was very special to Mattie; in fact, she'd been a mother to her.

"Come in, come inside," she said, tugging gently at his hand. "Don't stand out there on the porch."

Cole stepped into the room. "I'm sorry we have to meet this way, Mrs. Lovato. I know how much you and Mattie mean to each other."

"And you mean so much to her, too. Call me Mama T. Everyone does."

Another woman appeared, coming down the stairway from the second floor. She, too, was dressed in a terrycloth, pink bathrobe, wrapped around her rather stout shape and belted at the waist. She'd also braided her long, black hair for the night.

"This is Doreen," Mama T said. "She is another one of my children."

Doreen approached, looking from the sheriff to Cole as she extended her hand and introduced herself. She had a soft grip and kind eyes.

Doreen turned to McCoy. "Is there anything we can do to help?"

"Do either of you have any idea who could be responsible for taking Mattie? Any idea, even if it seems unreasonable," McCoy said.

Mama T held her clasped hands against her chest. "Is this related to her brother's death?"

"We don't know. We can't eliminate that possibility. Do you know anyone who might have done this?"

Distress lined the lady's face. "It could be anyone. Anyone she arrested before."

Cole knew how she felt. Mattie's work lent a fine opportunity for her to make enemies.

"She was here at your home tonight," McCoy said. "Did you notice anything unusual about her behavior this evening?"

Mama T paused as if thinking. "She was upset when she got here, wasn't she, Doreen?"

"Yes, she was. Even more upset than the night before."

Cole observed something akin to guilt cross the sheriff's face.

Mama T looked at Doreen while she spoke, as if for confirmation. "But she seemed to relax after she got here, and I think she had fun."

"She did have fun, Mama. She was laughing before she left."

"Did she say where she was going from here?" McCoy asked.

"She planned to go straight home. She mentioned she was tired and ready for bed," Doreen said, while Mama T nodded her agreement.

"Did you see her drive away? Or notice anyone following her?"

Mama T plucked the nap of her robe's lapel, her stress even more evident. "I didn't see her. We were in the kitchen, and I didn't watch her drive away. I should have."

"That's okay, ma'am," McCoy said, reassuring her. "Chances are there was nothing unusual for you to see anyway."

After determining that Mama T could provide no further information, McCoy made his way to the door. "I'm sorry we had to disturb you with this bad news. We'll keep you informed if anything changes."

"I'll be here," she said. "I won't be going back to bed."

They said their goodbyes and Cole followed McCoy out to the car. As they left the house, Robo's face popped up in the Explorer's window, panting and wild-eyed. Cole hurried to open the door, and saw what he'd been doing while they were gone. The entire carpet in the dog's compartment lay in shreds.

"Poor guy," Cole said. "I've got to get him out of this car."

McCoy raised a brow. "Is he distraught over Mattie absence?"

"That and everything else he's been through tonight. He's

always been an energy bomb ready to go off. Mattie works hard to make sure he stays well behaved."

McCoy's phone rang while Cole gave Robo some water. Distracted, Cole paid only half attention to McCoy's side of the conversation. As the sheriff ended the call, Cole closed the hatch and joined him inside the SUV.

"That was Detective LoSasso," McCoy said. "When she looked at the time frame of Mattie's disappearance, she could see both vehicles more clearly on the gas station surveillance video, so she called in Deputy Garcia to take a look. He knows his cars. These videos aren't recorded in color, but the sedan appears to be light gray or silver, maybe tan, and he thinks it's a Chevrolet. The pickup truck is probably dark blue, brown, or charcoal, and it might be a half-ton Ford. As in the other video, the truck was a few minutes behind the sedan, and it doesn't look like they're traveling together. They're both just headed west."

Cole leaned back in his seat, digesting the information, and his thought process stirred an uneasy feeling in his gut. "William's crime scene is west of town. We know that he was alive when he was taken into the forest. I hate to say it, but we need to consider the possibility that his killer is taking Mattie to the same area."

"I know. And we have to wonder if we have some kind of ritualistic serial killer on our hands. Let's go to the station. The satellite phone is there." McCoy started the car and shifted into gear. "I'll get on it and notify Brody. He can utilize the posse members who are up there to patrol the area between the upper and lower gravesites."

The sheriff's words made Cole's gut twist. He fought to maintain an even keel. "That sedan on the road was probably just someone headed west out of town. But the truck, especially a half-ton with four-wheel drive, worries me."

"Because?"

"A truck could be headed toward any one of dozens of off-road trails into the wilderness area. There are hundreds of square miles of forest out there. If he takes her up into that country, we're lost."

"There were horseshoe prints at William Cobb's gravesite. We speculate that he arrived there on horseback."

Cole expanded on the sheriff's statement. "If horses were involved in William's case, they might be in Mattie's. A truck could have been headed west to someone's property to pick up horses and a trailer."

"I need to update the bulletin to the state highway to be on the lookout for a truck and possibly a trailer on highways leading to all points west of Timber Creek. There's little traffic on the road this time of night. A rig for hauling horses would stand out."

"And we need to search for a dark-colored Ford pickup parked at trailheads on the west side of town," Cole said.

"I'll call in Rainbow to coordinate volunteers. They can do that."

As they pulled into the station parking lot, headlights of another car lit their SUV from behind.

McCoy opened his door to exit the car. "That's Detective LoSasso now."

When Cole opened the door on his side, Robo rushed forward and poked his nose through the mesh, trying to escape his compartment. His desperation mirrored what Cole was feeling, and it tugged at his heart. He spoke to the shepherd as he stroked his head. "I know, buddy. We're doing the best we can. We'll find her, don't worry."

Terrified that he might not be able to deliver what he promised, he almost choked on his words.

# TWENTY-NINE

Cole circled to the back of the vehicle and let Robo out, using the leash to transfer him into the station. Once inside, he set him free, and Robo rushed toward the staff office while Cole trailed behind.

The shepherd paced around the empty room to sniff, pausing at what Cole assumed must be Mattie's desk, given the large dog cushion lying beside it. Robo gave the chair a thorough once over, and then turned to trot back out into the hallway, panting with nerves. Cole snatched up the dog bed and followed him.

He hoped to settle Robo down to rest in the briefing room, which Cole knew from experience doubled as a war room at times of emergency, and that's where the dog was already headed. When he arrived at the room's closed door, he scratched at it, and Cole hurried to tap before opening it for him.

From inside, McCoy told them to come in.

Robo trotted over to the sheriff before doing a quick scent-scan of each of the chairs. Rick Lawson was seated at the table with McCoy, a laptop in front of him.

McCoy looked at Cole as he approached. "I've updated the bulletin and activated volunteers to search trailheads west of town."

Cole placed the dog bed on the floor. "Robo has become more agitated in the past half hour. I'm hoping the routine here might help him rest."

He called Robo to the cushion and told him to lie down. The shepherd obeyed for a few beats before popping back up. In a tone that would leave no room for misunderstanding, Cole told him to stay. He eased back down on the cushion, watching Cole with a worried eye. Cole sat in the chair beside him and began a firm, circular massage on the dog's shoulders and back.

Carrying her laptop, Stella entered the room and took a seat at the table. "Cole, tell us more about this drug Thianil. Where could someone get it?"

"From a veterinarian. It's a schedule two narcotic, so it would be regulated. A vet could dispense it to his clients. And with a prescription, a client could get it from a vet supply store, but in both cases it would probably need to be special ordered. The nearest vet supply store in this area is fifty miles away in Willow Springs. For that matter, so is the nearest vet, other than me."

"Could someone steal it?"

"Sure, but he'd have to know which veterinarian or supply outlet might have it on hand. I'm sure that not everyone stocks it. And those that do keep it locked up."

"Do you keep it?" Lawson asked.

"Never heard of it before tonight."

Lawson tapped the keys of his laptop. "I'll set up a search in the NCIC database for theft of veterinary drugs, see if I can turn up anything."

"What's the NCIC?" Cole asked.

"National Crime Information Center. It's a system maintained by the FBI. Local jurisdictions provide input for wanted or missing persons, stolen property, violent crimes, that sort of thing. I'll set this for both Colorado and California entries."

"I contacted Detective Hastings in Hollywood on his cell phone," Stella said, her attention focused on her computer screen. "Woke him up. He'll check in with his narcotics division about Thianil use and drug thefts in that area."

McCoy stood and turned a dry erase board on wheels so that it faced them. A photo of a handsome, dark-haired man wearing a grease-stained coverall and aping for the camera, his hands inside a car's engine, had been labeled William Cobb and pinned to the top. Cole swallowed against a sudden lump in his throat.

"Let's do a quick rundown on William Cobb and look for commonalities that might help us find Mattie," McCoy said.

Cole scanned the words written on the board, thinking it helped to see the information compiled in one place. The words "Labs Pending" at the bottom of the column struck him.

"Labs from William's autopsy should be screened for thiafentanil oxalate," Cole said.

"Requested," Lawson said, as he tapped the keyboard of his laptop.

He focused on the column headed "Persons of Interest," reading first those listed under a west coast subcategory: Tamara Bennett, girlfriend; Joseph Quintana, employer; gang friends; and Old Friend of the Family, unknown person.

"What's the status on these west coast persons of interest?" he asked.

McCoy answered him. "The girlfriend, employer, and gang friends have all been cleared. The Old Friend of the Family is a ghost as far as we can determine. Nothing solid on that."

"But that might be our guy."

"It's possible."

Cole continued to massage Robo and felt rewarded by the dog's response—he now lay quietly, his head lowered to rest between his front paws, his eyebrows twitching as he fought sleep.

He scanned the list under the "Local Persons of Interest" subheading which read: Gibson Galloway; Ed Lovejoy, sheep project; Tucker York, sheep project; shooter of bighorn ram, unknown; and Bret Flynn, near locale. *Riley's dad.* Cole remembered when he'd brought his horse to the clinic for sutures, bringing to mind the possibility that he'd been up on Redstone Ridge on Sunday.

"What about the local people?" Cole asked.

Stella brought him up to speed. "Ed Lovejoy can be eliminated for the ram and Mattie, and he has no known connection to California for William. Tucker York worked in California wildlife management five years prior to moving here, no alibi for the ram, and denies knowing William."

"No response to my attempts to reach him tonight," McCoy said.

"And most likely to have access to Thianil," Cole added with an even worse feeling about York. "Who is this Gibson Galloway?"

McCoy answered. "Mattie arrested him on Saturday night. From Bakersfield, California and denies knowledge of William Cobb. Threatened Mattie during the arrest Saturday night."

Stella spoke up. "She and I interviewed him yesterday. Says he was in Kansas during the time period for William's death, but alibi remains unconfirmed. I suggest we send Deputies Garcia and Johnson to bring him in for questioning. And let's get a warrant to test his rifles for a match with our slug and casing."

"Agreed." McCoy reached for his cell phone to set things in motion.

Cole came back to Bret Flynn. "Flynn's daughter Riley is staying at my house. She said he's tending bar in Hightower until two." He glanced at the plain-faced clock on the wall. "It's almost that time now, and he should still be at the Hornet's Nest."

Stella tapped the screen of her cell phone, evidently finding the number. "I'll make sure he's where he's supposed to be."

"Where does he live?" Lawson asked.

Cole heard Stella ask for Flynn while he answered Lawson's question. "He and his daughter live west of town, just beyond the city limits. His wife died about six months ago, and they moved here from Los Angeles."

Lawson raised a brow. "California—has anyone interviewed him yet?"

"Not yet," McCoy said. "Another one who didn't reply to a message today."

"Would he follow that westbound highway that we have on surveillance to get to his home?" Lawson asked Cole.

"He would."

Stella disconnected and came back to the table. "Flynn's not there. He was scheduled for work tonight, but he called in sick."

"What kind of vehicle does he drive?" Lawson asked, rising from his seat.

Cole tried to recall but hadn't paid attention. "I can't say. It was dark when he came to my clinic, but I know he has a pickup and trailer."

"Close enough," Stella said. "Let's go see if he's at home."

He looked down at Robo, who'd finally fallen asleep. He hated to wake him, but they needed the dog's special ability to indicate if Mattie was on the Flynn premises. Hoping that the dog's power nap had been enough to reset his nervous system, Cole stroked him gently and said his name. Robo's eyes popped open, coming into focus within seconds as he gazed up at Cole.

"Let's go, buddy," he said. Robo heaved to his feet and headed for the door.

Cole and Stella took the K-9 unit while McCoy and Lawson drove the sheriff's Jeep. Robo stood in the back, his eyes focused on the windshield, and Cole noticed with relief that he had stopped panting and bouncing around the cage. The brief sleep had done him some good.

Cole had never been to the Flynn place before, but he'd seen it from the highway. It took only a few minutes to arrive at the front yard and park. From this vantage point, the pickup truck in question was nowhere to be seen, and neither were the horses. There should have been two. Being curious animals, horses almost always came to the fence when people arrived, but there was no sign of a nose or a nicker. He shared his observations with Stella.

She opened her door. "You stay here," she said, and she wasn't talking to the dog.

"All right, but I want to get Robo out and make sure Mattie's not here before we leave."

"One step at time, cowboy." She exited the vehicle, shutting the door firmly behind her.

Robo stood rooted on his platform, his eyes fixed on Stella's back. Cole was glad to see that he wasn't trying to escape, and the frantic behavior that he'd demonstrated earlier seemed to have subsided. He threaded his hand through the heavy-gauge screen and kneaded the ruff behind Robo's ears while they waited, their front row seat helping to alleviate his own impatience.

Stella and McCoy went up to the porch, while Lawson remained down in the yard. McCoy banged on the door. He waited a half-minute and pounded the door again. Still no answer. McCoy continued to knock, identifying himself in a deep, booming voice. Cole didn't doubt that if Flynn happened to be inside asleep, the noise would have awakened him.

The officers exchanged a few words, and then Stella turned to head back his way. Cole took that as a cue that it was his time to play ball.

He tried to remember how Mattie always started a search and came up with: "Let's go to work, Robo."

Robo met him at the back hatch, where once again, Cole clipped on his leash and gave him some water.

Stella came up beside him. "No answer. We don't have a warrant, so we can't enter any buildings. See if Robo can turn up anything outside here."

Cole used Mattie's T-shirt to refresh Robo's scent memory and then told him to search. The shepherd surged forward. With no hesitation whatsoever, Robo put his nose to the ground and trotted up the steps to the porch. When he reached the door, he sat, turning his head to stare at Cole.

His excitement skyrocketed. "He's got a hit! He found Mattie's scent by the door!"

"I'll call for a warrant," McCoy said, heading for his Jeep.

Cole tried the doorknob and found it locked.

"Back off, Cole," Stella said. "Under these circumstances we can get that warrant verbally. It'll only take a few minutes."

Soon McCoy exited his Jeep. "I have a verbal warrant and permission to search inside buildings from Judge Taylor. Let's force the lock." He was carrying a small, leather kit with him, unzipping it as he approached. "I can pick it."

He extracted two tools before tucking the closed kit under his arm to free up both hands. Cole supposed that after years in law enforcement, the sheriff had learned how to breach locked doors without kicking them in. This particular knob appeared cheap, and McCoy gained entry within seconds.

"Timber Creek County Sheriff," McCoy shouted as he opened the door. "We're coming in."

Silence.

McCoy entered the room first, his flashlight held high and off to the side, away from his body. "Wait here, Cole."

Stella and Lawson followed him in, each drawing their weapon. Even from out on the porch, Cole could feel the stillness of the house, and he knew there would be no one home.

Lights shone through windows in turn as the officers went through and cleared the building. Stella came back to the door and gestured for him to come in. "See if Robo can pick up her scent inside."

Cole entered the living room, bringing Robo with him. What appeared to be new but inexpensive furniture clustered around a television, a coffee table in front of a couch and two upholstered chairs. Dirty dishes and discarded clothing littered their surfaces.

He directed Robo to search, following along as the dog put his nose to the floor, swept the room, and then trotted off to the kitchen. From there, Robo circled back to a hallway that led to two bedrooms—one obviously assigned to Riley, one to her dad—and a large, outdated, green-tiled bathroom.

No hits, no indication from Robo that he'd found Mattie's scent.

Confident that Robo was working for him, Cole rejoined the others in the living room. "He hasn't found her scent inside, but he definitely hit outside on the porch."

"I'll check to see if the vehicles are in the barn," Lawson said as he left.

"I'll back you up," McCoy said.

"Do we know if Mattie came here today for any reason?" Stella asked.

"No, but I can ask Riley." Cole withdrew his cell phone from his pocket, swiped to his contacts list, and dialed the teen.

It took a few rings for her to answer, and when she did, Cole could tell he'd awakened her. He gritted his teeth when she told him Mattie had come to the house to speak with her dad on Tuesday morning, little more than twenty-four hours earlier. Of course Robo would have found her scent on the porch.

"Have you heard from your dad?" Cole asked her.

"No."

"He didn't answer your text?"

"No, but when he's working, he doesn't always answer."

"Call me if you hear from him, okay?" After she agreed, he disconnected and shared the information with Stella.

"Damn it!" Stella said. "I thought Robo had a definite hit."

"He did. It just wasn't what we thought it was."

Lawson and McCoy sprinted back from the barn. "No vehicles out there," McCoy said.

Stella told them what they'd learned from Riley as she took out her cell phone. "I'll call dispatch to run a trace on Bret Flynn's truck so that we can get a description and plate number. We'll have Rainbow alert the volunteers to look for it at the trailheads."

Disappointed, Cole followed Stella to the Explorer. He glanced at his watch. Time was passing too quickly, and he couldn't help but think that for Mattie, it could be running out.

★

Mattie felt like she was finally getting somewhere. Sensation had returned to her hands enough to tell that her wrists were bound. Nevertheless, she flexed and released her fingers repeatedly, gaining progress in their strength by the minute.

She didn't dare move in a large way, but little shuffles of her feet told her that her ankles weren't bound like her wrists. The fact that her legs might be free gave her an inordinate amount of hope.

Robo. His doggie face with all its various expressions surfaced in her mind. But now, instead of the thought of him making her weak, it fueled the fires of revenge deep in her belly.

The gravelly crunch of footsteps returned, ominous as they echoed. The beam of a flashlight penetrated the darkness, and she caught a brief glimpse of stone streaked with veins of rose and green shale that surrounded her. *A cave*, she thought, before she closed her eyes to fake unconsciousness.

The toe of the man's boot connected with her kidney and pain flared in her back. She lay still as a wounded rabbit.

He grabbed her hair and pulled back her head, shining the flashlight in her face. "Time to wake up, girlie."

*Girlie.* The word dredged up a memory. Her father used to call her that.

Releasing her hair, he moved around to her front, sliding the light's beam over her body. He punched her shoulder, rocking her onto her back, and then slammed his fist into her belly, driving the breath out of her. Reflexively she drew up her knees and flopped clumsily onto her side.

"There you are," he said, his voice distorted by the mask he still wore. "It's about time."

The light blinded her. He appeared to be waiting for her to say something.

She forced an inhalation and spoke in a croaky voice that sounded nothing like hers. "What?"

"Now listen to me, girl. There's only one thing you got to tell me, or you'll find yourself in a world of hurt, just like your brother." He paused and she could hear the eerie sound of his breath whooshing in and out of the mask. "Where in the hell can I find Ramona Cobb?"

# THIRTY

Mattie couldn't believe what she'd heard. This guy was asking about her mother. "Ramona Cobb?" she echoed.

"You know who I'm talking about."

Still pulling for air, she curled around her belly to shield it. He shone the flashlight in her face, blinding her.

His knees popped as he knelt, and the scent of wood smoke clung to his clothing. Her mind frantically sorted through what she knew about her mother, but she couldn't come up with anything that would help her determine who she was dealing with—just the void from her past that she'd been trying to fill for months.

"Are you ready to talk?" he asked.

*Act like you want to cooperate*, she told herself. "Of course. I wish I knew how to find her, too."

"Don't act dumb."

"I'm not. I've been looking for her."

"I think you know where she is."

She needed to avoid getting into a "no, I don't" and "yes, you do" argument that would get her nowhere. "Let me tell you what I do know."

"That's why we're here."

"I haven't seen Ramona Cobb since I was six years old."

Striking as fast as a rattlesnake, he slapped her cheek. "Don't mess with me. You're a cop. You know where she is."

Her cheek stung. "I've looked for her. She's not in our database."

"Is she in prison?"

"I searched to see if she has a criminal record. She's not listed."

Gravel crunched as he rocked back on his heels away from her. He remained silent for a moment, as if thinking.

She ventured a question. "Why do you think she's in prison?"

"Ramona's not as innocent as she looks. She helped Harold with his business."

Was this about her father? "I can't remember much of anything from my childhood. I remember the night the cops came to arrest my dad, but memories before that are sketchy."

"Your dad, huh?"

*Odd response.* "He tried to kill my mom. The cops came to break up the fight, and they arrested him."

"And Ramona pressed charges?"

"The prosecutor did. From what I know, Ramona disappeared as soon as she was released from the hospital."

"Sure she did. She didn't want the law to catch up with her."

"I was raised in foster care. I have very few memories of my mother."

"It sounds like she dropped you when the going got rough. So there's no reason to protect her now, is there?"

"I'm not trying to protect her. I'm telling you what I know."

Without warning, he grabbed her shoulder and flipped her onto her stomach, trapping her arms beneath her. Sharp edges of stone cut into her bound hands as he straddled her back and sat on her hips. Grasping her hair, he slipped something that felt like a noose around her neck.

"You must need a little taste of how it went for your brother."

Her weak efforts to buck and kick resulted in nothing. She felt the rope tighten until it clamped off her breath. Her body went into survival mode, but her ability to fight seemed useless.

She searched for a way to save herself, but stars exploded in her vision, making it impossible to think.

Mattie coughed and sputtered as she came to, heaving for breath. Still on her belly with her arms pinned beneath her, she turned her face to the side. Sharp rock grazed her cheek, cutting into it.

"You want more of that?"

Unable to catch her breath, she shook her head no.

When he moved off her back to crouch beside her, she could draw fuller breaths. His rough hand gripped her shoulder, lifting to turn her. Without thinking, she palmed a sharp-edged piece of shale in her right hand before turning to her side.

"I'll talk," she gasped.

"What do you have to say?" For some reason, he still wore that mask, obscuring his face. Perhaps he planned to let her go if she gave him the information he wanted, but then she decided that was only false hope. She didn't have what he wanted anyway.

She had to keep her wits about her—it was the only thing she could control right now. She narrowed her eyes against the flashlight's beam.

"Where is Ramona?" he asked.

While he trained the light on her face, she wiggled the rock shard from her palm into her fingers. Grasping it so that it remained hidden, she tested the sharp edge against the rope that bound her wrists. She could barely reach it, but when she felt the piece of shale connect with the rope, she could have whooped with joy.

She couldn't recall abuse from her mother, but playing along suited her needs. "I wish I could tell you where she is. Ramona did us a favor when she abandoned us. She was always so mean."

"She's a lying bitch. And a thief."

"What did she steal?"

"Money."

"What money?"

"Back in the day, we were in business, see? The business of transportation of a certain type of goods from Mexico all the way to Canada. Fire power."

The cop in her knew he was talking about gunrunning. "But we were poor. Dirt poor."

"That's just it, girlie. There was more cash there than we could put in a bank. Harry and Ramona hid it. Buried it in the forest for safekeeping. Only it wasn't there when I went to dig it up."

*Can I believe any of this?* "Ramona took it?"

"Hell yeah, sweetheart."

"Almost twenty-five years ago?"

"Yep. She's probably blown through it by now, but I can't let a thief go unpunished. You know me. I'm the kind of guy that wants to get even."

She reached for something to keep the conversation going. "I remember that Ramona was Hispanic. Did she have family in Mexico? Or someplace here in the US? Could she have headed back to her home to live with her relatives?"

"I checked. Nada."

"What was she doing before she hooked up with Harold? I'm trying to think of different ways I could search a database. Could she have a criminal record under a different name?"

His feet scraped against stone as he moved away, a sign of detaching from the conversation.

Afraid that he was no longer focused only on her face, she kept her hands still. "I'm willing to try to find her again if I can get to my computer."

"I'm disappointed in you."

"Let me call one of my colleagues, a detective. I'll see if she can get you more information."

"That ain't gonna happen."

"What do you have to lose? Maybe a little time? You already have me as a hostage. That should motivate my colleagues to work faster."

No reply.

"If they have more information to search with than I did—where she was from, maybe a maiden name or a possible alias—they might be able to get something more out of our system."

He paused and she hoped he was thinking it over.

"Maybe a little fire would motivate you to talk."

He stood and walked away, lighting his path with his flashlight and leaving her alone in the darkness. She rolled to her back to watch him go, taking advantage of the light's beam to see what she could of her surroundings. The cave looked to be about twenty feet deep with ambient light at the opening. Once he went beyond the cave's mouth, he turned right and the slice of light disappeared with him.

He either felt confident that he'd immobilized her, or he'd forgotten that her feet weren't bound. She tried to sit, but her torso was too weak to respond.

After rolling to her side, she used the piece of shale to saw furiously at the rope around her wrists.

★

As Cole drove Stella back to the station from Flynn's place, a strong, westerly wind kicked up and buffeted the side of the K-9 unit. Dust and litter blew across the street in front of the headlights. Spring storm. He'd been too busy to watch a weather report for days, though catching a forecast rarely mattered. Spring weather in Colorado was hard to predict. One day could bring sunshine then snowfall the next. But the one thing Coloradans could count on this time of year—there would be wind.

After parking, Cole released Robo from his compartment and followed Stella into the lobby. He raised his hand to greet Mattie's friend, Rainbow. The dispatcher was speaking into a headset as he passed by, but she waved in acknowledgement, her face noticeably pale, the rims of her eyes reddened.

Stella stopped at Rainbow's desk to ask for an update on the volunteers' search of the trailheads, and Cole's hopes plummeted when the dispatcher said that no dark colored pickup nor truck and trailer rig had been found.

Bringing Robo with him, he entered the briefing room and sank into a chair. McCoy and Lawson were already there, each talking on their cell phones. A glance at the clock told him it was almost three AM. He settled Robo beside him and leaned forward to pet him, closing his eyes to rest them for a minute.

McCoy ended his phone call as Stella entered the room. The sheriff spoke, making Cole straighten in his seat to listen. "I have a report from Deputy Garcia. He found Gibson Galloway at his place along with his girlfriend. He's bringing them both in for questioning, but the girlfriend says they've been at Galloway's home since late yesterday afternoon, well before Mattie disappeared. Deputy Garcia thinks they were asleep when he arrived."

Stella sat at the table and slumped against it. "If that's true, we can eliminate him for Mattie."

"That leaves us with Tucker York and Bret Flynn. We have license plate numbers for their vehicles, and I've got the state patrol on the lookout for both of them." McCoy focused on his cell phone, swiping and tapping the screen as he stood and moved away from the table. "I'll try to reach York again."

Cole stared at what they knew about William's case written on the white board, his tired eyes focusing on the words "Old Friend of the Family, unknown" and then "Desert Eagle, registered to Harold Cobb."

McCoy dialed and redialed several times before giving up. Cole caught his eye as he came back to the table.

"What do we know about Harold Cobb?" Cole asked.

"Harold Cobb is deceased, killed in prison over twenty years ago," McCoy said.

"And we know that for a fact?" Cole asked.

"Yes, I confirmed it myself. I was a deputy working here in Timber Creek at the time. I responded to the call the night Cobb was arrested, and I'd taken an interest in the kids, so I wanted to make sure he was actually gone."

His words surprised Cole. He hadn't known that the sheriff had rescued Mattie the night she called the cops on her dad. He glanced at Stella, wondering if she'd known. Her face was unreadable.

"How did he die?" Lawson asked.

"Shiv to the back, right kidney area."

"Unusual except for in cases of organized crime or pedophiles."

"There was evidence of the latter, but the prosecutor shelved the case when Harold Cobb was killed. There was no reason to go forward after his death and put the victim through further trauma by having to testify."

Cole was shocked. Another quick look at Stella told him that her gaze had sharpened, homing in on the sheriff. But McCoy wore his cop face, and his voice had been smooth as butter. What did these two know about Mattie's childhood? What kind of torment had her father put her through? He could only imagine.

The urge to save Mattie spurred him. "Harold Cobb, William Cobb's death, the skeletons in the older graves—they've got to be connected to this old friend of the family who showed up in California."

Lawson's computer pinged, and he focused on the screen. "There's report of a break-in and burglary two months ago at a big game hunting preserve located between Los Angeles and Sacramento. Vials of Thianil and other narcotics were stolen from the veterinary office."

"How about the reversal agent, naltrexone?" Cole asked.

Lawton was reading the screen. "That, too. And some equipment used for administering the drug—a respirator mask complete with night vision goggles."

"To protect the airway and hunt down animals at night." Cole could visualize it. "Perfect for use on Mattie and Robo after dark."

Stella appeared to have renewed energy. "All right. So now we know where the drugs and equipment probably came from, and that points back to California. York moved to Denver from Sacramento, and Flynn just moved here from L.A. We've got to find these two men. One of them has to be our guy."

"One or both," McCoy said. "I have to wonder if our guy has a partner. The fact that we have no witnesses who spotted a rig parked at the Redstone trailhead during the time period of William's homicide makes me suspicious. A partner could have moved the rig after they unloaded the horses. That would decrease their visibility in the area and the risk of being discovered."

"That makes sense," Lawson said. "I've wondered about a

partner myself. A pickup and horse trailer is a big target for a witness to spot. It makes sense that our unknown subject would have someone move it away while he did his work."

"We've been assuming that we could spot a vehicle at a trailhead and that would tell us where to go," Stella said. "But if he has a partner, we can't make that assumption. Our bulletins for both York's and Flynn's trucks have given us nothing. Are they together now? Do they both have Mattie?"

That sat in silence, mulling it over.

A disturbing thought came to Cole. It was awful, but he decided he had to say it. "Flynn's daughter, Riley, has taken an interest in Mattie, and vice versa. Her friendship might be completely innocent, but what if she's involved some way?"

Stella frowned with concentration. "Working as a partner to help set up Mattie's abduction?"

"Maybe."

"Is Riley at your home right now?"

"She is." It was hard to wrap his head around the full scope of it, and he immediately began to backpedal. "But she was genuinely distraught when she found Robo in Mattie's yard, and she saved his life by calling me. That would point away from her involvement."

"What was she doing in Mattie's yard that late at night?" Stella mused. "I know they were texting and Mattie said she'd call and didn't, but why would the girl ride her bike close to a mile to go there in the dark to check on her?"

"I agree that seems strange," McCoy said.

"I need to talk to her." Stella's eyes narrowed. "At the very least, maybe she knows something."

The satellite phone beeped for an incoming call, making Cole startle.

McCoy answered it. "Yes, Deputy Brody." They sat in silence, listening to the sheriff's side of the conversation. "You're breaking up. Oh, it's the wind." Long pause. "All right. Take the phone with you and check back in."

McCoy placed the phone back in its cradle. "Deputy Brody is

taking two of the posse down the trail to search for campfires while the others stand guard at the crime scenes. It'll be slow going in the dark, but he's focused on the MO of these homicides, and he's hoping to spot a fire if there is one. They've ridden the area adjacent to the gravesites and found nothing. He's expanding the search down the trail and plans to include the backside of the ridge when he gets to the fork."

"The burning pit in our guy's MO is important to him," Lawson said. "It's logical that the ridge and fire are a part of his ritual, and he could be driven to return to that area." He pulled his cell phone from his pocket. "It's impossible to search the entire ridge by horseback in the dark, but a chopper might be able to find a campfire from the air."

Cole stared at him, his hopes rising.

Lawson swiped his phone. "I'll see if I can mobilize our chopper and do an air search of the ridge for a campfire."

Cole looked at McCoy. "I need to join the search on the ridge. We've done all we can here in town, and I want to take Robo with me. If we can get him within a mile of Mattie, he'll catch her scent and find her. Can you notify Brody that I'll meet him where the trail splits?"

"How long do you need to get there?"

"Within an hour."

Lawson ended his call. "They'll send up the helicopter, but they have concerns about the weather. Wind gusts in the mountains are forecasted up to seventy miles per hour. Wind of that speed could drive the chopper out of the area and back to the ground."

"Cole is taking Robo up to join the search on the ridge by horseback," McCoy told Lawson and then looked back at Cole. "Deputy Brody will have the satellite phone with him, so once you connect with each other, you can stay in contact with us here at the base."

"Can you put me on a horse?" Lawson asked Cole.

"I can arrange it. I have to run home to get my rig and pick up horses."

"I can communicate with the helicopter while we're on the trail," Lawson said to McCoy. "Once we connect with Brody we can loop you in on the sat phone and have three-way communication. If the chopper spots something, they can direct us where to go."

"I'll take you to your house, Cole," Stella said. "I need to talk to Riley."

"I'll wake up Mrs. Gibbs. She keeps her cell phone by her bed." Antsy, Cole stood, and Robo leaped up to join him, both of them more than ready to get started.

# THIRTY-ONE

Firelight flickered and danced at the cave's opening. *A fire pit like Willie's.* Smoke intensified, along with a growing sense of urgency. Mattie battled nausea brought on by the odor. She held the frayed end of the rope freed from her wrists, wondering how she could use it as a weapon. No doubt this guy was strong. Bracing a hand against the cave's stone floor, she pushed into a half-sitting position. Vertigo almost bowled her over.

She drew a breath, battling the dizziness. What was it Rainbow said during their yoga lessons? Breathe all the way to the bottom of your lungs on a count of three. Extend the exhalation for a count of six.

During the count, she pushed herself up into a tentative sit and crossed her legs. She gave each leg a brisk rubdown with her palms, thankful that her limbs were moving again.

*How much time do I have?*

She extended her legs, bending forward slowly at the waist, and lowered her head toward her knees. The spot where the dart had embedded in her back screamed in protest. Using her yoga breath to fight the pain, she continued her gradual movements, reaching forward to give her calves a quick pat down, welcoming discomfort if that meant her sensation had returned.

*How do I fight this guy?* The ultimate question. Grand prize for the right answer—you get to live.

She placed both palms on the stone floor and shifted into a

kneeling position, holding the pose until her head stopped swim-
ming. Regular breaths. Inhale, count to three, exhale, count to six.
Listen, ears straining, for footsteps. Watch the cave's opening for
return of the flashlight.

*Can I stand?* Moving in coordination with her breath, she ended
in a poor example of a forward bend, knees shaky and bent. With
caution, she began to unfold into a standing posture, catching herself when she felt her body tip forward. Dizzy and sweating, she
failed at several attempts before rising to a full stand, her muscles
trembling with the effort.

With Rainbow's count inside her head, she struggled to take in
enough oxygen for her body, imagining strength flowing into her
limbs with every breath. She stretched her arms above her head and
envisioned herself as a warrior preparing for battle.

The flicker of the firelight set the cave spinning. She fixed her
gaze straight ahead and knelt, lowering her hands to the firm stone
to steady herself.

Return to stand. Breathe in, breathe out. She repeated the process until she could stand without the threat of dizziness striking
her down.

Since forward movement made things worse, she decided
against trying to escape and outrun her captor. She needed more
time, but she wasn't sure she was going to get it. And fighting this
guy seemed all but hopeless.

*Breathe*, she told herself when she felt her chest tighten. *Think.
What are my weapons?*

She was dressed in light sweats, a T-shirt, and a hoodie. Nothing in the hoodie's pockets.

She had a frayed rope, the sharp-edged shale—and the element
of surprise. This last asset felt like her ace in the hole.

Sinking into a cross-legged sit, she searched blindly with her
fingers for a large piece of rock while she found the rope with the
fingers of her other hand. First, she came across the sharp piece of
shale that she'd used to cut her bindings, and she placed it in her
pocket for safekeeping. Finally, she found a hefty stone. After

wrapping the rope around the rock like ribbon on a present, she tied a strong knot, securing the rock at the end.

Then she remembered a weapon that Willie once made to hunt rabbits. A bola—a string of rocks tied together with twine. She hurried to duplicate it and managed to tie three rocks in a row along the length of the rope.

She'd lost track of time. How long had he been gone? Maybe fifteen minutes? A half hour? The pattern of firelight against the cave wall flared, and she could imagine the flames licking at branches and logs as this lowlife threw them into the pit.

Her mind flashed on a time when Robo had come to her rescue in another place where she'd been surrounded by walls of stone. Thinking of him made her heartsick. She would take strength from his fighting spirit, because this time she was on her own.

Still woozy, she gathered her energy to make the effort to stand. The drug that had been used on her was messing with her equilibrium. Dizziness and nausea threatened to overtake her. She appeared to have two choices: she could wait in ambush and fight him here inside the cave, or she could try to escape and run away from him outside.

Much as she wanted to bank on her ability to outrun the guy, she hesitated to stake her escape on a body she could barely control. She hugged her bola against her chest so that she wouldn't lose it in the darkness and continued to use breath and slow movement to recover.

The play of the flashlight's beam at the cave entrance told Mattie her time was up. She took the sharp-edged shale out of her pocket and grasped it in the palm of her right hand as she lay down on her side facing the back wall. In a fetal position, she tucked her hands close to her belly, the rope draped over her wrists, the rocks of the bola hidden beneath her upper leg.

His footsteps crunched as he approached. Smoke thickened the cave's atmosphere as if it came with him.

"Okay, girlie."

Did she actually hear glee in that eerie distorted voice?

"Look here what I got for you."

He circled near and stopped in front of her, this time directing the flashlight toward the ground rather than shining it in her eyes. In his other hand he held a stick that was about a foot long and a quarter inch around. He poked it forward, the end aglow with a red ember. Smoke spiraled off, wafting up to the cave's ceiling.

*This is how he burned and tortured Willie.*

He still wore the horrible mask. Maybe he hated the stench of burning flesh.

"Wait," she said. "I thought of something I should tell you about Ramona."

"What?" He sounded disappointed. She was certain that it was cat-and-mouse play he was after now, rather than information.

"Ramona had a sister that came to see us. She—" Mattie faked a spasm of coughing, which wasn't too hard considering the amount of smoke in the cave.

"What sister?"

She continued to cough, drawing up her knees. Between coughs, she sputtered, acting out an attempt to speak.

He leaned down, and she lashed out with the piece of shale, aiming for his neck. She felt it connect.

Gagging noises came through the mask, and he dropped the flashlight to grab at his throat. The flashlight tumbled and rolled, making the cave walls pinwheel around her dizzy head.

She stayed low to the ground. With the speed of a one-two punch, she recoiled and aimed lower—this time at his crotch.

The shale connected somewhere on his lower torso, and the mask on his face hissed with his sharp intake of breath. Bellowing with rage, he struck the back of her hand with his fist, knocking the shale out of her grasp.

Her hand stinging from the blow, she stayed on her side, drew back her right leg and kicked him as hard as she could on the ankle.

He stumbled, thrusting the burning stick at her like a blade. She raised her forearm to block her face, and the hot poker stabbed it, leaving a burning sting on her arm.

She didn't dare let him close in on top of her; she could never fend off someone his size. Rising up on one arm, she pushed herself backward about foot, dragging the bola with her.

Using a backhand swing, he whipped the hot poker toward her face. Instead of backing away, she ducked under and dove for his legs. With the heel of her hand, she popped a straight-arm punch to the front of his left knee, hoping to hyperextend it. He howled, kicking at her ineffectively with his right leg as his left knee buckled.

Grasping the end of the bola, she swung it sideways and forward, wrapping it around both legs. She yanked the rope, and he went down, landing on his back. Air whooshed through the speaker on the mask as the wind got knocked out of him.

She'd lost both weapons and played her ace in the hole. Time to escape. The cave spun around her, and she couldn't hold on much longer.

Grabbing a stone in one hand, she scrambled on hands and feet to get past him. Just when she thought she could make it to the cave's opening, he grabbed her by the ankle and dragged her toward him. Flipping onto her back, she allowed him to pull her closer, cocking her other leg at the knee while the sharp rocks on the cave's floor bit into her back.

When she felt she was close enough, she let loose with the most powerful kick she could muster and planted her shoe in the middle of that horrid mask, smashing it into his nose. She bent forward at the waist and whacked him on his bare head with the stone she still held.

He grunted, released her ankle, and she scooted backwards out of his reach. She'd stunned him, but he wasn't out.

Pumped with adrenaline, Mattie scrambled away on hands and knees and then rose up on two feet, lunging for the mouth of the cave and the open forest that now symbolized life and freedom—if only she could reach it.

She used the cave wall for support and stumbled along, gaining momentum while her captor roared. As she reached the cave's opening, she heard him regain his feet and charge toward her.

A huge fire blazed on the right, sparks popping ten feet into the air. *Run, run, run,* her mind screamed, and she turned left toward the shelter of the dense, black forest. She sprinted away, dodging boulders that littered the cave's entry. Her only hope was to get deeper into the trees where she could hide.

A gust of wind caromed downslope, slamming into her. She glanced over her shoulder and spotted her captor at the mouth of the cave, his flashlight beam swinging back and forth, searching for her. He turned off the light, and she wondered if the mask provided night vision, perhaps the reason that he'd kept it on.

The *whomp-whomp-whomp* of a helicopter resounded from high overhead—too high to offer help. She ran as fast as she could for the shelter of the forest.

# THIRTY-TWO

When Cole and Lawson arrived at the fork in the trail, they met Brody and two posse members, Garrett Hartman and Frank Sullivan, grim-faced men with determination etched on their faces. As they approached, Cole could hear Brody check in with McCoy on the satellite phone, telling him they'd arrived.

Robo bounded ahead to greet Brody, stopping at the end of the retractable leash. The leash had caused problems at first on the ride up, and Cole had been at his wits' end, not wanting to entangle Mountaineer's legs but fearful of losing Robo in the wilderness. Finally, Robo had understood that he was expected to follow, and he'd kept his place in their lineup. Until he spotted Brody. Cole figured the dog hoped he'd find Mattie with the chief deputy.

Brody returned Robo's greeting, thumping his side with a few pats. Sure enough, the dog looked beyond him toward the others, sniffing, searching for Mattie's scent.

"I'm glad to see he's none the worse for wear," Brody said, looking up at Cole. "This is bad business, Doc."

"It is that." Cole nodded at Garrett and Frank, standing hunched in the moonlight, their Stetsons pulled low and tight against the wind roaring through the pine trees. He projected his voice to speak over the noise. "Agent Lawson just heard from the helicopter."

Lawson filled in the details. "Because of the wind, the chopper needs to pull out and go back to base. They got in one pass before having to turn around, and they spotted a large campfire about a mile north of the backside of the ridge. I've got the estimated coordinates."

"This trail leads straight up to the top of the ridge, but it ends too far south to get to where we need to go," Cole said. "The campfire is farther north. Does anyone know an alternate route to get from here to the north side?"

"There's a game trail that heads north just beyond this fork," Garrett said. "It crosses some rugged country through a couple ravines, but I've hunted in there before. It can be done."

"There's another trail that leads to the north side, the Balderhouse off Soldier Canyon Road," Brody said. "Does anyone know the trail I'm talking about?"

Cole and the posse members acknowledged that they did.

Brody pulled a gadget from his coat pocket, evidently a GPS unit. "What are those coordinates?"

Lawson told him while Brody tapped them in.

"Here we go. It looks most likely he took the Balderhouse trail to get to this position. We need to split up and cover the lower part of the trail, too, in case we estimate wrong." Brody turned to Garrett and Frank. "Upon the orders of Sheriff McCoy, I'm going to swear you posse members in as special deputies. Do you accept the duties assigned to you by me and will you use anything within your means including lethal force to protect and serve, and to apprehend the person who is holding Deputy Cobb? Say I do."

They chimed in as instructed.

"Garrett, you lead the way across country to the upper part of the Balderhouse, and Cole, you come with us. Frank, you take Agent Lawson to the Balderhouse trailhead and head up from there."

Positioning Robo beside Mountaineer, Cole swung into the saddle and got ready to ride. Brody made a call to the sheriff to give him an update as they headed up the trail.

★

Mattie forced her legs to keep moving, digging deep to dredge up the muscle memory to run, an activity that usually came so easily to her but was now like slogging through mire. With the wind at her back, she headed downhill, knowing from experience that her low-to-the-ground build helped her outdistance larger runners on a downslope course.

Tall timber closed around, tempting her to stop and hide. But if her captor wore night vision lenses, and if she was still within his sight, she'd be lost. She had no energy left with which to fight.

Her head swam and the trees circled within her vision in cogwheel-like, freeze frames. Vertigo became as big a threat as the man chasing her. She didn't know how much longer she could keep moving.

After long minutes of putting one foot in front of the other, nausea forced her to stop and heave. Bile burned her throat. She spit to clear her mouth and moved on, trying to keep trees between her and her captor.

The density of the surrounding forest offered a new strategy— darting from one pine to another, from boulder to boulder, bush to bush. She hoped to stay hidden as she moved away. Dizziness made her disoriented, but putting distance between herself and her captor seemed more important than having a clear plan for where she needed to go.

She pushed forward, driving hard. The sharp edge of a half-buried rock caught the toe of her shoe and sent her sprawling, the hard ground knocking the wind out of her. Spent, she lay still, heaving for breath.

Her world gradually stopped swaying and she spotted the shadow of bushes off to her right. Staying low, she crawled into them, sharp thorns from prickly rose snagging her clothing and piercing her skin. She huddled inside the shrub like a rabbit brought to ground. Burning thirst made her yearn for water.

She rested for a few minutes, the shelter protecting her from the wind that roared through the trees. Gradually, another sound worked its way into her consciousness, and she raised her head to listen. An ominous thunder rose above the whistling wind, followed by a crack like the explosion of an oil drum.

Smoke seeped into her hideaway. An image of the huge, dancing fire her captor had built for her came into her mind, along with sparks flying from it, launching themselves into the wind like fireflies.

Forest fire. Her captor had set the forest on fire.

She eased through the thorny branches and stood. Blazing orange lit the ridge above her, rapidly feeding on timber and eating its way downward. Balls of fire leapt from tree to tree, the dry needles wicking flames into branches and sap, setting off booming explosions in the treetops.

And she happened to be right in its path.

Fear gripped her and she froze. She no longer had the luxury of hiding. She needed to run.

But where? She couldn't continue her downhill course. She'd never be able to outdistance the fire. It appeared to be spreading downhill and swirling off to her left.

*Don't panic.* Her disorientation cleared as she paused for a moment to think things through. Prevailing winds came from the northwest. She must be on the north side of Redstone Ridge. She needed to cut across slope to the right and head farther north to try to beat this dragon.

Relieved that her vertigo had eased a bit, she set off on her course, moving as fast as she could.

★

It had taken a precious hour to bushwhack their way through a deep ravine. When they reached the top of the other side, Cole became aware of a change in the wind. It was warmer than it had been before going down into the ravine's shelter. He caught a whiff of smoke.

Garrett shouted from up front. "Fire!"

Then Cole saw it through gaps in the surrounding pines, an orange glow in the distance. Blazing fire lit the horizon directly above them.

"Damn," Brody said as he rode up, reining in his horse beside Cole. "The son of a bitch has started a forest fire."

The fear for Mattie that Cole had felt earlier was nothing compared to that gripping his chest now. "Mattie's up there."

Garrett worked to settle his restless horse. "We've got to ride north across this slope until we intersect Balderhouse. By then, we can see which way the fire is going to spread."

Robo whined and barked. Head raised, he sniffed the wind. He gave Cole a stare and then stood with ears pricked, looking uphill to the northwest.

*Could he have caught Mattie's scent on the wind?*

Robo launched himself forward, hit the end of the leash, and then whirled and backed away, struggling to break free. Worried that he might slip his collar, Cole dismounted and grabbed hold of him.

"Robo, wait." Cole turned to the others. "I think he's found Mattie's scent on the wind. She can't be far from here."

Brody looked upwind. "She'd be directly northwest, possibly in the pathway of the fire. What's the terrain like in that direction?" he asked Garrett.

"No trail, about like this. There might be places we need to ride around, but we can make it."

"Fast enough to get north of that fire?"

Garrett shrugged.

Cole felt the need to keep moving. He checked the tightness of Robo's collar. If they lost him in this country, they'd never find him. "I'll follow Robo. You two keep moving north to the trail. We'll all meet there."

"No," Brody said. "Garrett, you go north, I'll stick with Cole."

"We'll all stick together," Garrett said. "Safety in numbers."

Brody considered it for only a second. "Cole, you lead the way."

"Let's go find Mattie," he told Robo as he swung into the saddle and reined Mountaineer off the trail. Robo bolted to the end of the leash, hitting it hard, and it snapped loose at the reel. Cole shouted for him to stay, but Robo paused only long enough to realize he was free, and then he turned and ran into the wind.

"Follow him," Brody yelled.

The wind that Cole rode into felt like a furnace from the depths of the earth.

★

Mattie traveled north, angling downhill with the wind to her left. Heat warmed her cheek, and as she ran, she checked the fire line whenever the timber opened up enough to see. It appeared to be gaining on her.

Smoke filtered through the forest making her cough, and she knew it could be just as deadly as the fire. An occasional deer bounded past, running in the same direction as she, giving her hope that she was on the right course. She struggled on.

Her ears filled with the combined noise of the wind and fire, but a new sound caught her attention—one she wasn't expecting. A sharp, staccato bark. A dog? Couldn't be. A coyote or a wolf?

She slowed, but the noise didn't repeat, so she couldn't determine its location. As she resumed her speed, she hoped the animal would find a safe spot to hole up.

Another bark stopped her. This time she could tell the bark came from behind, and it was close. She turned as a dark shadow lunged from between the trees, coming at her full tilt. The shadow was shaped like a wolf, but moonlight touched the tan color pattern. She thought she must be hallucinating—it couldn't be—but she recognized those tan markings.

"Robo!" She knelt, spreading her arms.

He tried to brake, but his exuberance made him thud into her chest, knocking her down. She grabbed onto him while he whined, licked her face, and wagged his whole body, snuggling as close as he could. She said his name over and over until tears choked her and all she could do was sob, amazement and joy filling her until it spilled over into the only outlet she could manage.

Robo licked her tears, and she pressed her face against his cheek and into his ruff as she hugged him close, stroking his fur, touching him to make sure he was real. Her hand came in contact with a cord, and she realized that he wore a leash clipped to his collar. Holding onto him with one arm, she tugged it toward her, recognizing the tough, nylon cord used in a retractable leash. It was frayed at the end.

*He must have broken loose from someone.* The guy who held her captive? Or someone else?

She used Robo's strength and size to help her kneel, keeping him close and leaning against him. She hadn't realized how desperately she'd been running on empty, and the fire had moved even closer. Time to run.

Robo began to bark, his front paws lifting with each effort as he faced the direction he'd come from.

Shadows of three riders materialized through the trees, and Mattie stood braced against Robo, her heart thudding with fear.

"Mattie!" She recognized Cole's voice, making her breath catch with a sob.

He swung down from his horse and hit the ground running, closing the gap between them and gathering her into his arms. "Thank God we found you," he breathed, his mouth against her ear.

Brody and Garrett Hartman were the other two riders, Brody shouting orders and Garrett holding Mountaineer steady while Cole made her let go of Robo so he could lift her into the saddle. He swung up behind and wrapped both arms around her, gathering the reins and nudging Mountaineer forward.

Hot wind washed over them as they headed straight across slope, trying to reach the north side of the blaze. Off balance, Mattie reeled in the saddle.

Cole steadied her, holding her against his chest and speaking close to her ear. "Did he dart you? Are you sick?"

"He did. Dizzy. Nauseous."

Cole slowed, and Brody pulled up alongside. "We need to stop and give her the antidote."

The typically stalwart Mountaineer danced in place, fighting the tight rein that Cole had on him and making Mattie's vision swirl. Fiery wind blew over them and smoke filled the air. Sparks landed in trees. Robo barked.

"We don't have time, Doc. We'll stop as soon as we've beat this fire."

"Go," Mattie said, not wanting to endanger the others. "I'm okay."

Cole hugged her tightly as he allowed Mountaineer to follow Garrett. "Hold on."

She gripped Cole's arms and stared straight forward, hoping to anchor herself to keep the swaying movement from making her sick. As they rode, the hot wind that beat against her left side gradually lessened, the air became cleaner, and then they broke into forest that appeared untouched by sparks. Soon the roar from the fire came from behind instead of sideways.

"Hold up Garrett," Brody called, and as they came to a halt, he said to Cole, "Okay, Doc, we can take a minute now."

Cole swung down to the ground and extracted a syringe and vial from his pocket. "Mattie, this is the antidote to the drug you were given. I already gave some to Robo and it reversed him within minutes. I can inject you with the same dose."

"Do it."

"Can you take this arm out of your sleeve?" Cole said as he drew the dosage into the syringe.

Mattie shrugged off the sleeve while Cole helped. Robo pranced at his feet, looking up at her. She wished she didn't feel so weak and could get down on the ground with him. She spoke to him soothingly.

"Now lean forward so I can reach you," Cole said. "That's it. Little sting."

Which was an understatement. The shot stung like a hornet as the medicine infiltrated the muscle of her upper arm.

Cole swung back up to sit behind her. "Let's keep moving. Tell me how you're feeling, Mattie. Keep talking to me so I know you're all right."

"I'll be all right," she said, as they moved off, Garrett leading the way.

Every thirty seconds, Cole asked her how she was feeling and after a few minutes, she could honestly say she was beginning to feel better. The trees had stopped circling in her vision, and Garrett and his horse had solidified into one image instead of morphing into double. Her nausea subsided, leaving her with a raging thirst. Cole handed her his canteen while they rode, and water had never tasted so good.

After a half hour, they reached a trail and turned to head down it.

"This is the Balderhouse trail," Cole murmured. "Do you know it?"

"Sort of." Then she called to Garrett. "Hold up a minute."

Brody rode up beside.

"If this is the trail he brought me up on, I was in a cave off to the south somewhere," she said to Brody. "It would be up where the fire started. He might still be there."

"Do you know who he is?"

"He wore a mask, a gas mask. It distorted his voice. I couldn't recognize him." She had another thought. "But I might recognize the scent of his cologne if I smelled it again."

"Great, Cobb. Your dog is rubbing off on you." The teasing note in Brody's words reestablished some normalcy.

"Let's go up there and look for him."

"You're not going anywhere except to the doctor," Brody said, and Cole made a sound of agreement.

"We can't let him get away. Robo can track him."

Brody studied her, as if taking her measure by the glow from the fire. She tried to straighten in the saddle.

"We'll pull up here and wait for the rest of our party to come up this trail," he said. "Then we'll decide."

# THIRTY-THREE

There was no way Cole would let Mattie head up that mountain to go after a killer. No freakin' way. The wind had pushed the fire southward, but still, it could shift back on them at any minute.

Sunrise glowed on the eastern horizon, providing enough light to see Mattie clearly, and she looked terrible—her pale face smeared with ash and bloodied from cuts and scratches, the whites of her eyes bloodshot, a reddened angry bruise around her neck from some type of ligature or garrote. Her voice was hoarse.

That monster must have strangled her, tortured her. When she'd taken her arm from the sleeve of her hoodie so that he could administer the injection, he'd seen abrasions at her wrist, dark splotchy bruises, and a blistered burn on her forearm.

The antidote had reversed the effects of Thianil for the most part, but occasionally he could feel a fine tremor course through her body. When he climbed down from Mountaineer and helped her dismount, she staggered as her feet hit the ground before catching her balance.

"You need to get to a doctor," he murmured, for her ears only. He'd start with trying to convince her before bringing Brody into the picture, but if he had to ask the chief deputy to pull rank, he would. "At the very least, you're dehydrated, and you need to be monitored for side effects from that drug."

"I just need more water," she said, reaching a trembling hand for the canteen. Robo pressed against her legs, looking up at her.

He handed his reins to Garrett and then led her to a small boulder a short distance from the horses. "Sit down here with Robo while we wait. I've got some energy bars in my pack. Do you feel like you can eat one?"

"Not yet. Maybe in a few minutes."

Which told him her nausea had not completely subsided. Her face and that burn needed cleaning and treatment. "Let me get my first aid kit from my pack."

Cole's eyes met Garrett's as he went to retrieve his kit from Mountaineer's saddle. His friend held Mattie in a special place in his heart, and lines of concern etched his craggy face as he untied a tightly rolled sleeping bag from behind his own saddle.

Garrett took the bag to Mattie, unzipping it as he went. "Here, stand up a minute, Mattie." He spread the bag open and wrapped it snuggly around her shoulders, tucking it into her hands in front as she sat back down on the cold stone.

She gave him a wan smile of gratitude.

Cole bent over her and used gauze pads and water to bathe her wounds, finishing up with touches of antibiotic ointment on the cuts and scrapes. Although there were dozens of them, he didn't think any of them would need to be sutured. At least that was something.

He dressed the second-degree burn on her arm with antiseptic and a sterile pad. As long as it didn't get infected, he thought it would heal without problems. The sleeping bag had helped, and by the time he zipped up his first aid kit, her shivers appeared to have ceased.

Brody came over to squat beside her. "Tell me what happened."

Garrett moved off a few paces as if giving her privacy.

"I remember Robo getting darted in the backyard. I tried to reach him, but then the guy darted me. I thought Robo might be dead." Her eyes met Cole's and he could read her questions there.

"Riley found him. She called me." There would be time later to give her more details if she wanted them.

Her eyelids fluttered and her breath caught as she looked away.

Cole could tell her feelings were raw and exposed. She bent and hugged Robo against her while she waged a battle to control her emotion.

Brody pressed on. "What happened after he took you from the yard?"

"I don't remember much at first." She told them about becoming aware that she was draped over a horse and being taken uphill, about awakening inside the cave with her hands tied, about being able to cut herself free while her captor built a fire, and then fighting him to break away and run.

Cole thought that her summary had left out some important details, and evidently Brody agreed. He touched his own throat as he posed his next question. "What about the ligature mark on your neck?"

Mattie touched it gently. "He was trying to get me to talk. To tell him where he could find Ramona Cobb . . . which is something I don't know."

"Your mother?"

"That was apparently his motive for taking me and for torturing and killing Willie. To find Ramona Cobb."

"Did he confess to killing William?"

"Not in those words. But he told me he was going to give me what he gave my brother, so yeah, he was the one who killed Willie."

"Just so he could get information about Ramona Cobb? Why? What all did he tell you?"

With complete emotional detachment, Mattie began to pass on the information she'd been told while being held prisoner. She told them how her captor believed that Ramona had taken money that was rightfully his, how he planned to track her down, and how he and Harold Cobb had been involved in a gunrunning operation decades earlier.

Though Mattie told her story without emotion, Cole wanted to plant his fist into something—preferably the face of the guy who'd taken her. He felt her slump beside him as she lifted the canteen to her lips, and he placed his arm against her back to support her.

Robo yawned and sank to the ground, nestling his head on her shoe. Mattie leaned forward and stroked the fur between his ears. He closed his eyes, looking exhausted but content.

Still squatting, Brody shifted on his heels. "We think the guy who took you is Bret Flynn."

Mattie's focus appeared to turn inward. "I never saw his face because of the mask, but his shape and size could be a match to Flynn. Why did you home in on him?"

Brody stood, his knees popping. "Lawson found a break-in at a hunting reserve near L.A. where the drugs and equipment used on you might have been stolen. The other possible suspect is Tucker York—he's from around that area, too. Flynn's horses and his rig aren't at his place, and he didn't show up for work last night. Was there anything about the guy that reminded you of either of these two men?"

She thought and then shook her head. "York strikes me as the right size and strong enough to be the one, too, but I don't have enough to identify either of them." She glanced at Cole. "What about Riley?"

"She's at my house. She stayed there after we took care of Robo." He wanted to reassure her but felt he should inform her of their suspicion. "Before we left the station, we speculated that your captor might have a partner who moved his rig away from the trailheads for him when he took William, and then you, up to the Ridge. We wondered if Riley could be Flynn's partner. Stella went to my house to talk to her. We haven't heard from them yet."

Mattie shook her head and gazed off into the distance. "Could I have missed something with Riley?"

"I need to call on the sat phone and tell the sheriff you're safe." Brody turned toward his horse where the satellite phone was tied to his saddle. "I'll see what Stella found out with the kid."

Cole sat with Mattie while they waited. After a brief interchange, Brody turned toward them to report.

"Stella said her interview was uneventful. She thinks the kid knows nothing and hasn't been involved."

The sound of shod hooves clicking on rock echoed through the forest, and Garrett stepped forward to peer down the trail. "It's the others in our party. Looks like they picked up a spare horse."

Robo awakened, rising to wave his tail as Rick Lawson and Frank reined to a halt, Frank leading a stout black gelding. Mattie left the sleeping bag on the boulder and moved forward to greet them. Their faces lit when they saw her, and a moment of quiet celebration followed.

"Where did you get the extra horse?" Brody asked.

"He came charging down the trail," Lawson said, "dragging a broken picket line."

"Is this the horse that carried you up to the cave?" Brody asked Mattie.

"I never saw either of the horses, the one he rode or the one I was on. It was too dark while we were moving, and I didn't see them when I ran off."

Cole didn't recognize the horse. "I don't think I've seen this gelding before. He's not the one that Flynn brought to my clinic."

"I saw two horses in Flynn's corral when I went to talk to him," Mattie said. "This wasn't one of them."

"Take a look at what's in the scabbard," Lawson said, gesturing toward the gelding.

Brody put on leather gloves as he approached the gelding and then pulled a rifle free from the scabbard before checking the ammo. "A Remington Model 700 loaded with .270 Winchester ammo."

"We'll send the rifle to ballistics," Lawson said, "but I'm willing to bet we've got the weapon that killed the ram."

"Was there a truck and trailer at the trailhead when you got there?" Brody asked.

Lawson shook his head. "Nothing parked there. What other trail could have been used?"

"This has to be the one," Cole said. "There must be a partner involved. Someone else had to have moved that truck."

The sun had risen, and Lawson scanned the blackened ridge. "I want to get up above the fire line and take a look. The wind has died down, and since there's so much devastation on top, I don't think there's a danger of it coming back on us."

Mattie straightened, and Cole knew what she planned to propose. In a split second he decided to play the card that he'd placed up his sleeve earlier. He spoke quietly. "Robo is exhausted, Mattie. We had to work him to find you, but now he needs to sleep. That's a powerful drug that was used on you both, and it acts on the nervous system. I think we should stay here and let him rest while the others go up on top. He's dead on his feet."

With a frown of concern, Mattie looked down at Robo standing at her left heel. As if on cue, the blessed dog gazed up at her, his sharp teeth gleaming as his mouth stretched open in a huge, squeaky yawn. *As soon as I can get my hands on a treat, he's going to get one for that*, Cole thought.

Brody stepped in. "You and your dog wait here, Cobb. We'll run a quick reconnaissance up above, and then come back for you. Rest now, so if we need you two for tracking, you can be ready to go."

To Cole's surprise, she yielded without argument, and she bent to stroke Robo's head and along his shoulders while the others divvied up roles. Frank rode away with Brody and Lawson while Cole and Garrett stayed with Mattie.

With a slow step, she returned to the sleeping bag, picked it up, and began spreading it beneath a pine tree. Cole hurried to help. She told Robo to lie down, and then she sank against him, pulled him close, and curved herself around him. Cole covered them both with the remaining half of the down-filled bag.

After Mattie closed her eyes, Cole glanced at Garrett who gave him a nod. They both picked spots where they could lean their backs against trees to rest while they sat and watched over her.

★

Gasping for breath, Mattie lunged upright to sit. Robo rolled onto his chest and stared at her. Cole came from a few feet away, soothing her with a gentle tone. "You're safe. It's just a slurry bomber making a pass."

She spotted the huge plane as it rumbled away, having dropped its payload of suppressant on the forest fire. Smoke lingered in the air, making her throat burn with thirst, and it hurt to swallow. She placed her hand to her sore neck. Cole handed her the canteen.

"How long have they been gone?" she asked, her voice sounding raspy and strange.

"Almost two hours. You slept?"

"Yeah." She tipped the canteen to sip, and the cool water soothed her throat. Cole's eyes were reddened, the lines around them showing his fatigue. "You were up all night?"

He shrugged and gave her a half smile. "I had a few things I needed to take care of."

His presence steadied her nerves, which she needed now more than ever. She rested her free hand on her dog's shoulders. "How bad was it for Robo?"

Cole winced. "Pretty bad. If Riley hadn't found him when she did, he would've died."

"You saved him."

He studied her for a moment, and then a slow smile flirted with the corners of his mouth. "You might say that. Will it earn me any brownie points?"

She felt unsure of how to respond. "I owe you."

He clasped her hand. "You don't owe me anything, Mattie. All I want from you is any spare affection you might toss my way."

"You have that."

"Garrett brewed some tea. Could you drink a cup?"

"I think so." She started to get up.

"Stay here. I'll bring it to you."

He arose, leaving her feeling uneasy. Her past was an embarrassment to her, and Cole knew only part of it. He didn't know the extent of the abuse she'd suffered at the hands of Harold Cobb. The life Cole had led was untouched by that kind of degradation—he wouldn't be able to understand that part of her that had been twisted when she was a child. And much as she wanted to, she had trouble allowing him past the wall she'd built to protect her feelings.

Before the others left to investigate the fire, she'd felt depleted. She'd had nothing left, and Robo looked like he felt the same way. She'd come to the realization that she couldn't do it all, and she needed to trust that others could handle things in her stead. It was a tough lesson for her—learning to let go—but thinking about Robo's welfare had tipped the balance.

Cole returned, handing her a steaming plastic cup. He held up an energy bar. "Can you eat this now?"

She realized she was starving. "Sure."

Robo watched, licking saliva from his black lips.

Mattie nodded toward her dog. "You didn't bring any food for him, did you?"

"Actually, I did. I bagged some before I left the clinic. C'mon, Robo, I'll feed you now."

Her dog looked full of energy as he followed Cole to the horses, which made her feel even better than her own sustenance. She sipped the strong, dark tea, the bitter brew replenishing her energy. While she nibbled on the sweet, nutty bar, she watched Robo scarf down a cupful of dog food. He came back to her, smacking his lips and waving his tail. He heaved a sigh as he plopped down beside her, everything right with his world.

She needed to take another lesson from her dog. You have food, you have water, you've rested; there's no reason to fret.

*But there is.* Her brother's killer was on the loose. And now that her battery felt recharged, she needed to take Robo up the trail to see if she could find him. After finishing the food, she scanned the mountain and spotted movement on a switchback up above. Riders. As they drew near, she could see that it was Brody and Frank, and they looked grim.

Brody stopped at the campsite and dismounted, while Frank rode on.

"He's long gone," Brody said, looking at Mattie. "Lawson stayed up there to secure the crime scene, and Frank's headed down to escort crime scene investigators up here. Looks like the fire pit got away from him and lit the forest. Horseshoe prints indicate the two horses panicked and broke their picket line. He caught one of them and rode north away from the fire. We tracked him far enough to see that he turned to ride downhill to the north of this trail."

"What trail was he on?" she asked.

"He wasn't on one. He just headed into the timber going downhill."

"If he has a partner, maybe he's headed down to meet up with him."

Garrett spoke up. "You've got a trail even farther north that he might hook up with, the one by Lowell Pass."

"That's the trail Flynn said he was on the day his horse got cut," Cole said, his voice edged with tension. "We need to make sure the volunteers have checked that trailhead for a rig, too."

Brody took out the satellite phone and dialed. After the few seconds it took to connect, he briefed the sheriff on the situation. "Did the volunteers check the Lowell Pass trailhead for a truck and trailer last night or today?"

Mattie felt edgy while she listened. She rolled up the sleeping bag and gave it to Garrett to tie back on his saddle. Robo picked up on her nerves and danced around her.

Still on the phone with the sheriff, Brody repeated what he was saying for the group's benefit. "No rig there, but this morning they've spotted a silver Tahoe at that trailhead with a stolen Colorado license plate. This might be the Tahoe that William's friend saw in front of his shop."

Brody looked confused—he'd been out of the loop while guarding William's crime scene—but Mattie nodded at him that she understood.

"What's your plan?" Brody asked the sheriff. Mattie watched his frown deepen while he listened. "Hold one minute."

Brody lowered the phone from his mouth. "They've got the Tahoe under surveillance, and they're watching Redstone and Balderhouse trailheads for activity. But Bret Flynn showed up at his place this morning with his rig and his two horses. Stella's in the interrogation room with him right now. He says he took his girlfriend on a night ride to the hot springs south of Hightower, and when they got back to the truck, it wouldn't start. His story checked out with the woman, and Riley has been at Cole's house all morning, so she couldn't have taken his rig to him." His face took on a sour expression. "Looks like he's not our guy."

Mattie felt a strange sense of relief. She'd found it hard to believe that Riley might be involved with murder and kidnapping. "So that narrows it down to Tucker York."

Cole spoke up. "Mattie, I took Robo into your backyard to make sure he locked in the scent of your attacker. I think he would recognize him."

"Tell the sheriff I want to bring Robo down to check out the Tahoe."

After Brody relayed the message, he held the phone out to Mattie. "Sheriff wants to talk to you."

She took the phone. "This is Mattie."

"Mattie!" The sheriff's voice boomed from the receiver. "It's great to hear your voice. Do you feel well enough to report for duty?"

"Reporting right now, sir. I can have Robo do a scent check on that Tahoe and see how he reacts."

"All right. One of us will meet you at the Balderhouse trailhead and take you over to Lowell Pass. It's good to have you back with us, Deputy."

"It's great to be here. See you soon."

While she and Brody spoke to the sheriff, Cole and Garrett had been busy breaking camp and tightening cinches on saddles. Cole led Mountaineer over to her. "You take him, and I'll ride the black horse."

She clenched her teeth at the thought of riding a horse again while Robo watched her expectantly. "I'll take the ground," she said.

"Are you sure?"

"I don't think I can stay on a horse if it's moving fast. This way, I can set the pace."

She didn't wait for protest. With Robo leading the way, she headed down the trail, figuring the riders would be hard pressed to keep up with her and her dog.

# THIRTY-FOUR

While she ran, Mattie thought hard about her captor. There'd been something familiar about his cologne, and she sorted through her memories, trying to put her finger on it. Had she first smelled it on Tucker York?

Finally, it came to her, along with the realization that the scent hadn't been cologne at all. The sweet blend of vanilla and cinnamon—she remembered where she'd smelled it. The ice cream shop. The odor had saturated the place and probably the clothing of its owners.

She stopped on the side of the trail, whistling for Robo to come back. "John Carter," she said as the others pulled up beside her.

"Who's that?" Brody asked.

"The new owner of the Happy Shack ice cream shop on Main Street." Her mind skipped to his wife. "The partner would probably be his wife, Violet Carter."

"That's the place that Riley hangs out all the time," Cole said.

"Why do you think it's him?" Brody asked.

"The cologne. It was actually the scent of ice cream and cinnamon. I remember smelling it in the shop when I went there to pick up Riley." She looked at Brody. "Call the sheriff. Have them locate Violet Carter and take her in for questioning."

"Do you have an address?"

"The ice cream shop is on Main Street. I don't know where they live." She looked at Cole to see if he knew, but he shook his head.

Mattie turned and began pounding down the trail again. She couldn't rest until she gained justice for her brother. Was she on the right track with the Carters? They owned horses. John had said he'd ridden horseback to go fishing. But how were they connected to Willie?

Her brother had referred to an old friend of the family, someone he didn't know existed but should have. Could he have meant a previous partner of their dad's? Willie had been two years older than she; perhaps he'd been more aware of their father's involvement in shady business.

When Mattie hit the parking lot at the base of the Balderhouse Trail, Stella was there with the K-9 unit. Cole and Brody trotted their horses over to a truck and horse trailer where one of the volunteers waited.

Stella exited the car and gave Mattie a thorough examination as she approached, her eyes dark with concern. When she reached her, she pulled Mattie into a hug, something completely unexpected. Mattie hugged her back.

Stella leaned away, still holding onto Mattie as she studied her face. "Are you sure you're all right to work? Do we need to take you to a doctor?"

"Cole gave me the antidote I needed."

"She should be seen by a doctor," Cole said as he joined them. "I'll take her to Doc McGinnis as soon as she'll let me."

Mattie held up her hand, signaling them to stop. "That's not necessary. Let's get loaded and go to the Lowell Pass trailhead."

When Mattie opened Robo's compartment, he jumped in and circled once on his dog cushion before plopping down. She noticed the torn up carpet. When she glanced at Cole for an explanation, he simply shrugged.

Robo looked at her and yawned. She stroked his fur and gave him water, which he lapped up eagerly. "You've made a mess, hmm? You must have been very upset."

Cole offered his canteen. "You need to drink water, too."

"Thanks," she said, taking it from him. She started to climb up into the back with Robo.

Cole clasped her arm lightly, guiding her a step backward. "Ride in front."

Mattie found she was too exhausted to argue.

Brody wound up in the back with Robo, and Stella took the driver's seat while Mattie and Cole shared the passenger seat. With his arm around her, his closeness felt natural, and she settled in beside him, her body weary and sore.

Stella opened the console and pulled out a handgun. She gave it to Mattie along with a half smile. "Your service weapon."

Her Glock. She took it out of the holster, popped the magazine to make sure it was fully loaded, and snapped it back into place. She racked the slide. Everything functioned as it should, and its weight felt good in her hands.

"The Carters are nowhere to be found," Stella said as she steered the Explorer from the lot, turned on the overheads, and accelerated to well over the speed limit. "We were able to get a warrant to search their place. No furniture in the home besides a mattress on the floor and a few folding chairs. They didn't plan to stick around. There's an old barn on the property where we found a silver Chevy Impala and a dark blue Ford F-150 with a horse trailer."

Stella paused and looked pointedly at Cole.

"The two vehicles you saw on the surveillance video," he said. Then to Mattie, "We suspected the truck in your abduction but not the car. They drove through town a few minutes apart, both headed west."

Stella resumed her briefing. "The truck had been reported stolen out of California and the Chevy up in Denver. Both have stolen Colorado plates. Tracks from a third vehicle with heavy tire tread are in the barn, too, most likely from this Tahoe we have our eye on."

Brody spoke up from the back. "So far all we have on the Carters is car theft and a whole lot of circumstantial."

"True," Stella said, glancing at him in the rearview mirror. "We can't even prove that those were their vehicles in the surveillance video. Too grainy."

"Chances are they know we've spotted the Tahoe," Brody said. "They've probably ditched it and won't come back."

Mattie agreed, but in the meantime she hoped she and Robo could come up with something. Anything.

They passed Deputy Johnson parked on the highway shoulder in his cruiser about a hundred yards from the Lowell Pass parking lot. Anyone could spot him. Brody was right. They'd be fortunate to find either of the Carters in this area.

Stella parked and they unloaded. Mattie changed Robo's collar to his search harness and began the chatter that told him it was time to work. She led him to the driver's side of the Tahoe.

He sniffed the door and the ground beneath, and his hackles rose. Mattie felt the back of her neck tingle as she decided to give the command used to search for an unknown fugitive. "Find the bad guy, Robo. Search!"

Experience had taught her that Robo's hair lifted when they were nearing their target or when he smelled someone he didn't like. This time she'd bet on the latter. He headed toward the woods, nose to the ground.

"Go ahead, Robo." The others had fallen in behind her, and she spoke to them in an undertone. "I think he's on the scent he found in our backyard."

Robo veered away from the trail, heading toward the forest. Mattie looked for footprints, but none were apparent in the dense grass at the edge of the parking lot. Without Robo's special detection system, they would have never known someone crossed this way. When they reached the trees, dried pine needles and dead foliage covered the ground, again blocking any sign of footprints. She depended on her dog's nose to lead them.

Robo charged through the trees and Mattie jogged behind, Brody at her back and Cole following. She wouldn't let Robo run blindly into another ambush, so she called out for him to wait. He stopped and looked back at her over his shoulder.

When she came up beside him, he trotted on, leading the way at a slower pace. But his back still bristled.

She was rounding a boulder when a gunshot blasted through the forest. The bullet pinged off the face of the rock near her head. Mattie ducked low, grabbed for Robo as she shouted his name, and dove for cover behind the boulder. Cole and Brody ducked in beside her.

"Robo, stay." She crouched behind the large rock, gripping his collar as he tried to break free. He settled at her heel briefly but then tried to wriggle free.

Another blast from the gun, and a bullet ricocheted wildly off the face of the boulder that shielded them. Keeping one hand on Robo's collar, she drew her Glock from its holster.

Robo barked and tugged in another attempt to break away. She'd never seen him so incensed, and she kept a tight grip on his collar. He'd faced simulated gunfire in training before, and it didn't bother him. It must be the fugitive's scent that had him so enraged. "Robo, stay! Easy. Heel!"

He pressed against her left side and she hugged him close.

His revolver in hand, Cole shielded both her and Robo. "We might be able to retreat down the trail. This boulder could block us."

"John Carter would be coming down from the mountain," Mattie said. "That has to be Violet that Robo tracked from the car."

"I'll see if she'll talk," Brody said before shouting uphill. "Violet Carter! We know it's you out there."

Another bullet splintered granite shards from the top of the boulder, sending them flying.

Mattie picked up a six-inch rock and tossed it to the right where it landed behind a pine. A gunshot rang out and the bullet smacked into the trunk of the same tree. The gun sounded like it was about fifty to seventy feet away, and the shooter seemed pretty damn accurate.

Brody tried again. "Violet Carter! Is that you? All we want to do is talk!"

A woman began to shout, but someone muffled her cries.

Brody frowned at Mattie. "That would be John Carter."

"See if he'll talk."

"John Carter!" Brody made a megaphone with his hands. "We've got you covered. Throw out your weapon."

A man's voice replied, taunting. "Hey, buckwheat! Looks like I'm the one that's got you pinned down."

Mattie recognized the voice from the ice cream shop, but she couldn't match it to the one distorted by her captor's mask.

"Keep him talking. Give him something to focus on," she said, edging out from behind Cole. "Robo and I are going downhill to circle around. See if I can get him in sight."

She heard Cole's protest as she told Robo to heel. She bent and edged down the trail, keeping the boulder at her back. Robo came with her, close to her left leg. She realized Cole was following, covering her back. Holding her Glock low, she sprinted down the trail until she was sure the terrain blocked them from view.

"Go bring Stella and Johnson for backup," she told Cole. "We don't know if we've got one shooter up there or two."

"I'll go with you."

"I need you to go for help." She reached out and squeezed his hand. "Be careful."

A perplexed expression crossed his face and his breath released in an exasperated huff. He touched her cheek before leaving. "Don't you dare get hurt."

Mattie cut off to the left, using the dense pine and spruce to shield her while she circled, running back uphill. She could hear Brody cajoling Carter but didn't pay attention to his words, not until the higher pitched tones of a woman's voice chimed in.

"Help! He's got me tied up."

A resounding slap stifled her call for help.

"You'd better back off or I'll shoot this noisy bitch!"

Brody called back, and his voice was now off to Mattie's right. She slowed, Robo hugging her heel. She slipped through the trees uphill, plotting a course to come abreast of the Carters before trying to get closer.

John Carter's voice came from on her right. Ten feet more

uphill and then she would cut back in. The steep incline shortened her breath, and she fought to silence her puffing.

This time Violet cried in a shrill bleat. "He's going to kill me!"

Mattie angled right, Robo silent and sticking close as she crept toward the two. She wanted to make sure that Brody would be away from her line of fire.

Robo stiffened and movement through the screen of pine boughs caught Mattie's eye. After maneuvering for a better view, she could make out John Carter huddled behind a boulder about thirty feet away. She grasped Robo's collar and whispered, "Quiet. Easy."

Sunlight glinted from the silver barrel of his handgun, held braced against the top of the boulder. His attention stayed riveted downhill.

Mattie inched forward, scanning the area for Violet, but trees blocked her view. Since she couldn't locate the woman, she couldn't fire her weapon. A stray bullet could create disaster.

She decided she couldn't wait. At any moment, John might spot her and the element of surprise would be lost. And if there was one thing she'd learned she could count on, it was the element of surprise.

She squatted beside Robo and hugged him close, every muscle in his body felt bunched and ready to spring. With more intensity than a shout, she whispered close to his ear. "Robo, take him!"

Silent and lethal, Robo's black form shot through the trees like a deadly shadow, picking up speed as he went. John turned. Robo hit the man at full speed, clamping his teeth on his arm. The gun went flying through the air.

Mattie raced toward them, shouting for Brody. Robo gripped John's right arm and tugged him along the ground, stretching him out in the pine needles. Mattie thudded down hard on his back, twisting his left arm until she heard him groan.

Brody came full tilt around the boulder.

"I've got him. Where's Violet?" Mattie shouted at him.

Brody beat around the foliage, looking for her.

"Over here," Stella shouted from a short distance. "We've got Violet."

John Carter bucked and tried to pull away from Robo. His efforts further angered her dog, and his fierce growls thundered through the clearing.

Despite a desperate need for revenge, Mattie fought to remain professional. "Be still and I'll tell the dog to let you go."

Carter continued to fight, which seemed to enrage Robo. With his jaws still clamped around Carter's arm, he gave it a mighty shake. Mattie clung to the man's back as he struggled to break free.

Brody strode near, leaned over, and placed his handgun where Carter could see it. "Give it up, Carter. Don't move," he shouted.

Carter stared up at him, his eyes full of venom, but he quit struggling.

Mattie decided it was safe to call off her dog. "Out! Robo, out!"

Robo dropped Carter's arm but stayed close, his neck bristled, his bared fangs gleaming. Saliva dripped from his mouth as he continued to growl. Mattie had never seen him so maddened during a takedown. Usually his tail was waving. Carter gave him one look and then buried his face on the ground.

"Stay still or he'll attack you again." Mattie shifted her weight backward off Carter's chest and cuffed him while Brody stood guard. Together they pulled Carter to his feet, and he stared at her, his gaze dark with malice.

Cole and Stella materialized through the pine trees, leading Violet Carter. Stella was breathing hard from the climb.

"We found this one making her way toward the parking lot." Stella held aloft a Ladysmith .38 Special with a robin's egg blue handle. "She was carrying this fancy gun, but she didn't put up a fight."

Violet cowered between Stella and Cole. "I'm a victim. He made me help him."

"We'll give you a chance to tell us all about it very soon," Stella said.

Mattie wondered if the woman's screams during the previous gunplay had been nothing but theatrics, or if she'd actually escaped.

Brody nudged John Carter forward. "Cobb, do you want to arrest this one and read him his rights?"

At that moment, Mattie could think of nothing that would please her more.

# THIRTY-FIVE

While Johnson and Brody transported the prisoners, Stella drove Mattie and Cole to the station. During the drive, Mattie told Stella everything that John Carter had said to her in the cave. Even though she'd been under duress, she felt confident that she could remember it word for word. Cole remained silent, and while his left arm stayed firm and still behind her shoulders, his hand clasped her upper arm gently.

"I want to be there when you question them," Mattie said.

Stella gave her a sideways glance. "I think that would work out well. I'll take the lead."

As they pulled into the station parking lot, Stella turned to Cole. "You can take my car if you want to go home."

"I'm staying with Mattie in case she needs me." Then to Mattie: "And I'll call Dr. McGinnis to make sure he can see you when you're done."

She knew she couldn't argue with him this time, so she simply nodded. Robo jumped out of the SUV and trotted to the station door.

Her eyes reddened and teary, Rainbow came from behind her desk in the lobby. Uncharacteristically speechless, she gave Mattie a long hug before releasing her to step back. With one hand, she held onto Mattie's while with the other, she gently traced a finger near the marks on Mattie's neck. She shook her head sadly.

Mattie tried to smile but felt it tremble on her lips. "We'll talk later," she told her friend. "I want to tell you how the yoga breathing helped me."

Gesturing for Cole to follow, she took Robo back to his bed in the staff office. "You can stay in here," she told Cole. "Use the phone if you want."

He stopped her as she turned to leave. "Wait a second."

Jittery about what lay ahead in the interrogation room but trying to put a lid on her feelings, she faced him.

"You've been through more than anyone should ever have to go through, and still you're the most kind and courageous person I know. Words can't say how much I admire you. I'll always have your back, Mattie, no matter what. Just let me in so I can help you."

His words made her throat swell and challenged the tight control she'd placed on her emotions. "I'm doing the best I can."

"I know it. We'll have time to talk about things soon. I just want you to know before you go in to face him—I might be waiting here in this room, but in spirit, I'm right there beside you."

Her breath released as she squeezed his hand. Unable to trust her voice, she nodded and turned to leave the room. She met Stella and Sheriff McCoy at the door.

McCoy took her hand in his large palm, pumping her arm while he studied her face. "Are you sure this is what you want to do, Deputy? Are you well enough for this?"

"Absolutely, on both counts."

"Let's go to it," Stella said. "We've got them cuffed in two separate rooms. We'll talk to Violet first."

Mattie followed her into the cold interrogation room. Violet looked every bit the worse for wear, her blond curls disheveled, her eyes reddened and lined with blotchy mascara as if she'd been crying. She avoided looking at Mattie and eyed Stella with suspicion. They took seats on the side of the table opposite the woman.

Although Stella had already read the Miranda rights, she started off with them again, this time presented from memory and ending with a question. "Do you want to talk this over with us right now so we can get the preliminaries out of the way?"

Violet stared at her for a moment and then nodded.

"For the recording, please say yes instead of nodding," Stella said.

Violet hesitated before speaking. "Yes, I'll talk to you, at least for a while. I want to talk about a deal."

Stella leaned forward. "It's not up to me to offer deals. The Timber Creek County Prosecutor does that. I'm the one you provide with information to see if you've got anything worthy of a deal."

"I'm a victim. I was coerced."

"How so?"

"John Carter had complete control over me."

Stella settled back in her chair and rested her forearms on the table as if she had all the time in the world. "Maybe you'd better tell me what you mean."

"He's been orchestrating everything we've done."

"Start at the beginning. How did you find yourself under John Carter's control?"

Mattie watched Violet's gaze chase around the room. The wheels were turning, and she had to wonder if the woman was fabricating lies as she spoke or if she was simply putting together her true story.

"I met him when he was in prison out in California. First I was his pen pal, and then I started visiting him. I fell in love with him and he told me he loved me, too. I found out later that he just said that so he would have someone to live with when he got out on parole."

There were some holes in the story already—Stella had told Mattie that they'd been unable to find a criminal record on a John Carter either in California or Colorado. But evidently the detective decided to let her talk rather than confront her.

"And then?" Stella prompted.

"We were fine at first. But then he left for a few days, and when he came back, he was a completely different person. Full of rage. That's when the abuse started." She slid a glance at Mattie and flinched when it connected. "He . . . he likes to choke people, women especially. Some of the stories he told me about how he tortured people—I didn't know if they were real or things he made up to scare me. But he threatened to kill me if I didn't do what he said. He choked me until I passed out. He burned my back with cigarettes. I knew he'd follow through on his threat to kill me if I didn't cooperate."

"We haven't found a record on a John Carter of his age and description in the system," Stella said.

"That's not his real name. Violet Carter isn't mine either. My real name is Virginia Carson, and I don't have a criminal record. You can look me up in your system."

"What's his name?" Mattie asked.

Her eyes slipped sideways to connect with Mattie's. "When I met him, he was doing time as John Cobb. He said he had a brother who was killed in prison here in Colorado."

*John Cobb.* Mattie's breath caught, and she had a terrible feeling about the answer to her next question. "The brother's name?"

"Harold Cobb."

*My father.* Heat flared in Mattie's cheeks, making her cuts and scratches sting. "What was John doing time for?"

"Drugs."

Not gunrunning, but a crime that could be related. Mattie's head was spinning from the news that the man who'd tried to kill her was her uncle. She fell silent, letting Stella pick up the questioning.

"How did you end up here in Colorado?"

"John hooked up with someone that he said he used to do business with. He trailered a couple horses out here to Colorado, and I drove the Tahoe. He brought this other man with him." She gazed at Stella with regret that might be genuine—hard to say. "I knew the man was unconscious, but I didn't know what John was going to do to him. You've got to believe me. John told me to move the truck and trailer, but I didn't know he was going to kill the guy. I found that out later."

"So you know that John Cobb killed the man that he brought here from California?"

"That's what John said."

"And the name of this person he killed was?"

"I don't know his name." She pointed at Mattie. "Her brother."

As horrible as her words were to listen to, they brought a sense of relief to Mattie. This witness could identify John Cobb as Willie's killer, and she'd be much more credible on the stand than the victim's sister. That should be enough to put him away.

"What was your plan for today?" Stella asked.

"John planned to meet me in the parking lot and we'd leave from there. Leave the horses and go." Violet looked down at the table. "He wasn't there when I got to the parking lot, and I was afraid someone would spot me. He would've killed me if I let that happen. I went up into the trees to hide."

A frown furrowed Stella's brow. "And what about Deputy Cobb? Was he planning to take her with you, too?"

Mattie figured Stella knew the answer to that question—John Cobb had planned to kill her.

Violet shifted in her chair. "I don't know what he planned to do with her."

"Hmm . . ." Stella paused, tapping a finger on the table. "Tell me. Why the attack on Deputy Cobb and her dog?"

"I'm not sure."

"He must have told you something."

Violet squirmed in her chair, her eyes cast away from Mattie. "He said she had information he wanted."

"About?"

Violet seemed to have trouble meeting Stella's gaze, and she looked down at the table instead. "I don't know."

Stella raised her hand to rub her cheekbone as if deep in thought, before turning to Mattie. "Deputy Cobb, had you ever met John Cobb before?"

"Not before I met him at the ice cream shop here in Timber Creek."

"Then why would John think Deputy Cobb had information that he wanted?" Stella asked Violet.

Her eyes narrowed. "He wanted to find her mother. He thought she would know where she was."

Mattie had regained her equilibrium, and she felt certain that Violet knew more about John Cobb's agenda than she was saying. Robo had followed Violet's scent into the forest, not John's. She wanted to know if the woman had been in her backyard during the attack. "A dog with scent training can find people by following their scent trail. My dog can remember the scent of different people and can lead me right to the person I want to find. It's amazing really."

Now she had Violet's full attention.

"In other words," Mattie continued, "he can tell me if a person has been in a specific area, like my yard."

"Tell us where you were last night around ten o'clock," Stella said.

Violet slumped lower in her chair. "Okay, I was there. Outside the yard. But I didn't shoot you or your dog with the dart gun. That was all John."

"Where were you exactly?" Stella asked.

"At the side of the house by the gate. John told me to blow a dog whistle when you let your dog out into the yard. One of those high-pitched things that people can't hear. The dog ran at me and John shot him. He planned to shoot you when you came outside to search for the dog. He didn't know you'd be right there at the same time. He almost missed you."

So the woman had helped execute the plan to attack a police officer and her K-9. Strange things could still happen, but Mattie was willing to bet that no one would be offering this prisoner much of a deal.

Placing her elbows on the table, Stella leaned forward and pinned Violet with her stare. "Would you be willing to testify against John Cobb?"

"I don't know. I don't know if you can protect me." Violet cast her gaze around the room as if for a way out. "I want to talk to a lawyer."

*Game over. Time to move on to John.*

Stella wrapped up with Violet, determining that the woman needed a public defender. Stella told her she would need to wait while they tried to reach him.

Out in the hallway, Stella clasped Mattie's arm and drew her close, speaking in a quiet voice. "Our research into Harold Cobb didn't bring up a brother as an associate."

"Neither of them served time for gunrunning. They must have stayed ahead of the law."

McCoy joined them in the hallway. He'd been watching the feed from the recording. "Found a California driver's license for Virginia Carson. Photo looks like her and prints are a match. She told the truth about not having a record. John Cobb does have a record for serving time for drug possession and dealing, but still no affiliation with Harold Cobb."

Stella acknowledged the information with a nod. "Mattie, are you up to talking to John Cobb now?"

"I have several questions for him."

"Let me take the lead." Stella opened the door of the next interrogation room, and Mattie followed her in.

John Cobb sat at the table, his hands in cuffs and chained to a steel eyebolt set in the floor. Deputy Johnson stood at the wall, keeping guard. A bright red cut adorned the top of John's nose where Mattie had kicked the mask, and bruises darkened both his eyes and his throat. The EMT that cared for prisoners at the station had wrapped his arm with a bandage where no doubt Robo had left his mark.

It pleased Mattie that she and her dog had been able to get in their licks.

The recorder had been running since they'd put John in the room, so Stella repeated the Miranda warning and began the interview. "John Cobb, are you willing to answer a few questions?"

He eyed Stella before giving Mattie an insolent smile. "Depends."

Stella placed her palms on the table. "We've spoken to Violet, also known as Virginia Carson. She wants to work with us. We've got your identity and your record, and we know you were responsible for William Cobb's death."

John shrugged, his cold eyes locked on Mattie.

"How did you find William Cobb?"

He gave Stella a scornful look.

"We know you killed him."

His snake eyes traveled back to Mattie and fixed on her.

Mattie wasn't afraid of him, and she wanted some answers. She leaned forward to take over. "Let's talk about the three skeletons we found up on Redstone Ridge then. The weapon involved in those deaths has been traced to your brother, Harold Cobb."

John tipped his head in acknowledgement. "Harold killed them. Three Mexicans that got caught up in his deal. I don't know their names."

"One was just a child."

He lifted one shoulder. "That's too bad, isn't it?"

"Were you there?"

He shook his head slowly in denial, but Mattie doubted that was the truth.

"What else do you know about their deaths?" Stella asked. "Why did Harold kill them?"

"Like I said. They got in his way. They were at one of the checkpoints at the wrong time. Saw too much. Had to get rid of 'em."

"What town were they from?"

"Don't know. Can't say."

"What else do you know about their deaths?" Mattie asked.

"Harold set the forest on fire that night."

"So he was the cause of the Redstone Ridge fire, huh?" If true, this little bit would give them a date to search for missing person reports. "And what is Ramona Cobb's maiden name?"

With a sly smile, he shook his head.

She was just about done with him and doubted anything more he might say would be useful. "Tell me, how does it feel to have murdered your own nephew and to have tried to kill your niece?"

The look he gave her was pure disgust. "You're not my kin."

"Oh yeah? So you're not Harold Cobb's brother?"

"You're not his daughter, you cocky little bitch."

The room looped around her, along with a wave of dizziness. How could this be true? Harold Cobb had been a lousy father whom she'd grown to hate, but he was the only one she could remember.

Stella picked up the questioning. "What do you mean by that?"

"Just what I said." John glared at Mattie and she met his black look straight on. "You and your brother are no kin of mine. Harold picked you up that same night when he picked up Ramona."

"What do you mean by picked up Ramona?" Stella asked.

"She was part of the bunch he took up to the ridge that night. He had to have her, and she begged to keep her kids. In spite of all her faults, Ramona was a real looker. And Harold was a fool."

Mattie thought of the vivid image of the burning child that had flashed into her mind when they exhumed the child's bones. She found her voice. "Are you saying that I was up on the ridge that night? I was there when those people were killed?"

John made derisive sound. "I've said all I'm going to say. I'm done talking."

Her mind tumbled with fragments of childhood memories. Riding horseback in front of a man she feared. Hearing the blast of a gunshot and her mother's scream. Watching the bodies burn until she turned away and buried her face against her brother. This man had been there. No matter what he said, she remembered that he'd been there, too.

Did Willie remember all this before he died? Did he remember being there the night the men burned the bodies up on the ridge?

Overwhelming fatigue washed through her, so heavy that she had to fight to keep her head up. She could barely hear Stella as she peppered John with follow-up questions, which he refused to answer.

Mattie braced against the table to push herself to stand, saying to Stella, "Excuse me for a minute."

She exited the interrogation room, closed the door, and leaned against it, looking down the hall to her office. First Robo and then Cole appeared at the doorway.

"Are you all right?" Cole asked, concern etched on his face.

She recognized that she'd hit the wall, and she had all she could take. She took the few steps needed to reach the security of Cole's strong arms, and she held him close, pressing her face against his chest. "I'll go with you now to see Dr. McGinnis," she said.

# THIRTY-SIX

Cole lingered at his bedroom door, observing Mattie from across the room. She slept soundly on his bed, her dark hair flared against his pillow, her breathing steady and regular. Robo lay beside her and he raised his head to stare at him, ears forward and alert. Even though he knew the dog would take his arm off if he approached, he'd never been so thrilled to see a protection dog on duty. Robo would guard her to his dying breath.

A breeze lifted the sheer, white under-panel away from the heavier, open draperies. Mattie had requested he open the window and leave the door open before she collapsed under the bed's comforter.

Assured that she was all right, he turned to pad downstairs on socked feet. After taking Mattie to see Dr. McGinnis and then setting her up to rest where he could keep an eye on her, Cole had dozed the rest of the day on his couch.

Dr. McGinnis had performed a thorough physical exam and then run an EKG to make sure Mattie hadn't suffered heart damage from the drug or her episode without oxygen. He decided the dosage of the antidote that Cole gave her was enough and didn't want to inject her with anything more, so he'd recommended sleep, nourishing food, and replenishment of electrolytes to help with her recurrent bouts of dizziness. Robo was making sure she received the first prescribed item on the treatment plan, while Mrs. Gibbs was taking care of the last two.

When they got home from the doctor's office, Mattie had showered and changed into a pair a sweats that Stella retrieved from her car. Then she'd gone to bed and fallen asleep.

Mattie's house was still surrounded by yellow tape, but Stella had promised she'd release the scene and clean up by evening. He knew that Mattie would want to move to her own home, though he planned for her to stay here where he could keep an eye on her, at least for one night. The thought of her returning to work gave him a chill, though he knew it was unreasonable to hope that Mattie might retire from her life as a K-9 officer.

*Could I handle being married to a police officer?* The thought startled him, and he paused at the bottom of the stairway to consider. To be honest, he'd examined the question a couple times recently, but not with the horror of last night's experience behind it.

Marrying Mattie would be a big step, and he wondered if any of them were ready for it. It would mean bringing her and Robo into his home and family. The kids already loved them both, and Cole figured their bond would only grow stronger if they all lived under one roof. But was it fair to expose them to the risk of losing Robo while on duty, much less the possibility of losing their new stepmother?

He cautioned himself not to overreact. Sure, police work was dangerous business, K-9 work even more so, but more officers retired from duty unscathed than those killed on the job. And this time danger had come out of Mattie's past rather than from her current law enforcement duties here in Timber Creek.

He didn't plan to let this incident change his future. Last night's terror had convinced him that he didn't want to live his life without Mattie in it.

★

Mattie's body jerked and startled her awake. She raised her head to study her unfamiliar surroundings. Pressed against her on the bed—where he wasn't typically allowed—Robo warmed her side. He gazed at her, ears pricked, as if anticipating her next move.

Instead of her own bedroom, she was in Cole's, where every-thing was big. King-sized bed, heavy oak furniture, large-screen television.

Safe.

She relaxed back on the pillow and cuddled against Robo. He rested his head on his paws while she stroked his silky fur, gently checking his rump and leg for sore spots. His lack of flinching reas-sured her that he must not have any significant tenderness. For her own part, she felt like she'd been caught in a cement mixer.

While she stretched her legs under the warm, fluffy comforter, she noticed movement at the doorway. Cole peeked around the jam, raising his hand in greeting when she looked at him.

He carried a tumbler of blueberry vitamin water and set it on the bedside table. "Do you feel any better?"

"I'll feel better tomorrow after I work some of the soreness out." She sat up, and Cole handed her the glass. The first few swal-lows hurt her throat but then felt soothing as she leaned against the headboard and sipped a bit more.

Cole sat on the edge of the bed, and Robo moved to position himself between them. Cole's dark eyes twinkled. "This dog gets the best of me every time."

"Will the kids be home soon?"

"In about fifteen minutes."

"I need to go. I can't let them see me looking like this— Frankenstein's bride."

He smiled. "They can and they will. It's not the first time they've seen a few cuts and bruises, although the redness in your eyes will create lots of questions from Sophie. Let's just tell her it was from being so close to the fire."

"I can go home now."

"Stella called. Your home isn't ready for you to go in there yet."

"What's taking so long?"

He made a vague gesture with his hand. "Not sure. She'll get to it when she can. I told her you were staying here for the night." He continued on with a rush, as if to stave off argument. "She also said to tell you that John Cobb shut down and asked for an attorney. Interrogation over."

"I doubt he'll provide us with anything more." Pain radiated from Mattie's chest as a coughing spasm gripped her.

Cole leaned forward to pat her on the back. "Remember Dr. McGinnis said to go ahead and cough. Your lungs weren't functioning at full capacity there for awhile and you might need to decongest."

When the spasm ended, she wiped moisture from her eyes, caused not only by coughing. Sometimes this man seemed too good, and she didn't want to sully his world with her dirty baggage. She pushed the comforter back so she could get up. "Cole, listen. It's really good of you to offer a place for me to stay, but it's not necessary."

"Wait," he said, taking her hand.

Robo stuck his nose between them, nuzzling her palm. He drew away to sneeze and then pushed his wet nose back between their hands, doing his best to separate them.

"Geez, Robo. Ick." Cole pulled a tissue from the box on the bedside table and wiped her palm, which she allowed, even though she didn't really care. "I don't want you to leave now, Mattie. We'll all rest better tonight if you stay here. Please do Mrs. Gibbs, the kids, and me this one favor and let us pamper you. At least for today."

She blinked the wetness from her eyes and turned away. "I'm not used to it."

"I know. You're always the strong one."

"I mean, I'm still trying to wrap my head around things. Everything I thought I knew about myself has been tossed into the air. I don't know what's real and what's not. I don't want to bring that into your home. I need time to sort things out."

"No, you don't. It's all in the past, Mattie. It doesn't matter in the present. There's nothing you can learn about yourself that would change the way I feel about you. Not a thing. I love you the way you are. I love the person you are. There's nothing out there that could change that for me."

Tears streamed, wetting her cheeks, and a sob racked her chest as Cole leaned forward to take her in his arms. Robo squirmed his way between them, and Cole embraced them both, her dog sandwiched in the middle. She gave up on trying to maintain control and sobbed unhindered until Robo's persistent nose nudged her arm and made her laugh while she cried.

"Robo. Move over, buddy. Give a guy a break." Cole tore more tissues from the box with one hand while he continued to hold her with the other, giving her several before he wiped his eyes and nose with another. "Okay. I know that finding out about yourself and your family is important to you, so here's what I think we should do. We'll send your DNA to an ancestry database to see if we can find your mother. Maybe she's trying to find you. Or maybe we can find other members of your family. No telling who's out there looking for you."

Her throat swelled, and she buried her face in a tissue. "Maybe no one."

"But maybe someone." He pulled her toward him, and Robo held the line resolutely, wedged between them. "The important thing for you to remember, Mattie, is that we're in this together. No matter what you discover, I'm with you."

It was a lot to take in, a lot to think about. The noisy bustle of the kids coming home from school drifted up the stairway, and Cole looked toward the open door. He leaned back slightly and looked into her face.

Unable to meet his eyes, she gazed down at Robo. It was too much emotional turmoil—love, sorrow, the joy of being alive and being with him. She might start crying again.

"I need to go downstairs and talk to the kids. A lot has happened since they left for school this morning. Are you okay on your own for a few minutes?"

She'd been on her own most of her life. "Sure."

"Will you feel like visiting with the kids later?"

All of sudden, everything came clear. Being with Sophie and Angela would be like medicine to her soul. There was nothing she would like better. "I'll splash some water on my face and get ready. Could you ask Mrs. Gibbs if she can loan me a scarf to put around my neck? The kids don't need to see this mark."

"Okay, but Stella wanted you to give her a call." He handed her his cell phone as he leaned forward and kissed her.

The kiss felt warm and gentle on her lips, loving but not demanding, normal and like it should be.

Cole straightened. "I'll get you a scarf and you can come down whenever you're ready."

She dialed Stella after he left. Her cell phone had never been found; it was probably smashed somewhere along the side of the road.

Stella answered. "What's up, Cole?"

"It's Mattie."

"Ah, glad to know you're awake. How are you feeling?"

"I'll be all right. Do we have any more information?"

"We sent John Cobb's rifle and ammo to the lab. We're certain he shot the ram, but we'll let ballistics prove it for us." Stella paused for a moment. "I tried to get a possible lead for Ramona out of Violet, but I don't think she knows anything about your mother. The good news is that after she talked to her attorney, it looks like she's decided to testify against John Cobb for William's death."

"That *is* good news." Mattie remembered her certainty that John Cobb had been on the ridge the night their three John Does had been killed. "Stella, do you think we can charge him for the deaths of our other three victims?"

"I think it's entirely possible. We can tie the murder weapon to Harold Cobb, and despite his denial, our taped interview gave us enough to place John Cobb at the crime scene that night. He knew too much. And the fact that he used the same MO and place to bury William is also damning. That has to be more than pure coincidence."

A thought crystalized in Mattie's mind, making her realize how happy she should be. "The discovery that I'm not related by blood to the Cobb brothers is a huge bonus."

"I hoped you would come to see it that way."

Cole returned with a green silk scarf in hand, which he waved at her before placing it beside her on the bed. "Join us when you're ready," he whispered as he left the room.

"Lab results were negative for recreational drugs in William's samples." Stella paused, and Mattie knew the other shoe was about to drop. "But they were positive for thiafentanil oxalate."

"So Cobb used the same drug on Willie that he used on me." She remembered how ill she'd been and realized that Willie had endured even more torture. It made her heart ache.

She wrapped up the conversation with Stella and then went to the bathroom to splash water on her reddened eyes. Her image in the mirror didn't look as bad as it had a few hours ago. Her physical wounds were already starting to heal, and the fiery redness from her cuts, scrapes, and bloodshot eyes had diminished.

And what about her ordeal's emotional impact? It might give her nightmares for a time, but as she gazed at her reflection in the mirror, she made a promise to herself. She would not let this experience come between her and the ones she loved. She'd learned that lesson the hard way, and she would not let John Cobb undermine her life.

In the past, she had let the focus on her "real family" blur the importance of reality. She'd slowly begun to take for granted the woman who'd loved her and cared for her since her teen years. Mama T. That sweet lady was as real as any mother could be.

And Doreen wanted to be her sister. Mattie would get to know her as well, and not just because her foster mom desired it, but because Doreen was family. Willie had found family in Tamara and Elliott, and she vowed to meet them, sometime in the not so distant future.

Family—that elusive web that shifted in shape, drew you in, and shored you up when you needed it most. Something Cole

Walker knew and worked for despite the different forms his own took during the past year. He'd opened his arms and offered her a place within his family for her to enjoy tonight, and she planned to take him up on it.

She draped the pretty scarf that Mrs. Gibbs loaned her loosely around her neck. Time to pay attention to those who meant the most to her, rather than dwell on those she'd lost. If meant to be, she would find her people someday. Maybe she already had.

# Acknowledgments

I want to express my sincere gratitude to the readers of the Timber Creek K-9 Mysteries for your support and encouragement. I appreciate that you allow me the opportunity to entertain, and I enjoy hearing from those of you who write to me.

Thank you to the professionals who shared their time and knowledge to assist with procedural content for this story: Tracy Brisendine, Medicolegal Death Investigator; Lieutenant Glenn J. Wilson (Ret.); Nancy Howard, District Wildlife Manager (retired); and Charles Mizushima, DVM. As always, I might have enhanced information they provided for fictional purposes, and any mistakes are mine alone.

Huge thanks to my agent, Terrie Wolf of AKA Literary Management, whose support is invaluable; to my editor, Nike Power, for her talent and skill; and to publisher Matt Martz, marketing associate Sarah Poppe, editorial and production assistant Jenny Chen, and the team of talented staff at Crooked Lane Books for suggesting the title for this book and for years of support for this series. I'm lucky to work with such a great team!

Thank you to readers Scott Graham (author of the National Park Mystery Series) and Susan Hemphill for their help with early drafts.

Thank you to friends and family whose encouragement and support means the world to me. Special thanks to my husband Charlie for help with housework and plotting; and to my daughters Sarah and Beth and son-in-law Adam for their input, love, and encouragement. You guys are the best!